TO: ROSIE,

Thank you for your support and for your kind words.

Peace,

JV

Rome Is

Burning

A Novel

Roy A. Teel Jr.

ROME IƧ BURNING

A Novel

Roy A. Teel Jr.

The Iron Eagle Series: Book Three

An Imprint of Narroway Publishing LLC.

Narroway Publishing LLC.
Imprint: Narroway Press
P.O. Box 1431
Lake Arrowhead, California 92352

This is a work of fiction. Names, characters, places, and incidents either are the product of the author's imagination or are used fictitiously, and any resemblance to actual persons, living or dead, business establishments, events or locales is entirely coincidental.

First Edition

ISBN: 978-0-9887025-3-0

Teel, Roy A., 1965-
   Rome Is Burning: A Novel, The Iron Eagle Series: Book Three /
   Roy A. Teel Jr. — 1st ed. — Lake Arrowhead, Calif. Narroway Press
   c2014.p. ; cm.ISBN: 978-0-9887025-3-0 (Hardcover)

1. Serial Killers — Fiction. 2. Police, FBI — Fiction
3. Crime — Fiction 4. Drama — Fiction
5. Mystery — Fiction 6. Suspense — Fiction. 7. Romance — Fiction.
   Title.

      Book Editing: Finesse Writing and Editing LLC.
      Cover and Book Design: Adan M. Garcia
      Author Photo: F. E. Arnest

"Every civilization creates its own destiny with disaster."

Roy A. Teel Jr.

Also by Roy A. Teel Jr.

Nonfiction:

The Way, The Truth, and The Lies: How the Gospels Mislead Christians about Jesus' True Message

Against the Grain: The American Mega-church and its Culture of Control

Fiction:

The Light of Darkness: Dialogues in Death: Collected Short Stories

And God Laughed, A Novel

Fiction Novel Series:

Rise of the Iron Eagle: Book One

Evil and the Details: Book Two

"This is the sorrowful state of souls unsure,

Whose lives earned neither honor nor bad fame.
And they are mingled with angels of the base sort
Who, neither rebellious to God nor faithful to Him,

Chose neither side, but kept themselves apart—
Now Heaven expels them, not to mar its splendor,
And Hell rejects them, lest the wicked of heart

Take glory over them."

The Inferno of Dante: Canto III-30
(Translation by Robert Pinsky)

MARK OF THE IRON EAGLE

Table of Contents

CHAPTER ONE

"Fine. I'll have Sam for dinner tomorrow night."

"**H**ands in prayer!" Ron Marcus was quoted as saying after finding the disembodied hands rising from the ground in front of the Griffith Park Observatory during his regular morning run. The media jumped all over the quote, and it was the day's headline even as investigators were arriving on scene trying to understand where the rest of the body was. Jim was called upon as the Sheriff of Los Angeles County to reassure a nervous public that everything that could be done was being done to find the killer. While the hands were a new touch, this was the fourth gruesome crime scene in three months and all were in Griffith Park. The media had nicknamed the killer the Griffith Grinder, and the notes left by the killer were as cryptic as the crime scenes themselves. Always a note written in blood on linen paper sealed with a maroon and black wax seal of the fleur-de-lis. If you were a football fan, you would recognize the symbol on the helmets of the New Orleans Saints. It was an ancient French symbol, and legend had it that it was displayed on the flags and armor of Joan of Arc's army in the battles against Britain; a beloved heroine who helped to free France, and in an ironic twist of fate was burned at the stake as a heretic.

When Jim arrived on scene, he was besieged by reporters all asking the same question, "What does the killer want?" If there was one thing Jim O'Brian was not, he was not a soft-spoken shoe tapping politician. "What does the killer want?" he bellowed to several reporters, "what you're giving the killer right now. Media attention.

Stop running articles and crazy ass news stories, and the killer won't get the prestige or attention." But that wasn't all. He knew the darker side of the story and the killer – that there was a woman in LA killing men. Her notes, while cryptic, always closed with the same message to law enforcement: "*To change the world, the blood of the innocent must be shed, the blood of all mankind.*"

John arrived on scene within minutes of Jim, and the two met out of the public eye to discuss this new killing and note. John had traded his pickup for a sedan. He wasn't a fan of the new digs, but it was what his new position as the head of the Behavioral Science Unit of the Los Angeles FBI headquarters required. He was promoted to Steve Hoffman's position after what the news media had dubbed the 'Barstow Feedings,' a headline both literal and factual. All of the people he worked with had advanced in their careers, leaving him as the head of a division he sometimes felt ill at ease overseeing. On top of everything else, his wife, Dr. Sara Swenson, had inherited a multibillion dollar estate from the late Walter Cruthers, who was, himself, a serial killer of young women. Sara had taken on the role of wealthy heiress reluctantly but had adapted quite well over the past several months. Money was no longer an issue for them but both insisted on continuing their careers despite their newfound wealth.

Jim was standing outside of a crime scene tent set up by the coroner where the latest victim's body parts had been found. His dress uniform and the five stars on his collar in the morning sunlight made him look like a decorated general. He ran for Sheriff after the Barstow case on the platform of changing the department; he was also both inspired and instructed to shut up or run after his wife, Barbara, had had enough of his bitching about the department. John walked up to him as he stood looking out over a knoll onto downtown Los Angeles, smoking a cigarette, and cursing under his breath. He saw John approaching. "Please tell me that this is now your fucking crime scene." He shook his head. "Oh, come the fuck on, John. Does Steve have his head up his ass now that he's running things at Quantico? All we have are parts, just fucking ground meat of, now, a fourth person. All victims are male and all killed to send us a message." "I agree with you a hundred percent, Jim. I called Steve on my way over, but he says it's still your baby. This has not crossed into our jurisdiction."

"Are you two idiots? The letters from this psycho bitch are threatening to kill the citizens of Los Angeles. That doesn't rise to the federal level?" "She has made no direct threats against civilian targets. Veiled threats are not going to get the federal cavalry sent in." Jim took a drag of his cigarette and threw it on the ground. "Oh, go fuck yourself! Did you read the notes she left?" John nodded. "John, this is domestic terrorism. This chick isn't working alone; she's part of something way bigger than we can imagine, and the people of Los Angles are in jeopardy." John nodded in agreement. Jim looked out over the skyline and asked,

"Where's The Eagle in all of this?" "I don't know, Jim." "Oh, fuck me. If anyone knows who The Eagle is and what he's thinking, it's you." John said nothing.

"Is Jade in the tent?" John asked. "Yea…she's lifting prints from the poor bastard's fingers to try and get an ID on him." John walked over to the tent entrance. Jade was in her coroner's jumpsuit placing fingerprint samples into a baggie when he walked in. "So," he said. She looked up from her kneeling position and smiled. "Well, if it isn't Special Agent John Swenson, as I live and breathe. Have you come to save me from this wretched place?" He laughed at her poorly executed southern accent and Scarlett O'Hara impression with a response of, "Frankly, Jade, I don't give a damn." She got to her feet and handed the samples off to one of her assistants. "What do we have?" he asked. "The same as the other three. He was put through a meat grinder." John shook his head. "What a way to die!" "He felt it all, John. Every inch of his body being ground into hamburger just like the other three victims." "Jim wants us to take over," he said. "I've only read some of the reports about the killer's notes, but I have to agree with him; you guys should be in the middle of this." "I agree, Jade, but my hands are tied by Washington." "You mean Steve Hoffman. If he were here in your position, he would be all over this, but he's not the one calling the shots here, is he?" John shook his head. "Well, based on this victim's placement and the contents of the note, I figure there's about to be an escalation in the body count." John's face sunk. "Based on what?" he asked. "A gut feeling I have. These killings are foreplay, John. This gal is part of something much bigger and much more ominous." He thanked her for her candor and walked back out of the tent where Jim was giving a news conference.

"Four killings do not a citywide panic make." He was doing his best to placate the media while at the same time poking the beast. John called for his team to come in and to get copies of everything that LA County had on the killings. He also ordered the notes be sent to the FBI crime lab in LA, so he could look them over. Jim heard him making calls and giving orders as he was finishing up his news conference. "Ladies and gentleman, I've just been informed that the FBI will be joining my office in investigating these killings. Allow me to introduce Special Agent John Swenson, the head of the Los Angles Field Office of Behavioral Science." John shot him a look. Jim knew he was bringing the wrath of Steve Hoffman and others down on John, but he needed a scapegoat. John muttered a few things into the microphone and handed it off to the public relations officer for the sheriff's department. He got over to Jim and said, "That was dirty pool, Jim. I'm going to catch hell for that." Jim smiled and said, "I know…welcome to the big league, kid!"

Sajahd Rasmush called out "number seventy nine" as he stood behind the counter at the California Department of Motor Vehicles in Canoga Park where he had been employed for ten years. He called the number again, but there was no reply, so he called out "number eighty," and a voice came calling from the back of the DMV office. Seth Markowitz was running full bore to the window, yelling, "I'm seventy nine; I'm number seventy nine." Saj wasn't in a forgiving mood. "You had your chance. Take another ticket." Seth was out of breath as Saj called for number eighty again with no response. "Please, sir. I've been here all day. I had an appointment but was late, and this is my second round with the numbers. I got a call while I was waiting earlier." Saj hadn't been paying attention, but Seth was dressed in an LA County Fire Department uniform. He took the ticket and the paperwork and started reading it over. "You didn't fill out the back of form 2225-55-3-T-Y-A." Seth looked at the form closely and said, "I don't have to. That form is only if I'm declaring the vehicle as non-operational to avoid registration. The truck is running. I need a new registration."

Saj looked over the paperwork and grabbed a stamp off his counter, hit the forms, walked to the back of his cage, and grabbed a set of license plates and registration tags. He typed in the data as Seth spoke, "Oh, thank you. I have had a hell of a day, and I'm still on duty. If this radio goes off again, I'm going to scream." Saj didn't react; he just kept typing. "Not the conversational type, huh?" Saj gave him a cold look and pressed the print button. He pulled off the report, handed Seth the plates and registration, and called out for number eighty again. Seth shook his head, grabbed the plates and the paperwork and said, "Fuckin' towel-headed termite asshole," and walked out. Saj didn't react; he just called out for number eighty again before moving on.

Colleen Bolton was finishing up paperwork at the LA County Assessor's office when Samuel Provost walked in. He had been her supervisor for just over three months, and he was a pig. She was leaning over the copy machine putting in paper as he walked by and slapped her on the ass. "You're hot stuff, babe. You give me what I want, and I will give you what you want." She walked back to her desk and pulled the reports she had done for him that were supposed to have been done by him and took them to his office. She laid them on his desk, and he asked if she had done them correctly. She nodded. "You better not have fucked them up. I have to present these to the board of supervisors tonight and practically every city office will be present." "These are the risk assessment forms you requested, Sam. I know you're new to this office and our procedures, but I assure you that these reports break down each disaster scenario the city and county could face. Fire, earthquakes, tsunamis, even terrorist scenarios, which are most unlikely. It's all there. You won't be embarrassed. I have been doing this for years. You'll be just fine." She was cold and indifferent to his attitude. "Well, hot damn. You're beautiful, sexy, and smart." She rolled her eyes as she turned to walk out of his office. He was only the county assessor because his brother was the Assistant Mayor of Los Angeles. He was huffing and puffing when he moved to block her from leaving. "I know what you're thinking, Colleen; I'm too sexy for you! I have a lot of influential friends in this city. I could make your life a lot easier not to mention a lot more profitable if you would play ball with me, or, more accurately, play with my balls." She drew in close to him and said, "Not if you were the last man on earth. If you touch me again, I promise you that it will be the last time you ever touch any woman including your wife." He didn't move. He laughed and said, "Women have been using that tired old line on me my whole life." She asked him to move. "I need you to work late tonight. I have the meeting at eight, and I need you to work with me on my speech and on the presentation maps before I go over there." She nodded, and he moved out of the way.

It was ten to five, and the office was starting to thin out. She knew that this was going to be another night of fighting him off as he made crude advances and rude sexual innuendoes. She sat down with the county maps for Los Angeles, as well as Riverside, Orange, San Bernardino, San Diego, and Ventura, rolled them up, and placed them in her bag to take home. It was five thirty, and the office was empty when Sam called her in. They spent the next hour going over the disaster preparedness report, and he never once made any crude or improper statements, gestures, or movements. "Okay," he said, "so, this gives us all the possible scenarios in the event of a major fire, earthquake, tsunami, or other natural disaster, as well as terrorist scenarios?" "Yes." "Outstanding! Great work, Colleen." He looked at his watch. "Shit! It's six forty-five; we don't have much time." She looked at him with confusion. "Time for what?" He stood up and started to unbutton his pants. "What the hell are you doing, Sam?" "You're going to give me head." "The hell I am. You have gone way too far this time, Mr. Provost. I'm reporting you for sexual harassment."

She got up to leave his office, and he cleared his throat. "You can do that, Colleen. You can file that complaint first thing in the morning after you have cleaned out your desk tonight and signed your letter of termination." She didn't flinch. "You have no standing here, Sam, and I will clean your clock; you will have no future in politics when this gets out." "And you won't have a future in government work or any other types of work either, Ms. Bolton. You see, I know you've been removing city and state-owned property from this building for over a year now. I also know and can prove that you lied to the board of supervisors three times in the past year about fire and water zoning reports, and I can only guess that the reason you did it was to advance someone's political agenda. I don't care who you're banging or who's banging you to get inside information from this office, that's your deal; however, you will fall to your knees and start sucking my cock, and you will swallow every drop of my cum, or I will terminate you with cause and turn over my discovery to the board of supervisors and the district attorney's office and let them decide what should be done with you."

She froze as the words came out of his mouth. A smile grew across his face. "Your ass is literally mine now, Ms. Bolton, so if you want to keep your job in this office as well as your reputation, and protect whomever you have been stealing detailed plotting and plan maps for all of this time, you will do I as I instruct." She looked over at the clock. It was five to seven, and he would be the first presenter, which she knew meant he had only twenty minutes before he had to be in his car to make it to the meeting on time. "I don't know where you get off, Mr. Provost." He smiled and said, "For the moment, in your throat. Take off your clothes!" "I have no idea what you are talking about and such allegations are unfounded and without merit." She could see that he was both watching the clock and her and was getting angry. "Okay, let me put it another way, Ms. Bolton. You have two choices. If there's nothing to my allegations, turn and walk out of my office. I will have your termination letter on my desk for your signature before you leave this evening, and you can adjudicate your allegations against me, and I will turn over the evidence I have against you. Or … you can do the smart thing and strip and suck my cock, and tomorrow we will work out our new private sexual agreement that keeps your secret safe and gives me what I want. You have thirty seconds to decide."

The look on her face said it all as she began to remove her clothing and knelt down before taking him in her mouth. His head went back in sheer pleasure. When she had finished him, he pushed her back and pulled his pants up. "Wear a skirt tomorrow. No panties, so I have easy access when I want it." He straightened his tie as he walked out the office door. She quietly picked up her clothing and went to the ladies' room to dress. "He has no idea what he's done!" she mumbled under her breath as the bathroom door closed behind her.

Saj and Seth were sitting in the living room of their secure apartment when Colleen arrived. She put her purse and bag down and pulled out the maps. Seth met her in the foyer and took the maps from her. "You look less than happy this evening, Colonel." She put her suit coat on the back of a chair in the living room and sat down. "Well, that's because I have a throat coated in Sam Provost's semen." "What happened?" Saj heard Seth ask the question, but he already knew the answer. "How much does he know?" "Enough that I'm going to be getting fucked by him for a while...and I do mean that literally." "Know what?" asked Seth. "That he's going to fuck me. Tomorrow, he wants me in a skirt for 'ease of access.'" "No, Colonel. How much does he know about what you've been doing?" "Oh...he only knows that I misled the supervisors, and that I've been removing maps and reports for more than a year. Don't worry; he thinks that I'm giving sex to another bozo in power. He has no idea what our real plan is." Saj got a grave look on his face. "How can you be sure?" "Saj...they could tie all the maps and falsified reports I've made over the past year to me, and they would have no idea what we're planning." "If this guy decides to throw you under the bus, we don't need the attention." "So ... what do you want me to do?" she asked, taking off her blouse and bra while walking to the bathroom.

"What the hell are you doing?" asked Saj. "I'm going to brush my teeth, take a shower, and then eat something to get the taste of dick out of my mouth. What do you suggest I do, Saj?" She had slipped off her skirt and panties and was stepping into the shower as he and Seth walked to the bathroom door. "Is this apartment still a safe zone?" Saj asked. "Yes!" she said from the shower while spitting water out of her mouth. "We need to call a meeting with the rest of the group," Saj said in a serious tone. "Don't tell me you're afraid for my virginity?" She peeked out around the shower curtain with a smile on her face. "Hardly!" Saj said laughing. "Your body hasn't seen virgin in a lot of years!" She shut the shower off, opened the curtain, and asked Seth for a towel. After drying off, she headed toward the small kitchen and stood nude in front of the refrigerator, grabbing a beer. She sat down on the living room couch with her feet on the ottoman and said, "I'm forty seven years old, Saj. I was a virgin once." He sat down on the couch next to her with a beer, and Seth sat down in a chair.

"Did you two get the registration on the last truck done today?" They nodded. Saj said with a worried tone, "We need to have a meeting of the council tonight about this new development." She swigged back the beer and said, "I can take a pounding and swallow some cum for a few more weeks until we have the rest of our plan in place." Saj dialed a number and put his cell phone on speaker. A man with a thick Mexican accent answered the phone. "Mr. Santiago? This is Saj. Is Valente there?" "Si." There were a few moments of silence, and Valente came on the line. "Hello, Saj. What's going on?" "I want to get Cathy on the line, too, before we talk." "So, get her on the line." He got Cathy Gutaree on the line as well. "This is a secure line, folks," said Raj. "Is this a formal council meeting?" asked Cathy. "Yes," responded Saj. "Go," Valente said, and Saj and Colleen explained the situation and Saj's concern. When they were finished, Valente spoke first. "Colleen, while I know you like sucking dick and getting fucked, literally, even by guys like Sam, you can't take this one for the fun of taking it. I know exactly what you want to do to Sam, and you get to do it, but I think you should do it now not later. He's already a loose cannon, and you can give him everything he wants sexually, but sooner rather than later he's going to say something, and he could destroy years of planning."

Colleen threw her hands in the air. "Fine. I'll have Sam for dinner tomorrow night. You're all invited. Be at my house at nine, so I have time to prepare the meal. I don't want to go fancy, so how about burgers?" Valente laughed. "That's fine." "I can let him fuck me, right?" Cathy sighed on the other end of the line. "Colleen, I know this is all a big game to you, and I know you're a sex freak, but don't get us into trouble here. Too much has gone into this." Colleen started laughing. "I just want a little … juice … for the fire tomorrow night, that's all." Saj grabbed her tit and twisted her nipple. She spread her legs and mouthed, "Do me, big boy!" He just laughed as Valente cleared his throat. "Okay. Colleen has dinner planned for tomorrow night. Do we have the last of the Southern California county maps?" "Yea. I brought them home tonight." "Great, Colonel. To keep things safe, if it's okay with you, I recommend that you call in sick tomorrow. You can invite Sam over and fuck his brains out all day; I don't care. I just want him taken care of by the time you put dinner on the table." "Oh, don't you worry about that. I'll let him grind me good all day, and then I will grind him good for the night. Dinner will be on the table tomorrow, and it will be on time and tasty."

"Seth and Saj, you two finished up with the last truck?" Saj spoke up. "Yea. We did it today, so we have the lot full." "Cathy, have you gotten the last of the fuel that we need?" "I have one more delivery, but that will come in next week, so we will be ready no later than next Friday." There was a moment of silence. "Seth, how are you doing with the fire equipment?" He had taken a sip of his beer and said, "I have rerouted all 911 traffic and air support as well as call centers going into all Southern California stations to our own center. I just need to input the override code, and every county from Ventura to San Diego will be routed to us. No one will know anything is happening until it's too late." "How many people do we have for staging when we're ready to burn?" Colleen spoke up. "We have three teams of four in each county; they already have their orders and are ready to go at a moment's notice." There was a pause before Seth spoke up. "And The Eagle?" "Nothing…not a word," Colleen said with a great deal of disappointment. "When you're done with Sam tomorrow night, you need to make a direct plea to him. This taunting isn't getting it done. He's either too stupid to get the hint or too smart to fall for it." "It's the latter," said Valente, "I've heard a lot of chatter from friends of mine who are cops and on the coroner's cleanup staff, and he's getting the messages. He's just not biting." "Then, as I said, Colleen needs to be more direct in her approach." "If we knew who the fuck he was, it would help," Seth heaved. "I know someone who might know who the Eagle is," said Valente. Angrily, and while swigging her beer, Colleen asked why the hell he hadn't said something about it before. "I just got the information the other night at the bar." "A name, please, sir!" "LA County Sheriff Jim O'Brian has said he thinks he knows who the Eagle is." Colleen said, "Well then, Valente, that's your job. It's your bar. It's police HQ when they're not working." There was a pause, and Valente said, "Yea. I'll talk to him. He should be in in the next day or so."

Colleen spoke back up, "According to the National Weather Service, there is a Santa Ana wind event expected in the next week. I think we push up our timeline to coincide with that event. All those in favor?" There was a resounding round of ayes. "Okay, we will discuss this in more detail tomorrow night at my house. Agreed?" The way she said it, it wasn't a request; it was an order. "Is the apartment still a secure location?" Seth asked. Colleen said, "Yes. No one in the world knows what we're doing here. The place is a fortress of security, and we have all incoming and outgoing communications encrypted. You could be standing at the front door with a mega-bugging device, and you wouldn't hear anything." "Your house is a safe zone, too?" asked Valente. "You bet. My dad set up the countersurveillance equipment there when I was a kid, and I have added to it and enhanced it since he passed away. I also worked out a deal with one of the privates at Pendleton PX; he felt really bad about what the Corps did to me, so I have a ton of upgraded military equipment at my home. We are fine there." Seth asked Colleen if she had spoken to Washington. There was a tense moment of silence.

"Yes. I have spoken to the supreme commander, and he will move as soon as we make ours." There was no response. Colleen said, "Okay, since there are no more comments or questions, good night to you all, and I will see you at dinner tomorrow." "What are you calling dinner tomorrow, Colleen?" Valente asked. "It's not what, Valente; it's who. Tomorrow, we're having Provost burgers and sausage!" There were laughs all around. "No trophies or murder scenes, Colleen. We need a clean kill and a missing person," Valente said. "I understand." The lines went dead. "Well, I don't know about you two, but I'm horny!" Saj looked at Seth and said, "No crossing swords!" They laughed as they followed Colleen into the bedroom undressing as they went. Seth said, "She really needs help with the sex compulsion she has." Saj had just taken off his underwear and was looking at Colleen on her knees on the bed waiting for them. "You want to bring that up now? Really?" The bedroom door closed behind Saj as Colleen was calling him to get the taste of Provost out of her mouth.

CHAPTER TWO

"I think Jim knows the identity of The Eagle."

John got home at half past nine. Sara was sitting in the solarium of their new home on the beach in Malibu. She called out to him when she heard the door. He walked in and sat down. "How are you doing, Sara?" She was reading a medical journal and put it down and walked over and gave him a big kiss. "I'm doing better now that you're home!" Sara called out to Maria and asked about dinner. After the windfall inheritance, Sara modified their lifestyle to make them more comfortable. Maria Espino had been Sara's housekeeper for nearly five years, and she trusted her with her life, so she hired Maria as her full-time maid and hired household staff to work under her direction. The accommodations for Maria and the rest of the staff were extravagant to say the least. Each employee had a four thousand square foot home with a private yard, pool, and Jacuzzi. The houses would eventually be connected by an elaborate set of breezeways to twelve employee housing units for full time staff.

The mansion sprawled over two acres and boasted every amenity known to man. The house was self supporting and relied on no outside services. It was an architectural wonder, and a litany of magazines had been vying to get access to the home; however, Sara refused them all. The whole of the property was connected to the Pacific Coast Highway by a main gated street entrance and a series of underground tunnels, and while the majority of the house and grounds were still under construction, there was a two mile tunnel that connected the Eagle's private section of the mansion to PCH. Two other underground roadways were in different stages of construction or development.

John had taken the extreme step of having the Parson's Trail home in Chatsworth destroyed. He had no need for it any longer now that The Eagle could do his work in their new home. He had the land cleared except for some storage containers that he kept there with extra vehicles and equipment. They purchased nearly ten thousand acres around it and set it up as a nature preserve. John designed, and had constructed, his own 'justice chamber,' as he called it, in a remote section of the Malibu house, and had it stocked for any needs that The Eagle might have in meting out justice when necessary.

Maria announced that dinner was ready in the small dining room overlooking the ocean. Sara and John adjourned for dinner and light conversation, but Sara could see that John was distracted. She left it alone until after the meal, and they went out onto the deck off the master bedroom to relax with a glass of wine. John had one, too. It took some doing on his part; he had given up drinking after his wife, Amber, had been murdered. They had both been huge wine fans and collected and tasted every chance they got. After her death, he went on a drinking binge that nearly killed him. He swore off all alcohol for over a decade. Sara brought not only love back into his life but the love of wine, and he allowed himself to enjoy a glass now and again but only with Sara, and he limited himself to two glasses.

When they were settled, Sara asked, "You're not here with me tonight. Where are you?" He took a sip of his wine and said, "I'm thinking of leaving the Bureau." He said it so calmly and so matter-of-factly that she was taken very much by surprise. "Oh… and what inspired this idea?" She sipped her wine and listened to the sea crashing out in the darkness off the deck. "I'm tired; I'm not enjoying what I do anymore." She didn't respond right away and sat quiet, lounging in a terrycloth robe and slippers. "Well," she said, "it's your life and your career, John. Money is not an issue for us. What would you do if you left the Bureau?" There was a long and awkward silence. "I'm thinking about making the work of The Eagle my full-time vocation." "What? Like Batman? This will be your cave, and you will fight for justice on the streets of Los Angeles. Superheroes are the things of fiction, John." He put his glass down and walked to the edge of the deck, staring out into the darkness of the Pacific Ocean as the surf crashed below his feet. "No. Nothing like that. I just feel that The Eagle could do a lot more good if he was stopping the evil before it started." She walked over to stand next to him on the balcony. "That's great in theory, honey, but without your work, you would not have the drop on the evil that's happening in this fine city or anywhere else for that matter. Have you considered that?" He looked over at her pretty face. "Yes. I know it's a foolish idea. I just needed to hear myself say it out loud."

She leaned her head against him and took a sip of her wine. "Life has changed a lot and fast; don't think that I haven't had thoughts of leaving the practice of medicine and just becoming an administrator or retiring altogether and traveling the world with you. I really think that we should set a firm retirement plan for the two of us, so we can quit the race and enjoy the money that we have received. But I also know, for me, I'm not ready to throw away years of education and the opportunity to make a difference in the lives of my fellow man even with the vast wealth we inherited. I feel that we are doing everything opposite of the monster who left this money to me. To us. We are a team, and I think together in our current jobs we can make a difference in the world." He leaned down and kissed her gently on the lips. "That's why I talk to you. You make sense to me. For me. You're a great sounding board, and you are a hundred percent right; however, I feel a change in the air, Sara. An ominous feeling that I have never felt before." She looked him in the eye. "Are you afraid?" He shook his head. "No... not at all. I don't know or understand fear, at least for myself. I worry about you, but I don't fear for you. There is something going on with these recent murders." "The Grinder murders?" He nodded. "This is a different breed of killer, not some nut job randomly killing people for the fun of it. I spent all afternoon in the office reading the notes left behind by the killer. She writes in riddles."

Sara pulled back, looking at John with astonishment. "She?" "Yea...it's a female killer, but she's not a serial killer." "If she's not a serial killer, then what is she?" He walked back over to the chair and sat down. "Well, the best I can glean from the letters, literally written in blood, she's a sadist and an anarchist." "Is she working alone?" "In the killings? Yes. In the big scheme of things, no way. Her letters have been goading The Eagle. She wants The Eagle to reveal himself to her." Sara sat back down in her chair and took another drink of her wine. "That's bold!" He nodded. "Why do you think she wants to flush The Eagle out?" He shrugged. "At first, I thought it was for some type of serial killer showdown, but I don't think so anymore. I think that she, and those that she's working with, view The Eagle as not just a vigilante but as a possible contact to help them further their cause or even assist in their plan." "Well, we know that they have The Eagle all wrong if that's what they think! Have you told Steve what you're thinking?" "No. Steve has become a politician. He's working with Ryan Skillen in Washington; he's of no use to me. In fact, he could be a hindrance." "You don't mean in need of elimination by The Eagle?" "No!" he replied quickly and empathically then took a sip of his wine. "At least I hope not." Sara got a scared look on her face. "You're on a slippery slope here, John. What's Jim's take on all of this?" He put his empty glass on the table. "I think Jim knows the identity of The Eagle, or I should say he has a pretty good handle on who it might be." She was both surprised and perplexed. "I don't recall you ever telling me that you thought Jim knew you were

The Eagle." "I know, but he does. He hasn't come right out and said it, but I know he has me pegged as The Eagle." "If he knew for sure, would he out you? Would you have to kill him?" "Neither. I believe that he would be relieved and would work his ass off to help me find the bad guys, and then, once I had them, he would forget my name… until the next case."

Sara sat quiet for a long time as the surf crashed on the beach. "If you're wrong, and Jim or anyone other than your victims discovers your alter ego, it would mean prison and the death penalty. I spent too many years without you to lose you again." He smiled. "I'm not going to prison, and you're not going to lose me again. I need to feel out this situation with this new killer. Jim thinks that it's a huge conspiracy of national importance; he thinks it's a domestic terrorism issue, and Steve won't listen." "And what do you think?" He walked over to the wet bar and grabbed a bottle of water. "I think he's right. I think that this killer has been giving us warning signs of impending doom for innocents. I also think that The Eagle needs to hunt her not communicate with her." "Well, how are you going to do that?" He was staring out toward the sea when he responded. "I've already started. If you think life has changed since you and I learned of what Cruthers was doing, and what he did to Amber and all those other girls, just wait. Things are going to get a lot freakier." She stood up and took off her robe and dropped it to the floor. She stood nude before him and said, "I suppose just when you think you've seen everything something new comes along. We will just take it one day at a time. Why don't you come, and we will get freaky in the bedroom together!" He smiled big. "You know how to end a conversation with a start!" She took his hand and started leading him to the bed. "Oh, honey," she said as they disappeared into the darkness, "you haven't seen anything yet."

It was ten p.m. when Jim showed up at Santiago's and yelled out as he walked through the door, "Bucket of beer, please, Valente!" He sat at one of the tables that he and Steve shared just before the Barstow case changed their lives and heard Valente crack the cap of a cold one for him. "Javier, I want to speak to Valente. Okay?" "Si," was the only response. He invited Valente to join him, and Valente didn't try to decline, which was out of character for him. He just sat right down. "Grab a beer," Jim told him as he took a drink of his beer. He did as he was asked and cracked one open and asked, "How are you doing, Detective O'Brian?" "Jim…goddamn it, Valente, call me Jim…I've known you since the day you were born. You're part of the family." Valente smiled and said, "I'm sorry. How are you doing, Jim?" "I feel like dog shit that's been boiled and poured onto hot pavement, Valente. How the fuck are you?" "Better than you, I think!" They both laughed, and Jim took out a cigarette, "Can I smoke in here, Javier?" He didn't even respond; he just threw his wrist in Jim's direction as he read the paper he had clenched in his old hands. "I'm telling you, Valente, the liberal fuckers in California have fucked this state and city up. What the fuck is the world coming to when a man can't smoke in a bar?" "An end?"

Jim looked at him with one eye half-opened and the cigarette between his teeth. "Yea…I'm beginning to feel that way." Valente smiled and said, "Shit, Jim. You've felt that way for a long time…you're just starting to see it?" He swigged his beer. "Why aren't you working for me or John? I know we have discussed it before, but you would make a great cop." "I don't think so, Jim. With all the shit going on in the world, I don't have the patience for it. I'm afraid I would take matters into my own hands like The Eagle, only I would get caught." Jim looked at him for a long time before answering him. "What the fuck do you know about The Eagle?" "Only what I've heard you say and read in the papers, which isn't much. Steve and John talked about him. Rumor has it that you know who The Eagle is or you know who does." Jim started laughing hysterically. "You're fuckin' kidding me, right? You think I know The Eagle or have an idea who The Eagle is? Well, if you were listening to me and Steve talk before the Barstow situation, you got it all wrong because everything I thought I knew about The Eagle or who he is went out the window on that one."

Valente's looked dejected. "Why do you care about The Eagle?" Jim asked, opening another beer. "I don't per se. I happen to admire what he has done, that's all. I take it you don't feel the same?" Jim swigged his beer and flipped his Zippo open and closed nervously. "I didn't used to, but the Barstow case changed my view of The Eagle. I wish I did know who he was or could talk to him because I'd like to shake his hand." "He did do a lot of good for your career," Valente said, taking a sip of his beer. "Fuck my career. He saved four little girls and who knows how many more. He also saved the city and the state from cannibalism. The man's a fuckin' hero to me." He paused and then whispered to Valente, "That's off the record. On the record, he's a cold-blooded killer that needs to be caught." He put his fingers to his lips then took another drink of his beer.

Valente took another sip of his beer and said, "I saw you on the news tonight. What's the deal with this new killer?" Jim had opened another beer and was finishing it off and said, "I can't comment on that. You know the rules." "Any idea who the killer is?" Jim laughed. "Ideas and theories are all we ever have, my boy … until we get rock solid leads. I can tell you, just between us, the killer's a chick!" That did take Valente by surprise. "A female serial killer? Now, you don't need a PhD in psychology to know that's unusual," said Valente. "Yea…and it appears she's trying to contact The Eagle." Valente again looked genuinely shocked. "Is it working?" Jim shook his head. "Nope. Nothing from The Eagle in months … poof … he just disappeared." "Do you think something happened to him?" "Who knows. I need to get home. Javier, Valente, thank you for the beers, and, Valente, thank you for the stimulating conversation. I'm going home to fuck my wife!" He started for the door when he noticed a look of disappointment on Valente's face. "Hey kid, relax. I'm certain that The Eagle is out there, and he's looking at this whole situation. He will make his move when he's ready."

Valente had a half-hearted smile on his face as Jim walked out of the bar. Cathy came out from the back and put her hand on Valente's shoulder and asked, "So?" "So…I have a feeling that the hunter is going to become the hunted," he said in a soft voice. "You think The Eagle is on to us?" He could hear the stress in Cathy's voice. "I hope the hell not…I would hate to have to kill an up and coming legend."

Sam learned that Colleen had called in sick when he arrived at the office at 10 a.m. There was a moment of panic when he listened to the voicemail she left for him, but then a smile grew across his face as she ended the message with, "I'm feeling ill, but I am here to play if you want. You know my address." He erased the message and pulled a flash drive out of his desk drawer. He downloaded all of the files related to Colleen and her misdeeds and put the flash drive back in the drawer. He didn't like keeping blackmail files on his government computer. He called Colleen back and got her voicemail. "I have received your message, Ms. Bolton. How about I drop by around eleven? If I don't hear back by ten thirty, I will take that as a yes and will see you at your house." He went to hang up but stopped and said, "Oh, when I arrive, I don't want you in a stitch of clothing." He hung up, called his secretary, and told her that he was feeling a bit under the weather, so he was going to finish up some work and then leave around ten thirty. His phone must have rang ten times in the half hour that passed. Each time it did, he cringed, thinking it would be Colleen, and that she was calling his bluff, but it was all business. Mostly congratulations for the very detailed and compelling talk he gave the night before to the board of supervisors. Even his brother in-law and the mayor called him. He was finally free of the calls, and it was close to eleven when he was able to make a break for it.

He grabbed his suit coat and briefcase and was pulling the flash drive out of his desk drawer when his secretary advised him he had a visitor. He told her, "I'm sick. I want to go home. Send whoever it is away. I will see them tomorrow." She told him he wanted to see this visitor. He hung up the phone and waited as the door to his office opened and Geoffrey Gillian, Assistant State Auditor, walked in, making an unannounced office visit. Sam invited him into his office, and the two men sat down. Sam closed the desk drawer with the flash drive inside and chatted nervously with Geoffrey. The meeting took only three minutes but the implications were huge for his office. Geoffrey had stopped by to let him know as a favor to the mayor that the governor's office had called for a site audit of all assessors in the state, and his office was to be audited starting the following morning.

"Sam, I'm here as a friend of your brother's and the mayor. Los Angeles County, as you know, and its taxpayers, is one of the largest sources of tax revenue for the state. The governor wants these audits, and he wants them now. I'm sending in auditors who are friendly to the mayor, but they won't cover up major discrepancies, so I'm just here to give you a friendly heads up that this is coming, and you better have your ducks in a row." That was the extent of his dialogue. Sam knew that that was the first and only time he would see Geoffrey; he was out of the picture. He did his duty to the mayor, whatever favor he may have owed him. He also knew that the friendship line about Geoffrey and the mayor was bullshit. The two men didn't like each other, which meant his office was fucked. He slammed his fist on his desk and yelled, "I'm gone for the day," and stormed out.

Sam pulled up at Colleen's house just before noon. She had a security gate at the entrance to her home and walls that surrounded the house. He pulled up to the gate, and before he could press the call button the gate opened. He pulled into the driveway. He looked up at a camera looking down at him and his car as he pulled his car next to the side of the house. The walls around the compound-style home were at least ten feet high and covered with ivy and red and pink bougainvillea. He walked around to the front door and went to knock, but the door opened. There, standing in front of him, was Colleen Bolton wearing nothing but a smile and holding a small tray with two drinks on it. She invited him in, and he walked in with a look of amazement on his face. "I had no idea you lived like this." She smiled and sat the drinks down and invited him to sit, which he did. She walked in front of him and bent over, her bare ass in his face. "This was my childhood home; I inherited it from my folks several years ago after they were killed in a car accident." He was startled and distracted by Colleen's sudden openness to his desires, her incredible home, and the impending audit. She sat down next to him and put her thigh over his and said, "So, where do you want to do me first?" Her voice was sultry and sexy; he was seeing a side of her he had never seen before. "You know where I want to do you, but first we have a problem."

She kept her leg over his and lay back on the sofa sipping her drink. "Oh…what problem would that be, Sammy?" He hated being called Sammy; he had made that clear, and she knew it, but he was distracted and didn't respond to the name. "Geoffrey Gillian showed up unannounced in my office an hour ago to tell me that we are going to be audited starting tomorrow." She slid her foot into his groin and moved her toes gently on his pants. She felt the rise of his penis. "So…we get audited all the time. Relax, baby. Let's play." He put the drink down and stood up abruptly. "What the fuck's going on here?" She sipped her drink lounging on her back, bare breasted, her hairless pubic region tan and slightly shiny in the sunlight. "What are you talking about Sammy? You wanted me. You now have me over a barrel. I'm just doing what you asked of me." "You hate me, Colleen!" She nodded. "You have always hated me, even before I became your boss. You're in on the audit, aren't you?" She lay back, her arms spread out with the drink in her right hand and said, "I have no idea what you're talking about, Sammy. I just want to have some fun!" The anger in his face was obvious. He grabbed her right arm, flinging the glass with its contents across the room, pulling her off the couch, landing her on her back on the floor. He smacked her hard across the face and asked, "What the fuck are you up to, you manipulative little bitch? You know more than you're telling!"

She got up off the floor holding the side of her face where he had hit her and walked over to a small mirror. "I don't know anything about the visit you received this morning, Sammy, and you're right; I hate your fucking guts. I had hoped to get a good fucking from you this afternoon before dispatching you, but I see the sex is not going to happen." He looked confused. "Dispatch me?" "Too subtle? Too complicated a term for a little mind and an even littler pecker? I'm going to kill you, asshole." His face took on one of humor, and he started laughing. "Little tiny you is going to kill me? Oh, that's rich, that's just rich." She spoke as she opened the door to the closet and reached in, "Yes, Sammy, I'm going to kill you. You annoy me, have insulted me, and made me suck your little dick and taste your horrible semen. Of course, in order to get the upper hand on you I will need an equalizer, but you understand that a little girl like me couldn't physically overpower you." She thought for a moment with her back to him. "Well, actually, I could take you down in hand to hand, but I don't want to break any of my things. There're a lot of rare vases and glass that would be knocked over if I dropped you with my skills, so I'll just use this!"

She turned quickly and before he could move or even see what she had in her hands, he felt a sharp pain in his groin. He looked down to see a dart sticking out of his pants. He looked at her with shock as the drug started to make him dizzy.

She smiled and said, "Oh, heavens. Did I do that?" She pushed him in the chest, and Sam fell to the floor. She stood over him as he became more and more sedated by the tranquilizer dart. "You're goddamn right I did, you miserable son of a bitch. Oh…Sammy. I'm looking forward to having some fun with you." She put the gun back into the closet and pulled his body off the white carpet onto the wood floor. She grabbed a towel that she had planned to use after sex and put it under his head. "Shit…I got to you just in time. You almost bled on my rug." She put a plastic trash bag over his head, pulled the dart out of his groin, and dragged him into the kitchen. She put plastic underneath his body and stripped him then took the bag off his head. He was breathing heavily, which made her smile. She opened the walk-in cooler in her gourmet kitchen, dragged Sam's body in, then shut the door and went to dress. When she came back, he was sitting up in the middle of the locker, his breath a vapor as he breathed. He was shivering; his nipples were hard from the cold, and his clothes were piled in a corner of the meat locker.

"What's going on? Where am I?" He was too dazed to resist as Colleen placed rope wraps on his wrists and put a steel hook in the middle of the restraints. She stood in front of him dressed in a red parka and cold weather pants and boots. She had a wired control in her hands, and she pushed a button, and he felt his body moving and rising off the floor into the air. In a few seconds, the pain in his wrists and shoulders was incredible, and he shrieked in agony. "Oh, Sammy. I have good news and bad news for you. The good news is you won't have to worry about the audit; I'll take care of it when I go into the office tomorrow since you won't be up to it." He shook his head, trying to clear the cobwebs. "You look here, bitch, your job is to suck my cock and get fucked by me anyway I want to give it to you. What the hell do you think you're doing? If you think that I'm keeping your felonious workings to myself now, you can kiss my ass." She started laughing. "The other good news is that I'm serving a wonderful meal to several of my friends this evening, as well as your wife and children, who are going to be receiving a box of fresh burgers and sausage to consume tonight. The bad news is that you are on the dinner menu for all of us."

He started screaming as the blades of the meat grinder began running. He could see the large stainless steel hopper of the grinder ahead of him as the pulley system pushed his body toward it. He stopped moving just above the rotating blades of the grinder. "You sick twisted bitch! It's you who's been killing all those men. You're the Griffith Grinder." Colleen just looked on and set the grinder to auto and left the meat locker. There was a large stainless steel bowl to catch the meat, and she had had the unit modified years ago, so it deboned the meat as it ground it. Most people had heard of the type of meat the unit made, which was nicknamed 'Pink Slime.' The knives started cutting into Sam's flesh as his feet went into the hopper. His screams went unheard as she was preparing her sausage seasoning. She had all of her herbs and spices ready when she went back into the locker a half hour later. It was quiet and cold. The unit had run its automatic cycle and had deboned and ground up Sam. All that was left was a pile of ground meat and a container of bones with his skinned and empty skull to the right of the unit where it kicked them out as it ground him up. She put on gloves and began to make burger patties. She separated out a large quantity of the meat for sausage. The unit had cleaned and separated his intestines, so she could use them for casings. She looked at the clock as she started her work. It was one fifteen, and it was half past four when she was done. "Damn…I really thought I would be finished by four."

She rolled two trays of meat out of the unit, burgers ready for the grill and sausage as well. She put together a care package for Sam's family. She prepared the meats in pretty packaging using a famous meat house's name on the label. She prepared it and then took the boxes to a drop location where a courier would ship the meats. She took the rest and started the grill in the backyard. She had made fresh potato salad, pasta salad, and even the buns were homemade. Her doorbell rang, and the smell of the cooking meat on the grill wafted through the house. Seth said, "I don't know what kind of boss he was, but he smells awesome." All five in her command came in and started fixing plates for themselves.

It was half past seven p.m. when the doorbell rang at the Provost home. Lisa Provost answered the door and was greeted by a delivery man with fresh meats. "WOW!" she exclaimed when she started opening the packaging. There was a typed note from Sam inside,

> *"Lisa, I won't be able to make it for dinner tonight; I have an audit to work on here at the office. I thought it would be a nice treat for you and the neighbors to have a little barbeque on ME! We have been planning it for months, but I just don't have the time. I will see you later this evening. I hope everyone will toast me in my absence.*
>
> *Love, Your Sam*
>
> *P.S. Save a burger and some sausage for me!"*

She called the kids to show them how thoughtful their father was. "Kids, call your friends and see who can come over. I will call a few of the neighbors. Daddy can't be here, but he sent this great meat, and it's fresh. I really don't want to freeze it." Within an hour, Lisa Provost had nearly thirty people at the house. Bob Andrews, their next door neighbor, did the grilling, and the neighbors threw together a little potluck and had a feast. Bob lifted a glass to the crowded backyard full of friends and neighbors and said, "A toast to Sam and Lisa, all around great friends and neighbors. And to Sam … for being so giving of himself." They all cheered as the meat slid down their throats filling their bellies.

Sam never made it home that night, and Lisa was worried, so she called the police. She filed a missing persons report the next morning. Sam was not at the office and had left early ill the day before, so it had been nearly twenty four hours, and an investigation was opened into his whereabouts. Jim O'Brian's new office was in the same building as Sam's. He received a call from the mayor's office asking him to put some resources into the missing person case, which pissed him off. He was on the phone with Tracy Bastian, an assistant to the mayor, who had called at his request. "You know what? This is bullshit. I don't have the time or resources to look for Sam Provost. He's an asshole, who is more than likely shacked up with some bimbo and will show up in a few days with some elaborate story as he has in the past." "You're probably right, Jim, but I just need this favor. The mayor needs this favor. The guy's wife is worried sick." Tracy pleaded with him. Jim shook his head and yelled into the phone, "Alright. I'll put someone on it…the best thing to happen to this asshole's family would be him disappearing. It would be good for the city of Los Angeles, too!" He slammed down the phone, enraged that they would waste his time and his office's time on a lowlife like Provost.

He was glad he didn't have to go far from his office to investigate. He called two of his lieutenants who were on desk duty and instructed them to follow him. He called down to Sam's office and asked to speak to Melanie Wilson, the assistant county assessor. He got her on the phone, and she was frazzled. "Hi, Mel. It's Jim." "Hi, Jim! What has you calling my little slice of hell?" "I've been asked to look into Sam's whereabouts." There was a sigh on the other end of the line. "Well, if you find him tell him to get his ass into the office. We're under audit by Sacramento, and I'm taking the heat along with his assistant." "Can I drop by and take a look around his office with a couple of my people? Nothing formal. I just want to nose around." She was curt. "Yea, sure, whatever you need to do, Jim. He's probably hooked up with some slut!"

"Yea, I already had that conversation with the mayor's office." "Okay…well, come down whenever you like. I will call Colleen Bolton, his assistant, and let her know you will be stopping in and to accommodate you with anything you need." "Thanks," Jim said as he hung up and called his secretary. "Do I have anything on my calendar this morning?" "No, sir. You have a pretty clear day." "Shit. Why is it when I want to do something I'm hammered into the ground with work, and when I don't want to do something there's not a damn thing going on?" "Karma?" she said laughing. "Yea, yea, very funny. I'm going down to the assessor's office; Sam Provost vanished again." There was a sigh on the other end of the line, "When will his wife get a clue and stop worrying about that dirtball?" "I don't know…she reported him missing, and you know who his relatives are." She sighed and told him that she would page him if there was anything that needed his attention. He was dressed in street clothes; he only wore the dress uniform when he had to make formal public appearances.

He walked into the assessor's office and was greeted by the office receptionist. "May I help you, sir?" "Yea. I'm Sheriff Jim O'Brian, here to see Colleen Bolton." She looked him up and down, "Do you have any ID, sir?" "You don't know me by my face?" She shook her head. "Huh." He flashed the badge clipped on his belt and the forty five millimeter handgun on his hip, but she wasn't impressed. He pulled out his ID and showed it to her. She got red-faced and said, "I'm sorry, Sheriff. Let me get Ms. Bolton for you." She dialed the phone and said, "Sheriff Jim O'Brian is here to see you." She hung up and told Jim she would be right out.

When Colleen Bolton entered the reception area Jim looked at her in awe. "You can't possibly be Sam Provost's assistant!" She smiled. Her green eyes sparkled, and her red lips and tan skin caught him off guard. She was dressed in a short black skirt and a low cut pink blouse. "I don't like to admit it, but, alas, I am, Sheriff. Ms. Wilson told me that you would be coming in. How can I assist you?" He knew he was staring, but he couldn't help himself. She had a great deal of perfect cleavage showing and that had his full attention. "Sheriff O'Brian? My eyes are up here, sir." He caught himself and looked into her eyes which were almost as distracting as her cleavage. "I'm sorry. How long have you worked for Sam?" "He became my boss about three months ago. Why?" "Oh, nothing. I've known Sam for a lot of years. I'm a little surprised that you're still working for him." She laughed as she invited him back to her office and said, "You mean because Mr. Provost is a male chauvinist pig and misogynist?" "Well, I don't think he hates women, so misogynist seems a bit strong… but yea!" "He hates women, Sheriff. I can assure you of that. How can I help you?"

He sat down in one of two office chairs in front of her desk. "I don't know if you are aware, but Sam's wife reported him missing this morning." She laughed as she sat down at her desk. "He's probably shacked up with one of his bimbos. I don't know why his wife puts up with him. I'm certain he will show up any time with some outlandish story about where he's been." Jim laughed. "You know, Ms. Bolton, you've only worked for him for three months, and you just quoted me verbatim." She smiled and batted her eyes and said, "His reputation preceded him. When he became the county assessor, I was warned." "And?" Jim asked. "He's hit on me all day every day since he took over the office." "And that doesn't bother you?" She smiled at Jim and said, "We just met, Sheriff O'Brian, and you were staring at my tits. It's the burden of being an attractive woman. Being almost middle age, beautiful, and having a sexy figure has its drawbacks." Jim laughed. "Well, I see that you're not shy about your looks!" Colleen laughed as well and said, "I don't apologize for my looks, if that's what you mean. I'm not a slut, Sheriff. I'm a well-educated and hard-working woman. I am in the position that I am in because of what's between my ears not who's been between my legs." He laughed once more. "Well, you are damn secure. Can you take me to Sam's office? I just need to do a little looking around." She rose from her chair and said, "Of course, but he's going to be pissed when he finds out you were in his office without a search warrant."

Jim looked at her strangely. "That's an odd statement, Ms. Bolton. There's no need for a search warrant. I've been asked to check on his whereabouts. This is an informal matter at this point." She walked him to Sam's office and opened his door. "Is there anything else I can do for you, Sheriff?" "No." She started to walk away. "Ms. Bolton?" She turned to look at him. "When was the last time you saw, Sam?" She got a thoughtful look on her face. "The night before last. He asked me to work late as he was giving a talk on public safety to the city and county board of supervisors. I had prepared his reports for him, and he asked that I stick around after the office closed to go over them with him." "I see. And which one of you left the office first?" "Sam did. Why?" "Do you remember what time he left the office?" "Um…about seven thirty. If my memory serves me correctly, he had to get downtown and was running late." "And that's the last time you saw him?" "Yes…I was out sick yesterday. I was having terrible cramps; it's that time of the month." Jim made a face. "Okay, thank you." "If you need anything else, please don't hesitate to come to my office. However, I wouldn't be surprised if Sam comes walking in while you're in there." Jim laughed under his breath and said loud enough for her to hear, "Nothing would make me happier. I've got better things to do with my time." She walked off, and he watched as she went. He hadn't seen a body like hers ever in his life. The black skirt clung to her hips and showed every curve, and they were all nice curves. "Well, I can see that Sam wouldn't get far with her. She might be gorgeous, but she's a stone-cold bitch."

Jim looked around the office. Sam had obviously just taken the job because he hadn't put up all the ornate shit people in Sam's position do when they get an appointment to an office as powerful as assessor. There were two cloth chairs in front of a faux wood desk. There were several book shelves with recorder books and plat map books, and the office had a nice view of the city. He walked around to Sam's side of the desk and looked over from Sam's vantage point if he had been sitting there. It was well organized, nothing out of place. He opened the drawers of the desk and didn't see anything out of the ordinary. The desk had a total of five drawers, two on each side and a long thin middle drawer. He opened each but didn't touch anything. He got to the final drawer of Sam's desk, looked around, and was about to close it when he saw a small flash drive that Sam had placed a white mailing label on with the initials, 'BMF.' "Hmm…BMF. What the hell does that stand for, and why is it in his drawer?" He put it in his pocket and finished looking around the office.

He walked back down the hall to Colleen's office and knocked. She had three other people in the office with her and was engrossed in what she was doing. She looked to find Jim standing there. He wasn't looking at her like before. She felt as if the luster had somehow come off. "Is everything okay, Sheriff?" "Yes, Ms. Bolton. Thank you for showing me to Sam's office. I'm finished for now." She stood up and walked over to the entrance to her office and stood in front of him. "Is everything okay?" she asked with concern in her voice. "Yea. He reached in his pocket and pulled out the flash drive. "Have you ever seen this before?" She shook her head. "Do the initials 'BMF' mean anything to you?" "No, sir. I've never seen it before and don't know what the acronym would stand for." "Okay. I'm sorry to bother you. I understand that your office is under audit." "Yes. I wish Sam was here as he knows these files backward and forward. We are having to wing it and not have issues." Jim was looking at the staff in her office rustling through documents. "What kind of issues?" She backpedaled a bit. "You know how it is. I'm not the assessor; Sam is. He works with a lot of files that I don't ever see, so I'm stuck answering questions basically blind, but we are getting through it. I just wish he would get his ass in here." "Sure, sure…well, good luck with the audit. I'm going to head back to my office." She thanked him and told him if he needed anything to call her. He left the office with the flash drive in hand and went back to his desk to see what was on it.

CHAPTER THREE

*"I'm telling you, Steve. There is
about to be a bloodbath in this city."*

John was working on the Grinder killer's praying hands case and reading over the notes from the other three crime scenes. The notes left by the killer confirmed to him that it was a woman and that she used poetry in her notes. Jim insisted that there was a pattern and that the killings were a distraction from a larger grand scheme. At first, he didn't see a pattern in the verse, but as he looked closer and carefully read the notes, a pattern started to emerge. The four pieces of evidence left at the scenes were all part of one poem. He did a comprehensive search using plagiarism software and literary correlations from the notes using word recognition for comparisons to any contemporary or classic poem. What came back interconnected enough of the killer's poetic verbiage to fill in the blanks. There, on his tablet, was the unmistakable terza rima of Dante Alighieri, the opening poem of Canto three from *The Inferno* to be exact.

Through me you enter the city of woes,
Through me you enter into eternal pain,
Through me you enter into the population of loss.

Justice moved my high maker, in power divine,
Wisdom supreme, love primal. No things were

before me not eternal; *eternal I remain.*

Abandon all hope, you who enter here.

The system underlined the words from the killer's poetry that connected to the poem based on word recognition. He ran it three times before he looked down at the tablet and said, "Shit! She was writing the verse herself interlaced with Dante's words from the canto recording the author's descent into hell." He called Jim and asked him to stop by his office. "What you got, John?" "I'm working your four crime scene letters. They're poems. Not separate poems, but a single poem…" There was a moment of silence, and Jim asked, "And do you know what the poem is?" John cleared his throat, "Are you familiar with Dante's Inferno?" Jim laughed. "Oh, shit yea. Hell, I read his shit all the time. Doesn't he write the sports page for the *Times*?" There was silence on the other end of the line. "John…you still there?" "Yea…you need to come to my office NOW! Your case has risen to the federal level. I'm calling Steve. I need all of your files. Bring them with you or have one of your IT people send me the electronic files." Jim was quiet for a few seconds and then said, "Listen, John. I want out of the case, but I need a little more than what you just told me." John got short and curt, "Get me the files and get to my office NOW, or I will have a group of agents in your office with a search and seizure order in ten minutes." Jim laughed nervously. "Jesus Christ, John. What's your fuckin' problem? You want the case, you got the case. I'm getting in my car right now. I will have the files sent to you electronically. You better have a good goddamn reason for becoming an asshole all of a sudden." John was hanging up the phone when Jim heard him say, "I do!"

Jim arrived at the federal building on Wilshire and parked in police parking. He had a box in his hands, and he was in no mood for any of the fed's shit. When he entered the building, two agents greeted him at the door, took the box, and escorted him to John's office. He walked in, and John was on the phone with Steve on speaker phone. "John, I don't give a good goddamn if the three notes from the killer fill in the third canto to some poem written hundreds of years ago. You're going to have to give me rock solid proof that this killer isn't a serial killer at all, and that she's a terrorist. I'm not going to be made a fool of with the administration. I have to have more to present to the president than a computer printout of some poetry lines that were arbitrarily put together. Jesus, John. You know those programs make mistakes all the time." Steve's voice was clear and irritated. John was not in a good mood either as he responded, "There won't be another single killing or note. She has delivered her message, Steve; it's loud, and it's clear. She plans to bring hell down on the people of Los Angeles." Jim was now sitting silent, listening to the argument as it unfolded. There was silence on Steve's end of the line. John slammed his fist down on his desk. The noise got the attention of those on other side of his closed door. Jim saw them through the window in John's office that looked out over the bull pen of field agents. The sheer power of the arm on the desk took Jim by surprise. In all of the time he knew John, he had never seen him angry, and in this moment, he knew if Steve were sitting where he was right now, he would have shit his pants. The veins in John's neck were bulging; his face was red with rage. "I'm telling you, Steve. There is about to be a bloodbath in this city, and we are going to be responsible for it. You might be a politician now, but I'm still a federal agent charged with a duty to protect the American people. This is coming, and if you choose to sit on your hands and mine you better pray The Iron Eagle rises to the occasion and gets into this before it happens. The blood of the people of Los Angeles will be on YOUR hands!" John slammed his fist down on the phone, smashing it to pieces.

He looked at Jim sitting in the chair staring at him … not afraid, more curious. "I'm sorry you had to see and hear that, Jim." Jim took a cigarette out of his top pocket and put it in his mouth and said, "Well, thanks for the fucking news flash, John. I've been saying what you just told Steve for over a fuckin' month. Why do you need me in your office?" "I want to go over anything else you might have." "You got my crime scene files?" "Yes." "Then you have everything that I have; besides, I can't get into this right now. I got drug into a fuckin' missing person case."

John stared at Jim with a bewildered look on his face. "What would the Sheriff of LA County have to do with investigating a missing person? That's like asking the mayor to oversee the janitorial department at the city parks." Jim laughed. "Nice fuckin' analogy. This was a special request that came down from the mayor's office." "The mayor? Who's missing?" John asked, sitting down in his chair. "Samuel Provost." John looked at him angrily. "The scumbag city councilman?" Jim laughed. "One and the same, but he's stepped down from the council and been appointed county assessor." John's eyes were huge. "Jesus, I didn't know that!" Jim laughed again. "You wouldn't for two reasons. One, you don't give a tinker's damn, and two, you don't follow local politics." "So, do you think he's really missing, or he's just dropped off the map for a few days?" "Who the hell knows? He was in his office yesterday morning and supposedly went home sick – wink, wink, nod, nod – but never returned home. The wife reported him missing this morning, and the orders to look for him came from above."

"I still don't get why they would ask you to get into it, that's what LAPD is for. It's not your area." "Tell me about it. The only bright side of the whole thing was meeting his executive assistant. John, she is one hell of a hot looking woman. Fuck, man, I get engorged just thinking about her." "You went over to his office?" Jim laughed. "No…she has a web cam and strips on the net at night…yes, you fuckin' moron. I went over to his office to take a look around." John was silent for a moment then asked, "And?" "And what?" "You've been a cop longer than I've been on the planet. Is he missing or not?" Jim laughed. "Jesus Christ, man. Do you have to remind me that I'm old?" Jim laughed and said, "I might be old, but I bet I fuck better than you. I have more experience." There was a laugh from John. "I have no comment. I'll take your word for it." That gave Jim a chuckle as he responded. "At first I thought he was on one of his humpabouts, but now I'm not so sure." "What changed your mind?" John asked as Jim sat chomping on the smoke between his teeth. "I don't know for sure. His assistant's a stone cold fox with a body that won't quit, but I'm pretty sure the Titanic ran into her." John cracked up. "That cold, huh?" "Dude, her personality makes ice feel warm." "Do you think she was involved? Do you think there's anything going on between Sam and her?" Jim laughed so hard that he started choking. "If that ugly bastard is hitting that, she's either brain damaged, and I know that's not the case because she's as smart as a whip, or he would have to have some big ass scary shit on her to get her anywhere near his junk."

"You said you met her. Did you take a look around his office?" "Yea…nothing really out of the ordinary. It all looked to be in order, except I found a flash drive in one of his desk drawers with the initials 'BMF' on it." Jim handed it to John. "Did you look at it?" Jim sighed. "Yea…I tried, but there was nothing on it. I plugged it into my USB port, and it came up with no files." John plugged the flash drive into the USB port on his tablet. He clicked a few buttons as Jim watched and then said, "It's not blank." "It's not?" "Nope. It's encrypted." Jim looked on as John kept typing. "Can you access it?" Jim asked. John made a few more keystrokes and said, "I just did. The reason I asked you to my office is because you're right. These killings are way more than we thought. There's a hidden message in the writing, and I believe that the woman who's doing the killing is only a small part of something much more ominous." He looked at John's face and his serious, almost dangerous look. John asked, "What's Provost's assistant's name?" "Colleen Bolton." John's face dropped. He looked at the information that was on his screen then looked at Jim and said, "The flash drive has a message." "And what's the message?" Jim asked. John cleared his throat. "Hell's coming to Los Angeles!" Jim laughed half-heartedly. "And I thought it was already here." John just shook his head as he looked down on the tablet screen and the contents of Provost's flash drive.

"Splinter cell," Saj said, looking out the window of the apartment in Hollywood. "That's how the Feebies and the D.O.Jerkoffs refer to terrorist groups in the U.S." He was staring off at the Hollywood sign on the hillside in the distance. "Here we are in an apartment on Sunset Strip, and they would call us a splinter cell." Valente was sitting in an arm chair in the middle of the room listening to Saj. "Ah...but we're not that, are we?" Saj shook his head. "They would call us 'home grown terrorists' or domestic terrorists, wouldn't they?" Valente asked. "Yes," Saj replied. "But we're not that either!" "Nope," Saj said very matter of factly. "If we are none of those things, what are we?" Saj turned from the window to face Valente. "Revolutionaries, patriots, liberators!" He walked to the kitchen for a beer and grabbed one for Valente. "Have you spoken to all units?" Valente asked, twisting the cap off his beer. "Yes!" "What's their temperature?" Saj took a drink of his beer and said, "Boiling over. They want to start moving; they have been training for this for over a decade. They want to hear less rhetoric from the leadership and see more action. They're tired of speeches about change. They want to put into action the plans they have been trained to execute." Valente sat quiet. The door to the apartment opened and in walked Colleen.

She saw the two men in the middle of the room and knew what they were talking about. "The natives growing restless?" she said, putting a shopping bag down on a small table in the kitchen and taking out some provisions for the weekend. "They want to hear from their supreme leader and their Joan of Arc, Colleen. When are you going to break your silence?" Valente asked calmly. "You are wise to be respectful, Valente; you are all wise to be respectful." She turned and put the groceries into the refrigerator. "This is no small task we are undertaking. Even now as we speak, the very words that come out of our mouths would have us imprisoned and killed. No judges or juries, just the swipe of a pen by a man behind a desk in the Oval Office. Poof! We vanish without a trace. Black ops abandoned by our government."

"Remember who we work for gentlemen. This is decades in the making. The last guy fucked up the attacks. Those who betrayed us must pay. That is the motive for this action, and it is and has been the motive of our supreme commander from day one. And as you both know, our commander is much less forgiving of errors and is more savage. We are but a blip on the American radar. All it takes is one moment of hesitation from those in power, and this thing dies, and all of our work will be for naught. It isn't every day you prepare to mount a coup, an end to the tyranny of Washington and its bureaucrats, a new era of true government of the people by the people." "Oh, shut the fuck up already!" Saj said with Valente seconding it. "This is what we were just discussing. You're right; the natives grow restless and weary of rhetoric and crappy speeches. If we don't make a move soon, they will move on their own. We will have no control over them then, and we will not have to worry about the bureaucratic machine. The very people we trained will be our executioners. They're tired of rambling diatribes, so get off your soap box and speak to the soldiers before we become a casualty of this war."

She stood in stunned silence; she had never had insubordination from her most trusted officers. "Your words are treason the two of you!" "No, they're reality. Those who follow you and us are talking about one thing and one thing only," Valente said. She turned around and folded the grocery bags. "Ignore us if you like, but you do so at your and our peril. You know damn well they are looking to you and the supreme commander to lead them. They also want to know why The Iron Eagle isn't rallying his support behind the two of you. He's their hero." She cut Valente off mid-sentence. "He's not a leader; he's a vigilante. He's a cop who's a killer … at least that's what the rumor mill says. You were supposed to have the inside track on The Eagle." He stood staring at her. "Well, I don't, and I don't think it wise that we try to get him involved." She took a beer from the fridge and sat down on the sofa a little more contrite. "Why not?" Valente responded, "I don't know who The Eagle is, but I can tell you that he's not just law enforcement; he's former military. The guy's definitely black op, either Marine Corps or Seal. This guy is well-trained in warfare, and if he learns of our plan, he will come up with a counter plan that will stop us dead in our tracks. I think you need to stop courting him, and you need to talk to our troops. We need to launch our offensive." "So, you think The Eagle is a patriot?" "I think The Eagle has his own agenda, and we don't want to get on it. He won't join us. We're wasting our time, and the troops are idolizing and talking about him as if he will lead the revolution."

She took a drink of her beer while looking around the room. "Okay, let's put some boots on the ground starting Monday. Let's dispatch all teams to their designated start locations. Next weekend is Labor Day weekend. The weather will be perfect; the Santa Ana winds will be blowing, and it's going to be hot. Set up a secure line. I will address the troops tonight at seven. We launch our attack next Saturday morning." The two men looked at each other in disbelief. "Well? You said we need to move, so let's move." Valente swigged the rest of his beer and said, "I will get with Seth to set up an encrypted frequency to send the message to the troops." Saj sat silent. "And what's your problem?" "I guess I never thought I would hear the order given." "Well, you have. This time next week Southern California will be a war zone." She finished her beer and said, "I have to get back to the office. I have one more thing to finish up." She grabbed her bag, and out the door she went.

Jim showed back up at John's office after running some errands and getting his people moving on Provost's missing person case. John was on the phone when he arrived and motioned for Jim to sit. There were a few moments of conversation, and he hung up. "So, first let me thank you for putting me in the hot seat with Washington. I've been on the phone with Steve and Ryan three times today." "Hey, any time I can be of ASS...ISTANCE you just let me know!" Jim let out a laugh. "So, Provost is missing...is it only your office investigating?" Jim shook his head. "No...formally, it's LAPD's case; neither I nor my office has any 'formal responsibilities' here." "So, your take is this guy is caught up with some chick and will show up sooner or later?" Jim nodded. "This guy is a known philanderer, and he can't keep his mouth shut or his dick in his pants to save his life. I'll be really fuckin' straight with you; I don't know how the fucker has kept out of a sexual harassment lawsuit." "Influence," John said flatly. "I suppose so." "I have been going over the data on the flash drive you picked up at his office." Jim laughed and said, "And?"

John pulled out a stainless steel case and put it on the desk top and opened it. When he opened the case, there was a screen on the top side and a keyboard on the bottom. It had all kinds of bells and whistles. Jim was impressed. "Shit, John, is that Fed-issued?" John shook his head. "It's my own unit. I did a lot of computer work in the military. What we use here and in Washington is tinker toy technology. This is state of the art technology; the government doesn't even know it exists, and given their archaic way of doing things, they will never catch up to us." "Us?" Jim asked. John plugged the flash drive into the laptop and started running diagnostics. In less than two seconds, the flash drive was opened and all files could be seen. "Well, we now know what the acronym 'BMF' stands for." He pointed to the title of the second document on the drive. Jim walked around to look at the screen. "'Blackmail File. Son of a bitch. Open it." John opened it, and it was password protected. "Jesus Christ! This guy really doesn't want anyone to see what's here," Jim said in disgust. John just smiled and ran a quick program, and the file opened. "How'd you do that?" Jim's eyes were fixed on the computer and the now open document.

"A simple algorithm. You see, there is little sophistication to the passwords and programs used for security in the cyber world. Society has been spoon-fed a lot of crap about Internet security." "What do you mean?" "You have a home computer, right?" Jim nodded. "You have spyware and malware and antivirus software on your computer?" "Yea!" "It's crap!" "I don't understand." "You can't...you're not expected to. The government uses propaganda through public, private, and government websites to get you using the latest and greatest 'security' software on your systems. The reality is that all of those programs are backdoored by the NSA." Jim was really confused and sat down in the chair across from John. "Say what? What's the NSA got to do with anything, and what's backdoored mean? Are you saying we're getting ass fucked by Uncle Sam?" John started laughing. "Yea, in a nut shell that's exactly what I'm saying." "How do you know all of this?" John laughed and clicked open the file on Sam's flash drive. "I can tell you, but then I will have to kill you." There was no humor in his eyes as John looked into Jim's eyes with a cold dead stare. "You're serious?" "You want to look at the data, or do you want to keep asking questions I'm not going to answer?" "Just one more question! What did you mean when you said us?" Jim asked. "I can't talk about it, Jim. Let's see who might want your boy dead!"

Jim walked around the desk and read down the list with John. It was a who's who of Los Angeles politics including the mayor and his brother-in-law, the assistant mayor. "Well, it's not who wants him missing; everyone wanted him missing." Jim laughed. John carefully read down the list and its information. One name jumped out at him that seemed out of place on the list – Colleen Bolton. John pointed to the name on the screen. Jim got a confused look on his face. "Colleen Bolton! This file says that she took some plat maps and county maps. That doesn't seem like much to blackmail her with." John read over in more detail what she had taken and more importantly when. "You might not think so, Jim, but Ms. Bolton may very well be the most dangerous person on this list." Jim walked back over and sat down in the chair. "Explain," he asked as he took a cigarette out of his pocket and put it in his mouth. "Well, according to Provost's files, Bolton has been removing original plat maps and county maps for nearly a year." "So...I'm good friends with Fred Reed, who was the county assessor before Provost, and he told me three or four years ago that the old paper mapping was being scanned into computer systems, so they can be used in the field by county and city resources including fire, water, and power, as well as police and military for everything from standard county work to disaster preparedness."

John looked at the list of maps taken and other reports on the flash drive. "Provost has it noted that Bolton lied to the county board of supervisors in reports to them on disaster preparedness at least three times over the past year." Jim was chewing on the cigarette like it was gum. "What purpose would lying to the supervisors serve her?" "What was the last thing Provost did before he disappeared?" "Um...said he was sick and going home." "No. The night before that?" "He had a board of supervisor's meeting and gave the keynote on the state of the county for disaster preparedness." "Did you ask Bolton about it?" Jim thought for a second. "Not about the talk, but she did volunteer that she worked late with Provost the night before he disappeared, and it was for that talk if my memory is right." "Jim, do you ever write anything down?"

John frowned as he picked up the phone. "Hey, I have a photographic memory." "Really? What county maps were taken by Bolton?" Jim fidgeted in his chair. "I only got a five second look."

John was on hold. He cupped his hand over the receiver and said, "Ventura, Los Angeles, Riverside, Orange, San Bernardino, and San Diego. Electric grid maps, natural gas pipelines, fire road and reservoirs, freeways and infrastructures, as well as beach and forest detail location maps." "Fuck you. You're reading the goddamn screen." John turned the computer toward Jim, so he could see that the screen was black. "You're a fuckin' freak, John…a fuckin' freak!" He uncapped the receiver. "Jenny, it's John Swenson. We have a situation that rises to the federal level here in Los Angeles. Is Steve in?" There were a few moments of silence, and he said, "Fine. Give me his voicemail, please. Thank you. Steve, it's John. I need you to call me as soon as you get this message. We have a terrorist plot being launched here in Los Angeles. I have physical proof now, and I think that it's already underway. This is extremely serious. We're going to need National Guard, FEMA, Red Cross, and the list goes on. This is a code 119; I repeat, a code 119." He hung up, jumped up, grabbed his coat and computer case and said, "Come with me." Jim didn't hesitate. He just followed John out of the building and down to his car. John said, "We need to get to Ms. Bolton and fast. Call the assessor's office and see if she's in. Don't say who you are, just ask for her." He called as John sped down the freeway at breakneck speed. He didn't have his lights or siren on, but Jim knew something was very wrong. "Hello. May I speak with Colleen Bolton, please? Harry Morrison calling for her." There was a moment of silence, and Jim closed his phone. "She answered; she's there. We have no grounds to make an arrest on her. The flash drive is inadmissible because I took it without a warrant, and I think you're running on nothing more than a hunch." John kept his eyes on the road and made a call. He had an ear bud in. Jim didn't get all of the conversation because he was talking in cryptic terms and ways he had never heard before. What he could glean from the conversation was that whoever he was talking to on the other end of the line had the same training and understanding that John had. "What the fuck was that all about?" Jim asked as they pulled to a screeching halt in front of Jim's building. "Just an old friend." Jim looked at John with a dazed look on his face. "What the fuck is going on, John?" "Provost is dead!" Jim jerked his head to the left nearly pinching a nerve as he turned to look at John. "How the hell do you know that?" They were running for the elevator bank as Jim asked the question. They entered and pushed the button for the eighth floor and the assessor's office. As they stepped into the elevator, the one next to it opened out to the street. Colleen Bolton was in a quick stride for the main entrance and her car. She was out of the office for good.

CHAPTER FOUR

"You called the fucking bomb squad? And you
want me to sit here and babysit this office?"

"119," Steve was yelling into his office phone at John, who was on his cell phone. "Are you out of your fucking mind, John, leaving a message calling LA under a 119?" Steve was furious. "It's a 119, Steve. I'm at the assessor's office. Are you going to be in your office for a few?" There was silence and then a stern, "You bet your ass I am." "I will call you back," John said as he hung up his cell. John and Jim were standing in the assessor's office, and Colleen Bolton was gone. Her office left neat and tidy; her computer on but locked. Her desk well organized. Nothing out of place according to her secretary. "Did Ms. Bolton receive any unusual calls today?" John asked. She scratched her head and said, "No, not that I recall." "What time did she leave?" "The first time or the last time?" John and Jim looked at each other. "She was here then left and returned?" "Yea…but that's not unusual for her. She's being called into meetings for city or county things all day long," the secretary said off the cuff. "What time did she arrive at the office today?" "She was here when I arrived at six thirty this morning." "Is that a normal time for her to be in?" John asked, probing the young woman who was really an unpaid intern. "I've only worked for Ms. Bolton for a few months. I came in with Mr. Provost's transition team when he was appointed interim assessor after Mr. Reed retired." "Okay, then since you have been working for Ms. Bolton, has that been a normal time for her to arrive?" She shrugged.

"Yea…pretty much. Most of the time she's here when I arrive at seven a.m." "You said she was here and then left and then returned and left again. What time was the last time she left?" There was a tone of concern in John's voice during this question and answer session. "Um…she left at eleven, which is her normal time to go to lunch. She came back at a quarter past two then just walked out the door about three minutes ago. You probably passed her in the hall." John looked at his watch. It was three thirty. "Did she take anything with her?" "Nothing out of the ordinary. Her bag, laptop, and a small box with some things in it." "Did you happen to see what was in the box?" She shook her head. Jim pulled John aside and asked, "Where are you going with this, John? There's no way I can help you if I don't know what's going on."

Jim followed John back into Bolton's office where he pressed the enter key on her keyboard. The screen lit up with a log in screen. John pulled a small black card from his pocket and plugged it into one of the lower USB ports on her computer. He typed a couple of commands, and the computer unlocked. What they saw on the screen made Jim's blood run cold. There, in bold red writing, were the opening lines of the poem in Canto three from Dante, which John had decoded earlier. Jim pointed a nervous finger at the screen and said, "Okay…that's not a good sign." John locked the computer and called his office. "This is Special Agent Swenson, 557514C. I need a search order for the Los Angeles County Assessor's office immediately. I need a tech team, bomb squad, and my CSI team in this building now!" He grabbed Jim and sat him in Bolton's chair. "Don't move a muscle and don't let anyone in this office or any other offices." Jim's face said it all. "Bomb squad? You called the fucking bomb squad? And you want me to sit here and babysit this office? Are you out of your fuckin' mind?" Jim got up, and John pushed him back down in the chair. "You will sit five minutes max. When my teams are on scene, get your deputies to lock down the building and secure the scene then meet me at Legion Park." John walked out of the office. "How do I do that, Mr. Wizard? My fucking car is at your office." "You're the sheriff of LA County … take one," John said as he walked out of sight dialing his cell phone as he disappeared.

Sara was between patients when she received a cryptic text message from John. "6 gsts 2nite at house, they will let selves in, no fear, meet me @ home ASAP!" She put the phone back in her pocket but had no idea what to think. She was already two hours over her shift. She called Marty and told him she was leaving, and that she would not be at the board meeting tonight. He didn't ask any questions. It was Sara's hospital, after all, and he worked for her. She didn't bother to change. She just got her stuff out of her locker and headed for the parking garage and her car. She dialed John's cell as she drove out of the parking structure but got voicemail. "Hi, honey. I got your text. I'm on my way home. Call me when you get this."

John called and left instructions with the staff at the house to allow six men in whose names he gave to his security detail on the premises. He instructed them to make them comfortable; he was en route. John's people showed up at Provost's office not three minutes after he left, and Jim jumped out of the chair and headed for the parking lot. He barked out instructions to his assistants and told them he would call them with further instructions. Jim's second in command asked what they were looking for. "I have no fuckin' idea. You have our people secure the building until the FBI gives us a heads up on what the hell's happening." "Where are you going?" Jim's watch commander asked in a stressed voice. "The hell if I know. I'm as in the dark as you are right now."

He called John's cell. "Swenson!" "What the fuck is going on, John? Where the hell are you? What the fuck is happening?" "Get to my house in Malibu. I will meet you at the front gate. I can't say anything more than that right now." "But you said to meet you at Legion Park." "I'm sorry, Jim. It was a distraction for those listening in Bolton's office." John was speeding through Malibu Canyon and crested the road near Pepperdine University's campus. The long green belt stretching toward the Pacific Ocean was so serene. He and Sara picnicked there every weekend. It was half past four when he turned onto PCH and headed north to Parson's Trail, the street name that he and Sara chose when subdividing the land they purchased and were building their estate on. It was an official street in Los Angeles County, and it was one of the newest additions to the county plat and street maps. It was even billed on Google Earth as the largest home on earth. He stopped at the front gate and waited for Jim who was surprisingly quick. He waved to Jim to pull in behind him, and the gate opened. Jim followed John's car in. They drove about fifty feet when the ground started to lower beneath Jim's car. He freaked and stopped the car. John saw him stopping in his rear view mirror and stopped only long enough to yell to him on his radio. "Keep moving forward, Jim. It's fine." "Fine my ass," Jim said to himself as he drove forward until his car was underground in a long well-lit tunnel. He followed John for nearly two miles before they pulled into a large underground parking lot. Jim put down the passenger window and said, "What the fuck is going on here, John? Are you fuckin' Batman?" "There's no time to chat. Park next to my car and follow me."

Jim parked and jumped out of his car; his knee buckled, and he cried out. John walked back to him and helped him stand up. "I'm too old for this cloak and dagger shit, John." He helped him through the entry doors and into the elevator. "Jesus Christ! How much fuckin' money do you have?" "I don't have a dime. It's all Sara's money. I just consulted on the design." John let out the first hint of a smile that Jim had seen in a long time. When the doors to the elevator opened, they opened and exited into a huge foyer and great room with walls that were nothing but windows that looked out over the sea. Jim was so taken by the view that John had to take his arm and pull him out of the room and into the hall. He walked him down a long naturally lit corridor with glass skylights then opened the door to a windowless room. "You will need to remain here until I clear you with the others." "Others? What fucking others? John, what the hell is going on here?" "You're just going to have to trust me, Jim. There's a fridge and wet bar in the corner with snacks. Feel free to have a beverage or two, but please don't get hammered. I need you to stay straight this afternoon, and you're going to want to be straight if I can get you into this meeting." With that the door shut, and he heard the distinct sound of a lock. He was locked in a windowless room with snacks and beverages and had no idea why. He slammed his fist against the door and screamed, "What the fuck?"

Sara parked and saw John's car and an LA County Sheriff's car parked in spots together. She didn't say a word. She got into the building and called for John, but only a member of the house staff entered to take her coat. She walked down the long corridor and saw that the guest waiting room was closed. "I guess John has invited Jim to his lair," she whispered softly. She walked down the corridor until she came to a conference room off The Eagle's private chambers. She put her palm on the lock pad and her eye into the retinal scanner, and the door opened. She walked in and saw John standing at the end of the conference table, but he wasn't alone. She recognized a couple of the men in the room, others she had never seen before. He walked over to Sara and said, "Gentlemen, for those of you who don't know my wife and much better half, this is Dr. Sara Swenson." There were nods all around but not much more. She saw Rick Park, John's Marine Corps buddy, whom she had met a few times. She waved at him, and he waved back. He was talking with Phillip "Philly Cheese" Sorano, another of John's friends from the Corps. Both men were now LA Firefighters. There were a few other faces she didn't recognize, so she sat down in a chair at the end of the table as the men chatted. The emblem of The Iron Eagle was lit prominently above the head of the table, and no one seemed to give it a thought. John called out and asked everyone to take a seat. He and five others sat down.

"There are supposed to be six men," Sara said. John smiled. "Yea, sweetheart. We are waiting on one more." "Is it Jim?" He shook his head. She sat silent as the milling stopped and everyone was seated. "I want to start this meeting by thanking you all for dropping everything to come out here on such short notice." Ricky spoke up. "If what you think is going on is true, we have you to thank." John didn't respond. There was a buzz over the intercom, and John picked up the phone and said, "See him in, please. Gentlemen, our sixth man has arrived. Allow me to get him, and we can get started." He walked out of the room, and the other men sat in silence awaiting John's return. It was only a few seconds, and the door opened and every one of the men stood up. Sara responded to their reaction by doing the same.

"At ease, men." They sat. Ryan Skillen walked into the room in a suit and tie and sat down at the far end of the table, and John sat at the head. "What do we have, John?" "Operation Nero is in action, sir." "How did you get this information?" There were about ten minutes of conversation. No one paid any attention to Sara, who had become a wall flower amongst these men. She only knew a little history on the men as a group. Ryan was their commanding officer when they were in the Marines. She would learn from listening that all of the men in the room were a part of a select black op unit that not even the government acknowledged existed. Each man served in the unit during and after they were discharged from the Corps, and all of them were highly decorated, though most of those decorations never saw the light of day. Every man had earned the Congressional Medal of Honor. John's was given posthumously as he was believed dead after a stealth mission in Afghanistan in 1998. When he popped up in Pakistan a few weeks later, he was brought back to life, but the record of the award had been removed from his permanent record. They were all a part of a sub sect of the military that the military either denied existed or thought was a myth. Outside of the six men in the room and now Sara, the only others who knew of their existence were the joint chiefs and the Pentagon … or so John thought. That was as far as their existence went to anyone either in the military or otherwise. They were a spook story you told your kids to keep them on the straight and narrow. They were all vigilantes, John being the most famous, and no one in the room was proud of it. He was belittled for what they called showboating, even though he assured the men that was never his intention. There was a long conversation about Operation Nero that Sara didn't understand until she finally interrupted by saying, "Excuse me."

The men fell silent; they forgot she was in the room. They had already shared too much in her presence. If she didn't remain loyal to John, she would be eliminated. John knew it; Sara knew it by the look on their faces. "I'm sorry to interrupt, gentlemen, but John has a long-time friend locked in what is the equivalent of a closet here at the house. Are you releasing him, or is he going to become a victim?" Ryan chimed in. "You brought Jim here?" Sara just sat in silence and whispered under her breath, "How the hell could he know that?" Ryan looked over at her and said, "I pay attention, Mrs. Swenson." She was mortified that he heard her. "Yes," John replied. "He has proven himself a loyal and faithful servant of the public trust. He has been through hell and spent over a decade searching for me as The Eagle. This is too big for us to do on our own. We need his help and resources." "This is a private club, John!" Ricky said. John pressed a button on a remote, and Jim's résumé and military file came up. The men sat reading it and studying it. John handed out file folders to each and allowed them to read over Jim's impressive résumé. "How long have you had this information on Sheriff O'Brian?" Ryan asked. "I only received the last of it a week ago." "Does he know anything?" Ryan asked. "No…and I can release him, and he will still not know anything." Heads around the table shook no, and when they were finished reading Ryan said, "Bring him in." "He earned the CMH," one of the men said as John went to get Jim. "He doesn't talk about it, guys. I don't know how he will react," John said as he was leaving the room. Ryan smiled as did the rest of them and said, "I know how Jim will react. I wonder how John will react!" There was some light laughter, but Sara was completely in the dark.

John opened the door to the room where Jim was being held, and he was leaning against the wall drinking an airplane-sized scotch. He had just swigged it down and said, "The Glenlivet 12 year aged nice…am I getting out of here alive?" "Follow me." He walked out the door, and Jim followed him down the hall. The doors to the room opened, and Jim saw each man seated at the table. John walked him to the front of the room and said, "Gentlemen, this is James Seamus O'Brian. Jim please meet..." He was interrupted bluntly and flatly by Jim. "The Brothers Grimm…Ryan, you asshole, what the fuck are you doing? I told John I hate this cloak and dagger shit. I'm too old for it." John sat down with his mouth hanging open. "Hey…I get to bust your balls for bringing the wrath of God down on me in D.C. with that news conference stunt." Jim laughed. "Yea, I guess I deserve that. So… what's up ladies? We wouldn't be standing in the lair of The Iron Eagle if there wasn't something way bigger than us going on." John sat silent. Jim looked over at him and said, "Sorry, kid…I've known all along who you are and what you were doing. Who do you think founded this little group?"

There was laughter all around, and Jim and Ryan explained that Jim was the last of the Vietnam generation to pass the torch of their order on in civilian life. He earned his CMH in Vietnam in the Tet Offensive, or to be more exact, for starting the attacks by the North Vietnamese. "Man, did they fuck that up or what? We had that war won before it ever started, and then Kennedy and dickhead LBJ stepped in and made a mess of it. Fuckin' Nixon…I wanted to kill that prick myself when he ended the war with a big giant 'L' for us. We had it won in '58 when Ike was still in office; he just couldn't wrap it up. Fuckin' term limits, that's what lost that whole conflict. If Ike had had one more term, we would have taken both Vietnam and Korea without ever having to fire a 'formal shot.'" Jim was rambling. Ryan interrupted him, "Yea, yea, nostalgia road. Are you in?" "Yea, I'm in. I don't know what I'm getting into, but I'm in. That okay with you, Mr. Eagle?" Jim asked. John sat mesmerized. "John, you're a good man. I support you a hundred percent, so we do this, and we take our direction from you."

Jim sat down. "Ryan will orchestrate things from Washington. He has the power on the senate's military appropriations committee to get what we need. The rest of you will work with me in the war room here at the house." John had just finished speaking when he looked over at his stunned wife. "Um…we will also have to get Sara a cold compress, a bottle of gin, and an explanation because she's never going to believe this." She sat in silence as they went to work setting up their command post in her home. "The most important thing right now is we have to figure out where Bolton is going to be putting boots on the ground here in Southern California. She will start with fire before she moves to infrastructure. We don't have a lot of time before all hell breaks loose," John said as they started mapping strategy. Sara asked, "Who is Bolton?"

Ryan responded, "That's a hell of a good question, Sara. John, bring up her file." Ryan stood up as he spoke. "Colonel Colleen Ann Bolton, United States Marine Corps, head of a MAD black op unit based out of Camp Pendleton, California. She's the youngest full bird colonel in Marine Corps history; she is also considered one of the most ruthless leaders and fighters. She and her second in command, Major Cathleen Gutaree, fought with their men in combat in engagements from Panama to Afghanistan and Iraq. Bolton is also very, very well known for her exceptional physical beauty. It is one of her greatest tools for disarming her male and sometimes female enemies." Several photographs of her were put up on the white screen in the back of the room including a couple of semi-nudes she had taken while in uniform. "WOW!" one of the men commented. Jim said, "WOW! Those are the last words or thoughts you have before she kills you." "You know her?" Phillip asked Jim. "Up until today only by reputation. I had no idea she was working in the same building with me. She flies low under the radar. I met her this morning but didn't put two and two together." Ryan chimed back in. "Colonel Bolton is a ruthless leader and an even more ruthless killer. She was raped by three of her men during a training exercise in Greenland early in her military career. She was found restrained to the ground, nude, beaten, and bloody. She didn't report the incident to her commanding officers; she took care of it herself!" John looked at Ryan and asked, "How?" "The official court martial verdict found her guilty of conduct unbecoming and humiliation of subordinate officers." "So, she has an axe to grind!" "Oh yea…her punishment was a dishonorable discharge. She was stripped of her rank."

"She was the victim," John replied. "Well, does the punishment she meted out to the three men fit the crime? She waited nearly a decade after her court martial, plotting her revenge, and when she unleashed it three men were made into ground meat. She stalked each man and meticulously captured, tortured, and then killed them. She then consumed their bodies over a period of months." Ricky piped up, "Well, she might be a hottie, but I will steer clear of her." Ryan continued, "Bolton was diagnosed with PTSD. She began to spiral into risky sexual behavior and became more and more violent. She was institutionalized for a brief period, was treated at the VA and released, then she dropped off the radar. In early 2000, she began to assemble a crack team of discharged operatives that were under her command." John said, "Let me guess. She started her recruiting with Cathleen Gutaree?" Ryan looked at him for a few moments then said, "John is correct. Major Gutaree is an enigma. We know very little about her. She rose through the ranks with Bolton and was not implicated in any wrongdoing in Bolton's court martial. She completed her hitch then retired and went underground. No one has seen or heard from her again." He paused. There were no comments, so he continued. "Bolton began to put together a campaign to humiliate the armed forces as well as the government that she felt betrayed her." Sara spoke up. "I can certainly understand her being pissed off, but she really brought it on herself by not reporting the rape to her commanding officers." Jim laughed. "You never served in the military did you, Sara?" "No." Ryan interjected, "I know that the media has of recent been shining a light on these matters, but if she had made formal complaints against fellow officers when this happened she would have been ostracized and raped again, physically at the will of her fellow soldiers and in the eyes of the public because the government and the military would have assassinated her character, which they ultimately did in her court martial. She did the right thing in the way she dealt with her attackers. It was what she did after that has brought us together here today. She was able to bring in her most loyal men and women from her unit. They are the best and the brightest of a new generation of fighting people. She has been planning a terrorist attack against American soft targets for over a decade, and now she has everything she needs to carry it out." "So, she's going to kill innocent people to get back at the government and the military?" Sara asked. John chimed in, "She's not going to kill any civilians directly; at least she doesn't think she is. She's going to use a combination of natural and manmade scenarios to bring the country's second largest city and adjoining counties to ruin." Ryan said, "The reason for the code name 'Nero' is that the operation is to use fire to destroy civilian targets and infrastructure; the scenario is one of the worst nightmares one could ever imagine."

CHAPTER FIVE

By five a.m., even the media stopped hyping
the story; they were running for their lives.

The desert landscape was desolate and barren. There was a new moon, and the only light was starlight, bright over the northern LA County landscape. It was just past midnight, and it was now Saturday, the beginning of the first full day of the Labor Day holiday weekend. Cathy was yelling to Colleen over the howling Santa Ana winds, now gusting over fifty miles an hour. "Boots on the ground are one thing, Colonel, putting our plan into action is another," she said as they walked along CA Highway 138 near Gorman. Sand and dust were blowing in their faces, and they covered themselves with black windbreakers as they walked. Colleen had an LA County fire assessment map in her hands, folded like you would fold a newspaper when reading it on a subway or bus. "Do you have any idea how long it has taken me to alter these maps?" Colleen asked without looking up. "No." "I didn't think so. The map you see here is the REAL fire danger mapping; the ones used in the stations are altered. We start fires in the following locations with these winds, and we will overwhelm all local and state first responders. There won't be enough resources to go around, and we're just going to keep on setting them fifteen minutes apart throughout LA County and then regroup to start phase two." Cathy looked down at the map and Colleen's finger pointing to the spot where they were standing. "You're in command!" Cathy yelled.

"You're goddamn right I am," she yelled back. "Call out these coordinates to our troops on the ground here in northern LA County."

Cathy grabbed her radio and called to the men in the field. "Attention, all units are active as of now. Here are your grid coordinates for Operation Nero." Colleen began calling off fire start points to Cathy to relay to the troops. Cathy called out, "LA County units listen up. Synchronize time. We're using civilian lingo for time. On my mark, current time, twelve fifty a.m. At one a.m. engage. Each group will start their zones fifteen minutes after the previous group. Groups one through three, you will start the first round of fires at one a.m. Each unit will burn one hundred yards for origination burn then move to your next assigned location. Do not engage civilians. Engage all non-civilian personnel you come in contact with and terminate with extreme prejudice. Unit one, start at 07N/17W; two, O7N/15W; three, O8N/13W." Cathy continued to parrot the coordinates from Colleen to the men until all three units were set with their coordinates.

Each unit was equipped with fire starters, which are used by the fire department to set backfires to cut off blazes but now were being repurposed to start a disastrous fire. The units were lit and throwing flames on the first set of grid coordinates. The men moved in a back and forth motion on the ground allowing the flames to dance in the dry brush and weeds, watching as they ignited into a fire ball and raced with the wind. Cathy called out over the radio, "Unit one, you will finish off with Southwestern LA County hot zones: Covina, Whittier, La Habra Heights, La Habra, and Hacienda Heights. That will start Orange County. LA County units will rendezvous at second base camp at Arrowhead off State Highway 18 in the San Bernardino National Forest to begin phase two at eight a.m. Those units who engage the enemy are to report such engagement immediately to base. Unless engaged in combat, we are in radio silence until eight a.m. Out."

Colleen looked off in the distance, standing on the highway, and watched as the first flames lit up the morning sky. The flames grew in size and intensity second by second, lapping at the darkness like a thirsty dog. "There's no stopping it now, Cathy. We have begun what we set out to do over a decade ago." Cathy watched the flames rise with a bit of pride in her eyes. "Will we make demands?" "Demands for WHAT?" Colleen yelled. "We are doing the bidding of the supreme commander. We can't stop what we've started. There are no demands. You have the twenty heavy hauler fuel rigs ready to roll?" Cathy smiled and said yes. Colleen put the map in the car and got in the driver's side with Cathy next to her. Colleen turned on her police and fire scanner. "Let's head for the depot in Long Beach. Once we hear that the fire is uncontrollable and that assets are stretched to their max, we will launch Operation Infrastructure. Twenty overpasses on all major freeways in LA County." She raced back to Interstate

5 south to stay ahead of the now fast moving flames and headed for Long Beach. "There won't be much time. We will overwhelm fire immediately. We need to have the rigs on the freeway at four a.m. with simultaneous detonations at six a.m. sharp for all of LA County. I want to keep civilian direct casualties at a minimum. Once this has played through, the death toll will be on the heads of the state, county, city, and, of course, good old Uncle Sam himself!" Colleen laughed in hysterics as the words rolled off her tongue. As she drove, she placed a phone call to the commander. Cathy couldn't hear the commander's conversation, but she did hear Colleen say thank you, and "I'm pleased that you are pleased. Operation Nero will transfer to your hands upon detonation of the trucks."

The first calls came over the scanners about spot fires at a little after one a.m. In under half an hour, it became obvious to firefighters that it was a lot more than that. The media started reporting it as Santa Ana fed wildfires. Colleen loved listening to the news and couldn't wait to get to Long Beach, so she could watch all of those reporters tell of the devastation with smiling faces and a gleam in their eye. Cathy told her that the 911 relay was working, and there was mass confusion on all levels of responders. Colleen just kept laughing as she drove and said, "Too bad we didn't save some of the meat from my dead. We could have had a cook out!" Cathy laughed. "Doesn't well-done citizen taste the same?" The smile left Colleen's eyes as she looked over at Cathy laughing in the passenger seat. "Citizen casualties are not our responsibility. Their public safety officials should have been checking their mapping. The civilian casualties are the direct result of their own mismanagement." The smile left Cathy's eyes, and the two went on to Long Beach listening to the scanners but not speaking.

The command post at The Eagle's lair was bustling. The police and fire scanners were overrun by confused and mystified firefighters and other first responders. There was mass confusion on the scanners, and the mood in the war room of The Eagle's lair was one of shock. Even they were taken by surprise with the speed with which Colonel Bolton and her men were moving. "We've underestimated Colonel Bolton, guys. The fires are burning. Operation Nero has begun. We know from the strategy mapping we have seen from Bolton that phase two is going to include truck bombs. We have to focus on the trucks," John called out as the map on the computer screen began to dot with fires. It was clear that if the weather cooperated and the fires grew and merged, they would take on a life and a weather system of their own. "The fires are being started in skirmish lines by Bolton's people. She has her troops deployed in sectors north to south." "Well, what about the fuckin' trucks?" Jim asked. "Do we know where the trucks will be coming out of?"

The screen started showing walls of fire being moved by the winds from east to west, moving toward the San Fernando Valley and all points of Los Angeles. "This thing is going to burn to the sea," Ryan said as he looked at the screen and the growing flames. The radio traffic had gone from sending in hotshot fire crews and working fire lines to retreating fire units and moving command posts. The scanner chattered with confused firefighters caught off guard by the ferocity of the fire. "Command, this is Battalion 52. We're surrounded by flames. There's nowhere to go. We're going to try to ride it out." Calls were coming from all over northern LA County, then there was silence. By five a.m., even the media stopped hyping the story; they were running for their lives. "Command, this is 47. We have moved down and are making a stand at Balboa Boulevard and Rinaldi. Everything above Rinaldi is burning. We have a huge loss of life. Where the hell are our resources?" "47, this is command. We have all resources deployed. You are in the inner ring of fire. Pull down to Balboa and Roscoe Boulevard. We're trying to get more air support." Ryan had been out of the room for a bit, but once he had his bearings, he got on the phone with Washington and was communicating directly with the White House and the president.

"Mr. President, with all due respect, you can dispatch every National Guard unit we have in the country; it's not going to stop these fires. Los Angeles is burning, sir. We need everything the military has to throw at this." There was silence as Ryan listened. They could see the anger. "No, you don't get it, asshole. There won't be a Los Angeles in twenty-four hours. We need all military resources, and we need them now. The United States and its citizens are under attack. This is going to make nine-eleven look like a car accident, Mr. President." A few more seconds went by as he held the phone to his ear. "I have been warning the administration and you, sir, of the possibility of a well-orchestrated terrorist attack. I have been warning you and your predecessors about this possibility for over a decade while at the FBI. There is no way to stop this now, sir. This is the perfect storm. The blood of the innocents in Los Angeles and elsewhere is on your hands." He threw the phone against the wall. "He's not listening. None of them are listening. The bombs will come next." He had John pull up a map of LA County. "Bolton will be going for power and intensity for maximum damage. She will either use fertilizer or fossil fuel to blow the bridges and overpasses throughout the county." There were five locations on the map that

Ryan and the men were looking at. Ryan looked at John and said, "I don't believe we can stop the bombings. We have to focus on locating and stopping Colonel Bolton and her troops." John nodded.

"This is a search and destroy mission, men. We have to cut off the commander's head. We have to kill Bolton and her people." He dispatched each of the men to locations in the outer counties in Southern California where it was most likely that Bolton would be trying to move the men and where chatter had been picked up for several months between Bolton and her men. John sent four of his men out into the counties and took off on a hunch for where he felt it most likely that Bolton could obtain the fuel she needed. John said, "My best guess is that Bolton will have each of the fire starter units in all counties from Ventura to San Diego. San Diego will be the last county she will move in." He left Jim in charge of the command center at the house with Sara.

Sara barked out to John that she needed to get to the hospital, and that they would need her. He took her arm as she was starting for the door. "There is no hospital, Sara. If it hasn't burned yet, it's going to. All you're going to do is die trying to get there. And even if you get there, you will never get back here." "I swore an oath, John." "So did I, Sara, but those oaths are off the table now. This is a whole new world, and it's going to need you when the smoke literally clears. You need to stay here with Jim and help coordinate our movements." Tears began to run down her face. "I don't know what to do. I feel helpless." He let go of her arm and said, "We all do. We can't stop what has been done thus far. We have to hunt down the enemies and eliminate them before they do more damage." She nodded and walked over near Jim and asked what she could do. She looked at John as he walked out the door and said, "Come back alive!" His tone was somber when he said, "I'll do my best. People are dying all over Los Angeles as we speak. Bolton and her troops will trade their lives for ours, so it's a matter of who kills who first. All of these men are going to try to stop the progression of this plan. I'm going to Long Beach to the refinery. She might use fuel trucks as bombs under overpasses to destroy them." He walked out the door, and she whispered loud enough that Jim could hear, "I love you." Jim looked at Sara and asked, "Can I call Barbara and get her here with us?" She nodded. He called Barbara's cell but there was no answer, and the house line was busy. "We have voicemail. The line would not ring busy…" There was a moment of silence between Jim and Sara, and he started to bark out orders to the remaining men in the room. Ryan announced that he was jumping a flight out of Santa Barbara back to Washington to see what he could do working directly with the administration. He told John and Jim he would stay in touch and be back at John's compound later that same night.

"Colonel!" one of her troops said saluting as Bolton walked past terminal one at Prudential Fuel Supply, Inc. It was two a.m., and one of the fuel trucks was rolling out the gates of the facility. She walked up to the dispatcher and ordered an update on movement. "Colonel, we have ten of twenty units on the road. Five are in position. We expect all units to be in position and ready for detonation by six a.m." "Carry on," she said as she walked back to the main office where Saj, Seth, Cathy, and Valente were waiting. "Update folks!" she asked as she put her coat on a chair and sat down with her feet up on a desk. Saj and Valente reported the fires were burning out of control across all of the northern LA County landscape. "Loss of life assessments?" she asked coldly. Cathy responded, "It's hard to gauge at this point, but based on the last census information for the county, I would estimate that we are in the thousands, maybe the tens of thousands." "Valente, I think it unwise that we remain grouped together. Sooner or later, the Department of Defense is going to release the dogs, and we don't all want to be in the same place at the same time." All nodded. "Let's disperse." Bolton put her feet flat on the floor and pointed her finger at a Southern California map that she had created with all counties and their safe zones. "Saj, you go to Oxnard. Wait for orders. The teams are ready up there, correct?" He nodded. "If you have had no direct orders from me by ten a.m., start Operation Ojai using the same fire parameters we used for LA." She handed him the Ventura County maps she had confiscated, and he left immediately. "Seth, you take Orange County. Our units are in Anaheim. Meet up with them at the Ramada Inn. The information is in your map kit. If you have had no instructions from me by nine a.m., commence with Operation Adventure using the same criteria." He nodded and left the building. The trucks had been rolling out the whole time she had been talking, and she called out to the dispatcher outside the room to see how many trucks were now on the road. Fifteen was the response, with ten now in position per her instructions.

"Valente, San Bernardino County is yours; the crew from LA County will meet up with you near Arrowhead Park at the base of the San Bernardino National Forest. This one will be a little trickier. I want you to deviate from our original plan there. As soon as all crew members are there, take them up Highway 18 through Big Bear until you reach Highway 247 in Lucerne Valley. Begin setting fires twenty feet apart toward the north northeast. The wind is perfect for a firestorm. That fire will take out everything from Crestline and Lake Arrowhead up to Big Bear and beyond. There will be no way to stop the fire, and with the winds, there will be no way that county officials will be able to get an evacuation order out, so the loss of life will be huge. They won't be expecting an attack to come from the desert and forest fronts." He nodded and left the room.

"Cathy, you take Riverside County. Our crews are ready down there. That's your old stomping ground, so...you will HQ at the old mission." Cathy nodded. "You and your crew will start fires at Interstate 10 and follow State Highway 62, starting fires all the way across the county line on my order. Once you have finished, take your team to Twentynine Palms and await further orders. If you do not hear from me by 11 a.m., proceed with phase two." Cathy saluted and left the building.

Colleen sat back as the last truck left the terminal and headed for the 710 Freeway, the same route all other units had taken. "Teresa!" Colleen yelled. Teresa Jensen appeared in the doorway. "All units have been dispatched?" "Yes, Colonel." "Okay, put up the screen and take control of the traffic cameras. Let's pipe it all in here." She walked out, and Colleen looked at the wall of monitors as each came to life with live traffic from all over Los Angeles County. "Teresa...blind them!" There were a few moments of silence, and Teresa announced that Los Angeles County was now blind. All of LA County street and freeway cameras were now under her control.

Harry Blyth was sitting in LA's central traffic center drinking his morning coffee and eating a jelly doughnut when the screens went to snow. "What the fuck?" He called for correction, but the response came back that they were dead. Someone had hacked the system; they were blind.

It was five-thirty a.m. when The Eagle started over the Vincent Thomas Bridge to Terminal Island. He knew it was a long shot, but he also knew that if there was any more corrupt city official who would sell his city into disaster, Robert Scossia was his guy. Scossia and his family owned and operated Prudential Fuel Supply, Inc. He was well-known for cutting crooked deals and barely kept from being indicted by a federal grand jury three years earlier on conspiracy and domestic terrorism charges for agreeing to sell loaded fuel trucks to an Iranian national who planned to blow up overpasses in LA County. The only thing that kept him out of prison was a tip that he got from one of his fellow city councilmen who happened to have an in with the LA U.S. Attorney's office who leaked him the information. Scossia contacted the FBI about what he thought were unusual requests from a man and ended up a hero instead of what he really was, a scumbag terrorist. The Eagle got to the terminal, and all was quiet. There were several dozen trucks all parked in a row and a few men moving around getting trucks ready to roll, but nothing that jumped out at him as unusual. He parked his pickup down near the federal prison that had been on the island for decades and walked back to the facility in full body armor with two gym bags. He moved quietly between trucks and pulled a nonlethal weapon from his bag and stowed the rest of his gear in an old steel storage container outside the main building. He surveyed the area but nothing seemed out of the ordinary. He heard the dispatcher's voice come over the PA and call for five drivers with routes for fuel delivery for the day.

CHAPTER SIX

*"You're an animal, but that's
thirty-five seconds. You pay up."*

ick Park spotted Sajahd Rashmush immediately entering the Holiday Inn in
Oxnard. "I can't get this fucking lucky!" he said to himself as he pulled into
the lot and watched Saj walk in. He and Saj went back a long way. Saj had
been in a paramilitary unit in Pakistan many, many years ago, and Rick had the
misfortune of running up against him and his men while on a black ops mission.
He was captured by Saj and his team. Saj took great satisfaction in methodically
breaking Rick's legs when he was captured. Patrick, Phillip, and John rescued him,
but not before he was almost crippled for life. It all came flooding back to him. The
sadistic laugh that he let out every time Rick screamed in agony as they isolated
bones in his legs to break. He got out of the car in full body armor and approached
a side entrance to the hotel. He moved down the hall and peeked through a small
glass window and saw Saj talking with another man. The two started walking to
Rick's position, so he hid under a stairwell. The door flung open, and the man
Saj was talking to burst through, checking out the area fully armed. Saj followed.
They started up the stairs and then stopped. "Colonel Bolton has given me orders
to command the Ojai attack. It is important that everyone be ready to go at eight
thirty a.m. It's five-fifty now. I'm going to nap for a few minutes in my suite. Have
the troops in my room at eight a.m." "Yes, sir!"

Saj walked up to the third floor and opened the stairwell entrance. Rick followed as the door closed. He was able to watch Saj through a small glass window in the door. Saj entered a room at the end of the hall, and as soon as the door closed, Rick entered the hall. There was no one around. He looked at the suite number. 331. He placed a small cellular device no bigger than a nail head in the upper right corner of the door. He placed it near the front top corner of the suite door for best reception and went back to the stairwell. He pulled out a small handheld unit and put a pair of Bluetooth devices into his ears. He could hear Saj in the room. There was no talking. The TV was on but not loud, so he knew that he was not hiding from anyone. He pulled out his cell and called Jim at HQ and told him he had Saj, but he wanted to take him alive.

"Ricky, I know you two have a history, but your orders are to kill him." Rick was listening to the sound of the now silent room. There was a soft snore coming into the ear buds. "I'm going to kill him, Jim…I just want to do it my way and extract information from him. Is there some place I can bring him to at the house?" Sara was looking at the map as the fires were spreading when Jim interrupted. "Sara, does The Eagle have a torture room here?" She nodded. "Can it accommodate more than one person?" She looked at him half dazed, "Yes. John, I mean, The Eagle has three rooms set up exclusively for detention and torture. Why?" Jim laughed. "I have a feeling that it's going to get a little crowded here before the day is through. Yea, Ricky, The Eagle has accommodations." "I'm bringing the bastard in, Jim. I deserve to extract my revenge. Killing him fast is too good for him." Jim held the radio in his hand. "How many others does he have there?" "One that I've seen, but I'm sure others." "What are you going to do to stop them?" "Take Saj and blow the motherfuckers up!" Jim nodded with a look of approval on his face. "Well, since you've thought it out, see you soon."

Rick slipped back into the hall. It was empty. He took a small card reader out of his pocket and slipped the keycard into the lock on the hotel room door. The red digital display began seeking random codes. The numbers started to stop and illuminate when he heard the elevator in the middle of the hall ding. He had two digits to go when four men stepped off the elevator. He looked around the corner to see that one of them was the man from the stairwell. "Fuck!" he said louder than he desired. They didn't react as the last red light went solid, and the lock on the suite clicked open. He slowly opened the door and slid inside, hiding in the first closet. There was a knock on the door, and Saj replied with a groggy voice, "It's not eight yet!" He rolled out of bed and answered it. He let the four men in and went back and sat on the side of the bed. "What's the fucking problem?" Saj asked. "We have the last two men coming, sir. I would like to address this with everyone present." A few moments passed before there was another knock on the door. Rick looked at his watch; it was six-thirty. They were allowed in, and the door was locked and bolted.

"Saj, Johnny here is having second thoughts about the mission. He wants out." Saj got more alert, and Rick watched from the closet. "Is this true, Johnny? After over a decade of training, we are starting the revolution, and you want to let these men, me, Colonel Bolton, and the commander down?" "Sir, I never signed on to kill civilians." Saj stood up and walked over to the TV and increased the volume. There was a reporter trying to keep her composure as she gave the news to those who could still hear or see her.

The LA fire burns out of control. Residents are ordered to evacuate immediately from Simi Valley through the central cities of the San Fernando Valley and LA.

She began to rattle off cities; cities that no one in a lifetime would imagine could burn.

If you live in these areas, emergency personnel are demanding that you evacuate immediately. Shelters have been set up by the Red Cross for those displaced. The death toll is estimated at two hundred thousand and is expected to go well north of that. We will stay on the air as long as possible.

Saj turned off the TV. "Is that what's bothering you, Johnny?" He nodded, and Rick saw Saj make a sudden move in the man's direction. Rick saw the kid hit the floor like a ton of bricks, a small pool of blood forming under his side. He was twitching on the floor as Saj leaned down to him, and a flash of the steel blade of his ST6 hunting knife caught Rick's eye. Saj laughed as he embedded the blade into the kid's abdomen and began to pull the blade from left to right, opening his bowel, allowing it to spill out onto the floor. Saj was whispering into his ear as he was cutting into him. "Johnny, Johnny...now we're having some fun, huh?" The diabolical laugh sent a blind rage through Rick.

"Okay, so Johnny is no longer a part of our group. Is there anyone else who wants out?" There was silence. "You are all part of an elite team of mercenaries hired to carry out these attacks. The men in this room represent the best of the best." Saj was wiping Johnny's blood off his field knife on the vest of one of his men as he spoke. "Now, I want to get some sleep before we execute our orders."

Rick pulled his nine millimeter with a silencer and slid the doors open. It was over in a matter of seconds. All the men were dead. Saj was sitting on the edge of his bed as Rick approached. "Well, I see that you're walking well. I should have broken your fucking arms, too." Rick shot him in the neck with a tranquilizing dart. Saj spoke as he slid down the front of the bed to the floor. "I'm going to have a bad day, aren't I?" Rick smiled as the dart paralyzed Saj. "No, not at all. What was it you would say to me before one of your torture sessions?" Rick had a thoughtful look on his face. "Oh yea…'we're going to have some fun!'" Saj went out. Rick picked him up and carried him to the stairwell and then to his vehicle. He restrained the unconscious Saj and radioed to Jim. "I have eliminated Bolton's Ventura County crew and am returning to base with one prisoner." "Roger that, Ricky. You got Saj, huh?" "Yes, sir. I have him." "He's going to have a bad day, isn't he?" Jim asked laughing. "That's exactly what he asked as he was going out. I am en route to base. Call The Eagle, and let him know what I've done. Once I drop Saj off, give me orders where to go next. Saj is going to be out for several hours." "See you back here, Ricky." Jim released the radio button.

Sara sat looking at him; Jim looked back at her void look. "Have you ever been involved in an Eagle killing?" She nodded. "So, you were the second pair of hands in the video on Marker?" She nodded again. "Well, Sara, I have a feeling there's going to be a very well-earned round of torture and confessions between today and tomorrow. You might want to prep your holding rooms for The Eagle and his friends. They are going to be very, very busy." She got up, and without saying a word, went out into the hall and started opening rooms. "It's going to be a noisy day. This woman and her men have killed nearly a half million people, and the fires rage on. The Eagle will deal with them. Yes, The Eagle will deal with them." She muttered it over and over as she prepared the rooms. "These rooms are to become the seat of justice. These people are cold-blooded killers." She was putting a rubber sheet on one of the gurneys, and as she did she said in a clear and defiant tone, "I want to assist The Eagle in meting out their punishment. A long death is deserved by them."

The Eagle moved quietly to a back entrance of the terminal office. It was locked with a keycard lock. He pulled a key reader from his vest and slipped the card into the lock. The red digital display started searching for the code, while inside, Colleen was about to do the unthinkable.

Patrick "C4" Martin isn't a patient guy. He received a tip through his contacts in Orange County that one of Colleen's units was in Anaheim at a Ramada Inn off Garden Grove Boulevard. He made his way to the hotel and the front desk. He checked in under his own name and took a room on the twentieth floor. The clerk asked if he needed any help with his luggage. He had a military duffle bag over his shoulder and smiled at the desk clerk and said, "No thanks. I travel light," and walked off to the elevator bank and on to his room. He called his contact and asked for everything he had on the terrorists. "They are on the twentieth floor, suite 2010. It's a corner suite." "How many in the attack party?" he asked. "Eight plus Seth." Patrick laughed. "I can't believe that pussy is leading a terrorist cell! Jesus Christ! Now I've seen everything." "Well, you know him well!" the male voice on the other end of the line said. "You know it, kid. I served with him for a very, very short time in Afghanistan in ninety-nine. I remember we had a lead on the guys that would become known as the nine-eleven hijacker pilots. I was ready to blow the building they were in when he disappeared. I lost my eyes and couldn't complete the mission. I found out later that the fucker gave the leader of the group the heads up that we were on to him and the others, and they escaped to Jordan." The voice on the other end of the line said, "Well, you have him now and his co-conspirators. This is hard for me, Pat, but I know it has to be done. I wish, in a way, that I could be there. Give Seth my regards. Let him know I won't miss him. What are you going to do?" Patrick laughed. "Blow the motherfucker to hell with his friends!"

He hung up the line and opened his duffle bag. He pulled three units of C4 out of the bag and molded the clay-like explosives into the shape of airplanes. He set a radio frequency for the firing caps to Seth's cell phone carrier given to him by his contact and placed them into the explosives. He put little American flags on each and walked down the hall to the suite. He pulled the fire alarm while walking the hall then hid in the stairwell as the hotel emptied out including Markowitz's room. He counted the men as they exited. There were nine with Markowitz. When the room was cleared, he entered and placed the explosives in very obvious spots. Once the hotel was empty, he sent Markowitz a text to tell him the hotel was clear. Patrick remained in place as the rest of the guests remained outside waiting for the fire department. The hotel manager yelled at the men as they entered the hotel, but they ignored the calls and went back to their suite.

Patrick watched as all nine men entered. He moved to the other end of the floor. Seth was intent on the mission and didn't notice the three makeshift airplanes that looked like they were made out of Play-Doh. He sat down in a chair in the corner of the suite near a large picture window and began shouting out orders. One of his men noticed one of the small planes sitting on the back of one of the couches in the room and commented on it. Patrick was listening to the dialogue in the room. "Who's been playing with Play-Doh?" he asked. Seth looked over at the object his man was speaking about when he noticed a second one on the desk on the other side of the room. "Oh, son of a bitch. We've been made. We have to get out of here now!" The men started moving rapidly only to end up tripping over each other. Seth fell to the floor in front of the sliding glass doors that led to the balcony. He lifted his hand to pull himself up as Patrick called Markowitz's cell phone. The explosion rocked the neighboring buildings, glass and debris rained down on guests in the parking lot, and the body of one of the men came crashing down on a car parked in a handicapped spot beneath where the corner suite, now in flames, had been.

Patrick walked slowly down the hall, his nine millimeter with silencer in hand. The room had been destroyed, but he had to make sure he had a full kill. He entered what remained of the suite to find body parts everywhere. He was about to exit when he heard a moan coming from the bathroom. He entered to see Markowitz sitting against the wall near the toilet. He was bloody but alert. The explosion had blown him across the room. Seth looked Patrick in the eyes as he approached him and said, "You...but how?" He snarled as Patrick raised the gun. "Your son and I became good friends after the nine-eleven attacks. He learned of Bolton's plan a week ago and has been trailing you ever since. "My son betrayed me?" Patrick released the safety on the weapon and pointed it at Seth's head. "Yea...I guess when you set his uncle up to be murdered on a plane sitting in first class on nine-eleven, he took it personally. He wanted to be here to see me take you out, but he's finishing up his training at Quantico with the Marine Corps. He sends you his worst. Oh...this is for letting those sons of bitches kill Americans and for what you have done to America yet again...rot in hell." He pulled the trigger, blowing Markowitz's head off, then walked out of the building with his duffle bag over his shoulder and cell phone in hand.

"Jim, it's C4. Markowitz's brains have painted the walls of the head here in the hotel. It looks like a Rorschach inkblot test on the walls of the suite. 'Hmm, it looks to me like an asshole, doc.'" Patrick laughed out loud. Jim said, "He committed suicide?" Patrick laughed on the line, "Yea...he didn't know it, but it was about eleven years ago!" Jim laughed. "Good job. I know Ryan will be happy to hear that." "Where to, Jim?" "Come back in. John is still out. Ricky got his man. Literally. He just brought him in." "Who'd he get?" "You're never going to believe it. Saj Rashmush!" "No fucking shit...oh, Saj is going to have a bad day." "That's the consensus." "I'm on my way in, Jim." "Roger that. There's fire everywhere. Be careful."

Lance Coswalski was on Interstate 10 east when his scanner intercepted a transmission from one of Bolton's men calling to Valente Santiago. He listened as the caller called out coordinates. Lance pulled over to the shoulder and plugged the coordinates into his GPS. "Santiago, I'm en route. Is everyone there?" There was a moment of silence, and then Valente's voice came on over the radio. "Mike, this better be a secure line. Colonel Bolton gave strict instructions to maintain radio silence, and why the hell would you use my full name?" There was a laugh on the line. "Who the hell is listening? They're all trying to fight a fire that's engulfing LA." A few more seconds of silence followed, and Valente came back on the radio."Yes. All of LA's fire starters are here and accounted for but you. Get your ass here ASAP. We're in a cabin seven miles off Route 18 and Waterman Canyon. Follow Waterman and the arrowhead on the side of the mountain. We are waiting for you to start phase three."

Lance picked up his radio and called in to Jim. "Jim, I just picked up radio chatter and coordinates for Bolton's third strike team." "Good! Where are you at?" "I'm on Interstate 10 just past the junction of the I-15 and 215 interchanges." "How far are you from the coordinates you intercepted?" "Ten minutes. I'm en route." "Do you know who the leader is?" "I've never heard the name before, but one of Bolton's soldiers called in and spoke to the man in charge. His name is Valente Santiago." There was silence on the other end of the radio. "Jim? You there? Over." "Yea…yea, I'm here. Are you sure you heard that name as the commanding officer?" "Loud and clear. He was pissed off at the caller. He said Bolton had given explicit instructions to maintain radio silence. Do you know this Valente guy?" Sara was back in the room, and she was listening to the conversation. The look on Jim's face said it all. "Yea…I know him very well. I've known him since he was a kid. It doesn't make any sense. I was just talking to him the other night." "Well, I don't know what to tell you, but he's the one running the show in San Bernardino County." "How many men in his unit?" "Well, Valente said that all fire starters from LA County were with him less the caller. Based on the skirmish line fires, I would say there are six to eight men, not including Santiago and the caller." "You're going to need back up." "Who do we have near me that's not engaged with the enemy?" Jim looked at the release chart for all of the men. "I can get you Phillip." "Philly Cheese! Perfect." He gave Jim the coordinates for the location of Bolton's men and told him to have Phil meet him near the entrance to the cabin. Jim radioed Philly and gave him instructions to meet up with Cosmo. Jim sat down for a few seconds then raised Cosmo on the radio. "Lance." "Yea." "I want Valente alive!" "I'll do my best. I don't know what we're going to walk into here. Give me a description." Jim gave him a description of Valente and said, "Look, I know you want to eradicate these guys. We have two of Bolton's units down and one prisoner here at base camp. I want Valente alive, Cos. It's a big deal." "Like I said, Jim, I'll do my best, but I make no promises. I'm not going to get dead trying to save your guy." There was silence on the other end of the line. Cosmo knew he wouldn't speak to Jim again until the mission was done.

Cosmo arrived at the location at ten to seven with Phil right behind him. The two men broke out their assault gear and body armor and moved through the thick forest to the cabin. There were two men stationed outside. "Lookouts? I thought they weren't afraid of being followed or found?" Cosmo just shrugged his shoulders and pointed in the direction to move. When they reached the opposite side of the cabin Phil said, "I will take up the rear of the cabin, and see if I can get a count. You stay here and keep an eye on these two dweebs. If they move in my direction, call out our signal." He fell to the ground and began to crawl on his stomach. Cosmo watched until he disappeared near the rear of the building. The two lookouts just sat at opposite ends of the cabin's entrance looking off into space. "These guys aren't pros that's for damn sure," Cosmo said to himself. A few minutes later Philly came back. "Well?" he asked. Phil pulled out a small camera and showed Cosmo the shots. "Great close-ups. You should be a photographer." "I am smart-ass. That's what I do when I'm not killing people. We have nine men total, seven inside and the two dipshits on the front porch." Cosmo pointed to one of the photos and said, "That guy is Valente Santiago. He's the leader of Bolton's merry band of would-be soldiers. Jim wants him alive." Phil looked at the picture and shrugged, "Okay! So, how do you want to hit them?" He looked at the photos closely. "You go back to the back where you took these shots and wait by this back door. Wait three minutes then break the back door in and throw in a flash grenade. I will take out the two in the front then enter through the main entrance; you enter the rear. We should be able to kill all of them and take Santiago in forty-five seconds." Phil laughed. "I bet I can take my guys and Santiago in thirty seconds." "You're on! The usual wager?" "Of course. See you on the porch in three minutes."

Phil moved back to his position at the rear of the cabin. Cosmo pulled out his nine millimeter with its extra capacity clip and body armor piercing bullets and slowly screwed on the muzzle silencer. He looked at his watch and stood up and started walking toward the cabin. One of the guards spotted him and ordered him to stop. "I don't think so," he said, raising his weapon and dropping the two men before they could say another word. The sound of their bodies hitting the front porch of the cabin coincided with the flash grenade. Phil came in the back door, methodically executing every man in sight. Cosmo entered the front door and took a bullet to the chest but returned fire. It was over in twenty-five seconds. Valente was under the bodies of his men. He was covered in blood and screaming, "Don't kill me; don't kill me." Cosmo grabbed him from the pile and threw him against the wall. Phil made it to the middle of the room, tugging at his body armor. "You okay?" Cosmo asked. "Yea. One of those little fuckers shot me in the chest." "Well, you're still talking, so they weren't using cop killer bullets." "Good thing, man." He looked down at his watch. "Twenty-eight seconds. Pay up!" There was a moan from a corner of the cabin, and Phil shot the man rolling on the floor." "Man!

Clean headshot. You're an animal, but that's thirty-five seconds. You pay up." Valente lied on the floor of the cabin covered in blood, shaking as he saw one man hand the other a dollar bill. "Okay, let's get Mr. Santiago here in your truck."

Phil picked him up and threw him over his shoulder. Valente hung over his shoulder like a sack of potatoes." "Where are you taking me?" he said in a groggy voice. "Our boss wants a few words." They got to the trucks, and Phil tied up Valente and threw him in the back. As he was closing the bed cover Valente asked, "Who's your boss?" The two men laughed. "That's a surprise. I don't want to take that away from you," Phil said, putting a piece of duct tape over Valente's mouth and then hitting him with a tranquilizer dart. "Jim, this is Phil." "Go ahead." "Cosmo and I have taken out Bolton's team here." "And Valente?" "I don't know why you want him. He's a pussy. The best thing for him would have been a bullet to the head, but I have him. He's asleep in the back of my truck." There was a moment's pause and then a quiet and deliberate response from Jim. "Bring him to me!" "You got it; do you want us to do any clean up?" "No...leave 'em to the buzzards." "Roger. We're on our way in."

Cathy didn't know it, but she and her men were all that was left of Bolton's team. It was eight a.m., and she called her troops together for one last briefing before breaking radio silence. What she also didn't know was that Blake Stroud was waiting in the parking lot of the hotel where she was hole up with her crew. Blake and Cathy had a history. They had once been a couple and had worked together for several years. He knew she would be in Riverside County because that was her home county. He also knew where she would hole up, the same place they used to hole up when they were off duty and spending sweaty weekends away from their spouses and work. He checked with the front desk clerk, and she confirmed that Cathy Gutaree was registered in the hotel. He told the clerk he had a special delivery for her and got her room number. She was on the first floor, room 1010. He walked out the front doors of the hotel to his truck and radioed to Jim. "I've got Gutaree and her crew." Jim came back over the radio. "I know you didn't pickup radio chatter on her. Where are you?" "An old hangout of ours in the heart of Riverside." "What the fuck would she be doing there?" "That's a hell of a good question. This was a hangout that she always came to when she was in trouble or needed privacy." There was silence. "You used to fuck her there as I recall!" There was a light but serious laugh. "Yea...that's ancient history." "Blake...you have a lot of history with her. Are you going to be able to pull the trigger?"

There were too many moments of silence for Jim, so he said, "Oh…fuck you. I'm sending in backup. Don't even think of moving until the guys get there." "Who are you sending?" "Cosmo and Philly. They just cleaned up in San Bernardino and have a prisoner, but he's knocked out. I'm routing them to you." Blake cleared his throat, "Thanks, Jim." Rick was standing in the room with Jim listening. Jim handed the radio to him. "You sure you're okay there, bud?" Rick asked. "Yea…I want her alive. We need more on the plot, and she's Bolton's second in command. Jim's worried I won't pull the trigger. I'm worried that I won't stop pulling it." "The guys are en route." There was a pause and Rick said, "Blake…if you have to move before they get there, you have to take her out." There was a moment of silence. "Roger that." "We want Gutaree alive, so let's hope she doesn't make a move before Cosmo and Philly are on scene. They are really, really good at hostage rescues. Tell them to treat it that way."

There were a few moments of silence, and Blake came back, "Yea…okay. Hey, Jim. Have the guys meet me at 6th and Orange Street at the hotel garage." "Roger that, Blake." Jim closed off the radio, and Sara looked at Jim and asked, "What was that all about?" Jim sat down in John's chair at the end of the table and said, "A potential problem, Sara, that's what that is. A real potential problem." "Explain!" He took a cigarette out of his pocket and put it between his teeth, "Can I smoke in here?" "Usually, no, but under the current circumstances, yes!" He pulled out his Zippo and lit the cigarette when his cell phone rang; he looked at the caller ID and smiled. He pressed the answer key and said, "Please tell me you're all right." Sara mouthed, "Barb?" He nodded, and Sara left him alone in the room. "Jim, what the hell is going on? It's hell out here!" "You're not far off. Where are you?" "I'm at the house, but they are telling us to evacuate. I don't know where to go." "Get in your car and get to Topanga Canyon Boulevard. Head west on Topanga and take it through the canyon until you come out at PCH. Turn right on PCH and take it through Malibu. Just before you start into no man's land between Malibu and Oxnard, you will see Sara out on the street. She will wave you in to the compound." "Compound? Where the hell are you?" "Fighting against the people who started this hell. Now get going. I will bring you up to speed when you get here. Drive safe." There was a moment of silence and Jim said, "Barb?" "Yea?" "I love you." She laughed under her breath. "I love you, too, you lughead. Don't worry. I will make it to you. I will see you soon." The line went dead, and Jim knew that the cell towers in the valley were going down. He would not speak to her again until she was with him … if she made it at all.

He called out to Sara. She called back that she heard the conversation and walked back in and said, "We have a few minutes before I go out looking for Barbara. What's the deal with Blake?" He told her the story of Blake and Cathy. He and Cathy had both been in the FBI together after they did their hitches in the military. They had had feelings for each other for many years but never acted on them. They were both married and in ninety-eight they were assigned to a terrorist threat in California. Cathy was from Riverside, and when they weren't working, they struck up an affair to end all affairs, until their spouses found out and dumped them both, taking everything. Jim said, "It turned out that Colleen Bolton and Cathy Gutaree were childhood friends. When things started going south for Bolton, Cathy jumped ship, leaving Blake alone on a stakeout of a terrorist cell that was operating out of San Diego. The FBI had received a tip that there were several foreign nationals attending flight schools in Arizona and San Diego. They also had several credible tips that they were planning to attack the U.S. using civilian airliners. Cathy and Blake were teamed up on the surveillance of eight of the would-be hijackers and were bouncing around the country tracking the plot that would end up being the nine-eleven terrorist attacks. The person the government has convinced the world was responsible for the terrorist attacks isn't who they say it is." "You mean Bin Laden?" Sara asked. "Yea. Long and short was that Cathy bailed on Blake, leaving him open to the real enemy of the state. Blake was captured and tortured until he was located and freed by an elite Marine Corps black ops team."

"That's what John was doing in late ninety-nine and two thousand?" Jim nodded and continued. "Cathy sold Blake out to this mastermind, and Blake wants payback." Sara sat for a long time pondering what Jim had told her then asked, "John's unit was activated, and he ended up missing for several months, so he was in on this?" Jim nodded again and said, "There is a lot of bad blood, not just between Cathy and Blake but between John, the government, and the real mastermind of the nine-eleven attacks. John and his team had the information and ability to stop the whole thing from happening, and...let's just say that certain high up individuals in government stopped a military and federal task force from killing the plot." Sara sat dumbfounded; she had no words. Jim laughed slightly under his breath and said, "This is too big for you to even begin to comprehend, Sara. You just have to trust that John and the men out there still love this country, and they are doing everything in their power to stop what's going on. They can't save everybody, but now that John and his men know who's responsible, heads are rolling and going to continue to roll." He paused and took a drag off his cigarette and said, "I don't think that it's going to end with this small group either. This is a huge conspiracy. It's going to get worse before it gets better. John won't lose this time. He's The Iron Eagle. He will get all those responsible. The newly-elected president learned about it through his own intelligence channels and had Gutaree and Stroud pulled off the case."

He looked at his watch and asked Sara to go out and see if she could flag down Barbara. The radio hissed for a moment and Blake was on. "The men are here. We're moving in." "Roger that. Call when you're done."

Blake, Phil, and Lance had already cased the room. As with the others, Cathy had a suite on a corner of the first floor with an entrance off sixth. "What's our total count?" Blake asked. "You mean terrorists? Eight including Gutaree." He nodded. "You want her alive?" Blake nodded again. "You know that if you take her back to The Eagle, she will be tortured and killed for information?" Phil said to Blake. He nodded. "I can put a bullet in her head, and you don't have to go through all of that." "I want to go through all of that. If the bitch had kept her mouth shut nine-eleven would never have happened, and we could have taken out the terrorist teams without the world having to ever hear the name al-Qaeda." He paused. "Besides, the bitch sold me out." Cosmo laughed. "She's not going to be happy to see you!" Blake smiled. "I know! Let's do this thing." Cosmo and Philly told Blake how they took down Valente and his group; it sounded like a good plan. Blake said, "Philly, you take the inside entrance. We will take the street. Same thing, baby... flash grenade, then kill everyone but Cathy. Time?" Cosmo laughed. "Oh...shit... sixty seconds." Philly laughed and said, "I want my buck back."

All three moved into position. It was over in less than forty-five seconds. To add insult to injury, Cathy was on the toilet when they engaged her team. Blake walked into the bathroom where she was sitting nude on the toilet. "Hello, Cathy!" She frowned. "Hello, Blake. So Colleen's dead!" "Who knows? You might be reunited." He held the muzzle of his gun against her forehead." "I'm a traitor to the nation. I handed the keys to your plan over to the enemy. I handed you over to the enemy, and I'm responsible for the nine-eleven attacks. You have me. What could be more humiliating for me than to have my brains blown out on the toilet?" He laughed. "Having your ass in the hands of The Iron Eagle!" Her face went sheet white as he shot her in the neck with a tranquilizer dart. She was sliding off the toilet onto the floor when she said, "Not The Eagle. Jesus, Blake, do you hate me that much?" The last word she heard before she blacked out was, "Yes!"

CHAPTER SEVEN

*"I don't like the government's history
when it comes to these things, John."*

olleen Bolton sat in front of the monitors unaware that The Iron Eagle was only a few feet away working to break the lock code and enter the facility. "All trucks are in place, Colonel," called her dispatcher. Colleen picked up the radio and said, "Phase two, 'truck stop,' initiate." She had wanted the attacks at six a.m., but it wasn't possible. It was eight a.m. when her orders were carried out. The explosions were perfectly timed. Twenty eighteen-wheeler fuel tanker trucks fully loaded exploded under twenty critical freeway overpasses throughout Los Angeles County simultaneously. The shock wave could be felt as far south as northern Mexico and as far north as Santa Barbara. In Los Angeles, buildings in the vicinity of the blasts had windows blown out, structures collapsed from the sheer power of the explosions. Fourteen of the twenty overpasses that were estimated to take severe fire damage that would weaken them simply disintegrated in the blast, leaving freeways covered in rubble. There were holes where trucks once sat, and fiery fuel rained down on the freeways and adjacent structures. There were no police or fire units to respond. They were all trying to fight the fires that had started on the northern edges of LA County and had grown and consumed every community in the county from Lancaster and Palmdale through the San Fernando Valley and Pasadena and all surrounding areas. What was left of the remaining fire units were now staging from Santa Monica, south to Irvine in Orange County. Everything above the fire line had been or was being consumed by flames. The media was not only overwhelmed, they had lost all of their field reporters. The dead outnumbered the living.

There were millions lost in the havoc and flames, and the fire could be seen clearly from the international space station. The City of Los Angeles would never be the same. Colleen sat laughing hysterically as station after station went off the air; The Eagle made entry but too late to stop the truck bombs. He killed three guards outside the door to her command post and walked in on Colleen in his full armor. She didn't turn around. She just sat there staring at the snowy screens and said, "The Iron Eagle and his team is too late again!" He shot her in the neck with a dart then tied her hands and feet, picked up her body, and threw her in his truck. He radioed to Jim that he had her. "It's a total loss, John," Jim said over the radio. "I got Bolton, but I was too late to stop phase two of her plan. What about Barb? Have you heard from her?" "Ah…yea. She just got here. Sara led her in. What's it like out there, John?"

He looked to the east as he drove PCH from Long Beach back to Malibu. The sky was dark black, and he could see flames in every direction. There wasn't a car on the road, but there were people in the ocean, hundreds of them, some moving some not. There were thousands more on the beaches and smoke was blowing out to sea at a high rate of speed. "It's what I imagine hell looks like, Jim. It's the canto from Dante that Bolton used in her letters. I'm en route. Is everyone back?" "Blake, Philly, and Cosmo have made it out of Riverside. They have Cathy. We also have a surprise guest here, but I will wait for your arrival for you to meet him." "Terrorist?" "Oh, yes, and a surprising one at that." "Did we suffer any casualties?" "No. Everyone is accounted for. We need to interrogate Bolton and Gutaree. I have a feeling that this is only one small part of a hell of a lot larger plot by Bolton." John was speeding down PCH as he spoke, "I guarantee you that this is only the tip of the iceberg. The question is can we get the information out of these people fast enough to stop it? And even if we can, can and will the White House assist in stopping the furtherance of this plot?" "I don't like the government's history when it comes to these things, John." "Yea, neither do I. I'm out." Jim looked over at Sara and said, "He's coming home." She looked at Jim and said, "Home? Home to what?"

John pulled into the underground garage and saw that all vehicles were there. He took Bolton and threw her into one of the observation rooms in the house and went to the command center. "The clock is ticking, gentlemen. I have a feeling that there is a larger group of cells waiting for her instructions, and if they don't hear from her very soon, they will execute on their own." It was nine-thirty, and Bolton and her LA team had successfully pulled off the worst terrorist attack in world history. Jim was staring at several split screen TVs and watching news from other parts of the country and the world. He pointed at a monitor that had Aljazeera America on it. He also was watching a feed from Aljazeera global. "Well, the good news is that no one is taking credit for this attack. Hell, the hebes and camel jockeys are praying to Mecca that whoever did this doesn't do it to them."

"The world is on high alert, guys." John sat down at the table. "Let's worry about our own country right now. What's the status of the fires?" Jim pulled up a statewide screen, and Lance patched them into U.S. central command and NASA. Jim asked, "Has anyone hacked the NSA and the CIA?" "Yea…they had their joke encryption. I broke it ten minutes ago but grabbed a sandwich before bringing it online. Everyone use your laptops and tablets. I did a cross patch, so all agencies can be monitored from one website. Ping 87.212.911.13." They typed in the domain, and all government agencies popped up on their screens. "Who can see this?" asked John. "Just us." "Can it be traced back through any DNS or ISP server?" Lance laughed. "Sure, John. I used Google. No, man. If anyone tries to ping this IP it shows up as: *'IP address: Error: Host not found. Host name: 87.212.911.13 Alias: 87.212.911.13 is from () in region.'* I'm bouncing it off the government's own servers. If they even had the time to try to trace the DNS or ISP, the algorithm I used for the encryption would take them a thousand years to decode. I call it the 'tail chaser.' It's awesome." He said it with a devious and playful laugh. "Okay, so we have it all. The White House, Pentagon, CIA, NSA, FBI, DOJ, DHS, and NORAD. It's like having the federal version of NFL Sunday Ticket," John said. That drew a few laughs.

"Has anyone spoken to Ryan?" John asked. Jim piped up, smoking his cigarette. No one said a word. "He called about an hour ago and said that the president has called for an emergency meeting of both houses; he's also met with the joint chiefs in the SIT room at the White House with the president." "And?" "That's all he told me." John grabbed a satellite phone from the rack of chargers on a credenza in the conference room and called Ryan's secure cell. Ryan answered immediately, and John asked, "Ryan, so what does the government know?" "Not much, John. They are all freaking out. No one knows what to do. There's never been anything like this before." "Well, Ryan, why don't you go tell your boss that he needs to get assets here at once. He needs to get the fires out. The city and county can't be saved. The loss of life is going to be staggering, but there needs to be some sort of effort on the part of government to make it look like they tried." "Is the worst over, or is this just the beginning?" Ryan's voice had desperation in it. "Just the beginning. We have Bolton, Gutaree, Sajahd, and one other… Jim, who's the fourth?" He didn't respond. "We have four of the six leaders." "Have you interrogated them yet?" "Ryan, we've had them together for less than an hour. Don't let the administration or any of its cronies know we have them. I don't know how far up this goes." "Agreed. I will grab a flight out tonight. I will land in Santa Barbara and take a car to your place." "Okay. Call me and let me know when those assets are going to hit the ground here. Based on my observations at this point, it looks like the fires will be out when they hit the ocean." "Yea, we're watching what we can of media coverage of the fires. It's one giant inferno." "You don't have to tell us. We're living it." John went to hang up when he stopped and asked, "Ryan?" "Yea." "Your bosses stopped us on nine-eleven when we had the evidence and the advanced notice to stop the attacks. We didn't get the heads up here that we had in those months leading up to the attacks. While this is worse than that day on a grand scale, we won't be thwarted in trying to root out the rest of the cells to eliminate them. You're going to have to tell your boss he is going to need multiple black op teams to hit hard and fast where we tell you when we tell you. You better start putting them together now, so when we have the information those teams are ready to move to kill this thing." John hung up the cell and called the men together.

"All right. It's time to wake up our guests. Each of you take one of the prisoners and use normal interrogation techniques on them. I will take Bolton." Jim laughed. "Um…John. About that third terrorist." "Yes, Jim. Do I know the third?" He nodded. "Who is it?" "Valente Santiago." John stood dumbfounded. "What the hell?" "I had the same reaction…I have known this guy since he was a kid. I will talk to him and see what I can get from him before I turn him over to you." John nodded. Sara stood up and asked, "What can I do to help. It sounds like we don't have much time. What do you need from me?" John said, "Have a crash cart ready and prep four IV bags." Rick took a bag out of a backpack he had and handed it to Sara. In the bag were numerous vials with small white powder cakes in the bottom. "Sara, this is a very, very rare truth serum. If you would mix eight vials, please. You need 80mg of diluent for each vial. You don't need to shake the cakes; they will dissolve on contact, then fill four syringes with sixty mg of drug using twenty-three gauge needles," Rick asked. Sara started laughing. "Truth serum? You're kidding, right? There's no such thing. What is this? Sodium pentothal?" Rick got a serious expression. "There is such a thing as truth serum, and you're holding it. No, it's not sodium pentothal. It's a drug called SP-117. It was developed by our friends in the former Soviet Union during the cold war and used widely by the KGB. The CIA got a sample of it in the late 1950s and made some modifications to the drug, and it's perfect. It's odorless, colorless, and tasteless. It can be administered orally or by IM or IV delivery. The best part of using this drug is after it wears off the victim has no idea that he ever had a conversation about anything."

Jim grunted at Rick, then addressed Sara, "Cloak and dagger, Ricky. I'm too old for cloak and dagger. Sara, the drug is real, it works, and we need it mixed ASAP." She looked at John, who just nodded his head.

She took the vials and mixed them as directed. When she was done, she brought them back on a tray and placed them on the conference table. "How stable is the drug?" she asked. John responded, "Very, and it has an indefinite shelf life." "How are you going to get it into these people?" Phil spoke up. "That's a hell of a good question. How are we going to do it, Mr. Eagle? If they see it coming, they're going to fight it, and I know that Colleen has been through the ringer with this to build up a tolerance." Sara got a strange look on her face. John answered before she could ask. "When we were going through training, one of the things that the government did was use these drugs on us on a daily basis in higher and higher doses in the hopes of building up immunity or at least a high tolerance to it." "Did it work?" "That depends." "On what?" "Which drug was used on you to build the tolerance or immunity. All of the people we're holding would have been exposed to the CIA and KGB versions of the drug." Sara smiled and asked, "Let me guess. You guys have your own version." Lance and Phil smiled. John pointed to the two men. "They are both pharmacists and chemists ... they were able to make a few tweaks that, so far, no one can resist." "And do these people know about your 'tweaked drug?'" Sara asked. John smiled and shook his head. He took a syringe as did the others, and they left the room.

Bolton was still out when The Eagle came into the room. He restrained her to a gurney and gave her the injection. The prick of the needle roused her, and he put it down on a steel tray next to the gurney. "Ah…SP-117. You guys never give up." He offered her water, which she was grateful for. She took a sip and said, "Thank you, John…I tried to get to you before I made the move." He nodded. "After the events of nine-eleven, your government killing your team's ability to stop the attacks, and literally killing one of your teams, you still want to defend this joke of a nation?" "I swore an oath, Colleen, as did you." "Oh, kiss my ass. I really do mean it; if you want my ass, you can have it. The government made us swear an oath that they broke before they ever took it." "So, you decide to single-handedly start a revolution?" "I see you read the notes, and you're just now getting it." "I didn't see all of your notes together until it was too late." "I thought something was wrong. You never made a move. I was sure you would make a move. Now I know why you didn't. Well, you can't stop this one. It's already in motion, and there's nothing you can do to stop it."

Her speech was starting to slur, and she recognized that something was wrong. "You didn't inject me with SP-117?" "No, Colleen. I gave you a hybrid of the drug in the water you just drank." "Fuck...I won't talk, John!" "Yes, you will, Colleen, so let's get started. How many cells do you have awaiting orders and where are they?" She didn't respond, and he grabbed a sealed bottle of water off the counter, opened it so she could hear the seal crack, and he took a drink." She licked her lips. "Would you like more water?" She nodded, and he put the bottle to her lips, and she drank down the liquid quickly. "You're thirsty?" She nodded. "So, you want to answer my question?" She shook her head. "Either way you're going to kill me, John. I know that, and you know that. I would rather die knowing I took a few million others with me." He took a swig off the bottle that she had drunk from and said, "You would make my life and your death a lot less painful if you just answered my questions now." "Yes, I would, but you know that I'm not going to do that. So, what's it going to be, Iron Eagle? I never got the nickname, John. Your team's whole profile is 'to keep a low profile,' and you're a famous vigilante serial killer." "That was not, and is not, the objective of my mission in private life. But we're not here to talk about me. Where are the cells?" "You know, John, I always admired you. The government shit all over you, a billionaire hospital mogul rapes and murders your beautiful wife, and you keep on plugging along under the yoke and whip of your federal master." The Eagle didn't react. "Oh, come on. The fact that I know who killed your wife doesn't surprise you?" He sighed. "Colleen, there is nothing about you or your knowledge that would surprise me. Now, I ask again. Where are the cells?" She started talking about the weather, the fires, the truck bombs, the perfect execution of her terrorist plot. She wasn't responding to the drug, which was quite a surprise to him.

He picked up a razor knife from the table next to Bolton and walked down to her feet. She was wearing a skirt and a light blouse, hardly what one would expect from an ex-military leader. He slid the blade out as she kept talking and cut her clothing from her body. She had no bra or panties. She was ready for action. "I see that you were planning to play," he said, "Well, shit, John. Fuck me. You know you want to. I can destroy a nation and get laid at the same time. You know I want it, and I know you want to. Give it to me." He put the knife back on the table and said, "You are right, Colleen. I do want to give it to you, and I'm going to." He took out a pair of copper nipple clamps and clipped them onto her breasts. She cringed a little then smiled and said, "I love it rough and dirty." He smiled. "I know you do, but I also know the things that you're afraid of, Colleen." He spoke as he moved down her thighs to her feet. He pulled out a pair of jumper cables and crimped her feet with them and hooked the other end of the cables to two leads coming out of the floor. She kept chatting, though more animated, with a quiver of nervousness in her voice. He paid no attention and grabbed her right breast and attached an electrode to the copper clamp, followed by the left. He plugged the cables into the electric panel in the wall with the ankle electrodes and smiled at her. "So, are we going to have a shocking time?" she asked, wincing when she tried to move her ankles. He didn't respond. He grabbed a bottle of conducting gel from the table next to her and squeezed the thick, clear, cold liquid onto her breasts and ankles.

"I think you're losing your torture touch, John. You're supposed to put that on before you put on the electrodes." He took out a copper plate and lifted her from the middle and placed it under her back just above her ass. The copper rolled like a belt over her mid section, and he clamped it down and put gel on the outer edges. "You're doing it wrong, John." "Not really, Colleen. I'm looking to do some serious skin damage. When I flip the switch, I will have 220 volts of electricity available to use on you." He held up a small white remote with a dial on it. "The great thing about this device is I control the current. I can make it gentle and tingly to get your orgasmic regions flowing, or raise it slowly and carefully, burning away your skin while watching you convulse from the increasing current. No, I'm not going to waste my time asking about your other terrorist cells. I'm going to give you a little taste of my new toy, then we'll talk again." She lied still. He walked out of sight and came back with a five gallon bucket in his hand. "Oh, I forgot to mention it. I've gotten really, really good at this stuff." The bucket contained ice water, and he poured it over her body then turned the dial on the remote and watched her body twitch and fight against the current running through her flesh. She convulsed as he turned the dial down.

"I have to admit, Colleen, you have a really, really hot body. I do mean that literally and figuratively." She was still shaking from the electricity that had been coursing through her body. "Your ankles! I'm amazed. I've used this on a lot of people, Colleen, but you're the first one whose skin started to burn with the first low volt of current. You're going to have nasty scars on your breasts and ankles." "Fuck you!" came her response. "Okay, let's give it another shot. Let's make those perky double Ds look like boiled chicken." He poured more water over her and watched as he ran a higher voltage of electricity through her body. She convulsed and screamed with the pain of the increasing voltage. The Eagle took another pair of copper clips, spread her legs, and clamped one on each side of her labia. She got aroused and started squirming with excitement. "Now, that's what I've been waiting for." She smiled. He turned the remote, and the smile left her face as the current passed through her body. "The vagina is very, very wet. It makes its own lubricant, and the best part is if it gets dry I just give you a little extra JOLT, and you'll piss yourself." The back and forth went on for over an hour when Colleen started to break. "Okay, okay. Please, no more. I'll never have sex again. You're turning me into hamburger." She laughed, and The Eagle asked, "Where are the other cells?" She got her composure and asked for water. He gave it to her, and within minutes, her speech was clear as was her mind. She looked John in the eye and said, "There is no grand plot, Iron Fucking Eagle. You're looking at it. You killed my men. They were it. All I wanted was to pay back the government for what they did to me." "So, the fires and the truck bombs were just you and your people, and then you were going to finish off the rest of the infrastructure, water, gas, electric, phone, etc.?" She nodded. "Who are you working with, Colonel. I'm not buying it." There were a few too many moments of silence, and The Eagle poured more ice water over her nude and burned flesh, and she screamed in agony. "I gave you what you want. No more, please, no more!" He grabbed a collar from the wall and placed it around her neck, strapping it to the table over her throat. "I'll be back to discuss some other things, Colonel. Just relax." "I'm freezing…at least give me something warm." He held up the white remote. "No…no…no." He hit her with a straight high shock that knocked her out. He checked her for a pulse, and she had a good strong one. When he exited the room, he asked Sara to check on Bolton's vitals. She nodded and went in to check on her.

John returned to the room with the other men and handed Rick a midi recorder with Bolton's confession. He played it for the room, and each of the men listened intently. "Jesus, John. She's working for someone else. This is a distraction she has put into motion for something even bigger," Lance said. Rick looked around the room and asked, "How are you going to get the rest out of her? She is resisting the truth cocktail." They all looked at the clock; it was two p.m. Jim asked, "When will Ryan be on the ground in LA?" John told him not until after eight. "Something smells fishy here, guys. Ryan bugs out when he knows that we are dealing with a terrorist threat, and he hasn't gotten back to us with the government's countermeasure?" Jim said with a sinister voice. John looked on at the men in the room and said, "I need to have another conversation with Colonel Bolton." He walked out of the room and went back to Bolton. She was sweating and swearing as he held the remote in his hand. "Colonel, you look like you could use a drink." "I'll take a beer if you have one." He shook his head. She looked at him with both terror and rage in her eyes. "You're going to kill me, so just get it done." The Eagle walked past her gurney to a large object covered by a tarp. She followed him with her eyes and saw him looking at the tarp with his hand on his face in deep thought. "Colonel, I am going to kill you; you deserve that, but you know that I can't do that until I know what you know. How about I make you a deal. You tell me the name, rank, and serial number of your commanding officer and the details of this whole plot, and I will kill you quick." She was staring at the tarp in the corner of the room as The Eagle turned to face her. She said in a nervous voice, "It's Operation Nero, and you already know who is spearheading it." She could see it on The Eagle's face. It was as if a light came on. He walked out of the room telling Bolton only that he would return. When he got back to the men, he took a satellite phone and said, "I'm calling Ryan. I'm going to bait him with an outlandish story. Bolton claims that I know who their leader is. Let's hope I'm not right."

CHAPTER EIGHT

*"She wanted to get back at the men and
women who hurt and dishonored her."*

Ryan was sitting in a meeting when his cell rang. He took the call in an outer room; it was John. "Ryan, we have Bolton and three of her other lieutenants." "How big is this thing?" he asked nervously. "Huge. I've dispatched C4 to San Francisco to terminate one of her next sleeper cells, but they are all across the country in every major city, and they aren't going to be sleeping for very long." "What do you want from me?" "You have to get the president to order units to the locations of the other cells, or the blood bath that has taken LA by storm is going to start taking the country." "Do you have coordinates on the cells?" "Yes." "How many are we talking about?" "A thousand men spread out over the contiguous U.S. as well as Alaska and Hawaii." Ryan's shoulders slumped. "Oh my God!" "When C4 takes out Frisco, we have twenty hours before a chain reaction starts. The only person who can stop them is Bolton, and I don't see that happening." "Email me the information. I will present it to the president." "Where's Steve, Ryan?" There was a hush. "He's here." "Here as in at the White House with you?" "Yes." "You need to impress upon our political leaders that this is not a game. Los Angeles is merely the starting point of something bigger than anything you or they can ever imagine. The U.S. government trained us; you now have a divided military. I'm not ruling out the possibility that Bolton might have sympathizers in uniform with their hands on tactical and conventional weapons and the ability and clearances to use them."

"Are you telling me that all of this might be but a distraction for a military coup?" "Yes." "How the hell do we stop that?" Ryan asked. John was silent for several minutes. "John? John, are you there?" "Yea…I'm here." "Well?" "If this is the run up to a coup by the military, then there is someone waiting in the wings to take the helm of a new America. We need to find that person and remove his head. I can tell you right now it's not Bolton." "Do you think she knows who it is?" "No!" "Seriously!? She's running this terror plot against America, and she doesn't know who the leader of the coup is?" "That's right…I gave her the truth cocktail, and she claims that she didn't start this as a coup. She started it to teach the government a lesson. She wanted to get back at the men and women who hurt and dishonored her." "By killing millions of civilians?" "She's really twisted, Ryan. I mean really, really twisted." There was a sudden pause on John's end of the line. He got a thoughtful look on his face looking down at the phone in his hand.

"What time are you landing in Santa Barbara?" "What?" "You're flying in tonight to Santa Barbara, right?" "Yes. Why?" "Do you need me to send a car?" "No. I have a car waiting at the airport. I will drive down. Are the roads passable to get to you?" "Yes…the fire rages on in LA and Orange Counties. Our place is off the grid; we are self-sustained, so you can get here." "How are you going to find this mysterious leader of this coup?" Ryan asked. "You let me worry about that. Talk to the president. Let me know what he says about putting boots on the ground to stop the escalation. Once you have his attention, you can conference us in, and I can give the commanders in the SIT room the coordinates for the other cells based on what Bolton has told me." "Will do. I'll call you as soon as I have spoken to the president." "Yes, sir."

John hung up and called Steve Hoffman's office. "Hoffman" came the voice on the other end of the line. "I don't suppose that you have your office phone forwarded to your cell?" "John? Are you okay? What the hell's going on out there?" "You probably know more than me, Steve; we don't have a lot of media coverage. Right now, the city's on fire. How's the conversation going with you and Ryan and the president about getting boots on the ground for the terrorist plot we just uncovered?" "Huh?" "You haven't even spoken to Ryan today have you?" "Why would I speak to Ryan?" "Tell me what you know about what's happening here in LA." "Not much. They're calling it terrorism. The media is stating that the fires were started by an unidentified group out there." "What are the president and the joint chiefs saying?" "Um…I got a call first thing this morning when the fires started, asking for any and all information the FBI has on terror groups under investigation in Los Angeles and the surrounding areas. The same orders went to the rest of the intelligence community." "Anything else?" John asked. "The president is going to address the nation tonight at six p.m. eastern time on the disaster. He's dispatched both full military and National Guard resources to assist in the firefight; he's saying he will do whatever it takes to bring those responsible to justice." "I need to speak to the president!" "What?" "There isn't a lot of time, Steve. You have to get me on the line with the president NOW!" "What the hell is going on?" "I will explain it only to the president. Get me connected to him, Steve. The future of this nation depends on it." "I don't have a direct line to the president, John. For that one, you should call Ryan." That response was met with silence.

"Steve, can you make contact with the president on your own?" "I'm an advisor. I can't just call the Oval Office and ask his secretary to put me through." "You didn't answer the question. Can you get to the president?" "Yes, but given the scope of the day's events, it's going to be difficult." "Have you had any interaction with Carl Daly, the president's chief of staff?" "Um…yea. I have met with him a few times, but for the most part President Hernandez wants direct contact with me. Why? Do you know Carl Daly?" John held the phone close to his ear; those in the room were only getting one side of the conversation. "Yea," John responded. "So, why don't you just give him a call?" Steve asked. "It's a long story, one too long to tell right now. You need to contact the president. When you speak to him, tell him 'Rome is Burning.'" The faces in the room sank when they heard those words come out of John's mouth. "What the fuck does that mean?" "He'll understand." "Then what?" "That's all you need to do. He'll take it from there." There were a few moments of silence, and Steve finally agreed to contact the president.

John was about to hang up when Steve said, "The person who can get to the president faster than any of us is Ryan. I'll call him and have him pass on the message." "NO!" John yelled into the phone. Everyone in the room knew what was happening except Jim. John had forgotten for a few seconds that his unit was sitting with him. "Whatever you do, Steve, DO NOT CALL RYAN!" "Why the fuck not?" "Just do what I've asked. Don't say a word to Ryan. He's coming out to see me later this evening." "Okay, okay, shit, John, I feel like I work for you." "Steve, right now you do. You will understand the whole thing very soon. Please make the call to the president, and call me when you have spoken to him. DO NOT GIVE THE MESSAGE TO ANYONE. YOU MUST SPEAK DIRECTLY TO THE PRESIDENT! Are we clear?" "Yea. You don't have to yell. I'm not fuckin' deaf." "Call me when you have passed my message on to the president." "Will do." As soon as John hung up, he looked around the room at the faces of the men. Ricky spoke up, "You can't be serious. You're really calling out 'Rome is Burning?'" "I never in my life thought that I would, but yes, gentlemen, 'Rome is Burning.' We need to get to Jouqhin Ranch off of Browns Canyon Road in Chatsworth, Michael D. Antonovich Regional Park." There was some murmuring, and Jim spoke up. "You want us to go to a park in the Chatsworth hills above my old office? What the hell for?" "Blake, you want to field this?" Blake stood up and started talking.

"Antonovich was part of a Nike missile range that the government set up in the 1950s. In all, there are twenty-two underground missile silos between Oat Mountain and Rocky Peak. In 1986, the silos were said to have been abandoned, and the ICBMs inside removed due to an automation project started by the administration. The automation occurred due to a failure of launch command to launch their nuke after NORAD called the code in October 1986. The men were removed and replaced with computer operated systems." Jim started laughing. "That was a fuckin' movie!" Blake looked at Jim with dead eyes, "This was no fucking movie, so listen and listen good." Jim stopped smiling.

"After NORAD pulled the plug on manned silos, they decided they needed to drive the silos into secrecy. The cold war was at its peak, and the silos were vulnerable to attack in a first strike scenario. The decision was made through the Pentagon to start a propaganda campaign using state and local media to announce the closure of the Titan bases and the abandonment of the silos. The Pentagon had nicknamed the San Fernando Valley 'the ring of fire' because the silos ran all around the local mountain ranges, and nukes could be deployed quickly to strike the eastern or western hemisphere. What the world and the people didn't know is that the Pentagon and the next four presidential administrations worked in secret to reinstall and secure the silos. They did get rid of the Titan missiles because they were obsolete and not as accurate as the military thought. They were replaced and have been upgraded several times. The most current missiles used in the silos are the LGM-30G Minuteman III intercontinental ballistic missiles. These missiles have a longer range, better reentry from low earth orbit, and can carry three war heads from three hundred kilotons and up. They are also remotely guided, which makes them extremely accurate, and the missiles can be launched in a matter of minutes – under three as opposed to the old Titans which could take up to an hour to prep and fire."

Jim interrupted, "Okay. Thanks for the history and national defense class, but what the hell does this have to do with what's going on and this whole 'Rome's Burning' shit?" John responded. "Jim, what we're discussing here is so highly classified that we could all be killed for treason. The term 'Rome is Burning' was coined in the early 90s when a military commander who shall remain nameless lost it and, with the help of several computer hackers, was able to gain access to the keycodes for three rockets armed with warheads and tried to issue a strike order. He was thwarted by an elite team of Marine special forces fighters who nicknamed the mission 'Rome is Burning.' Since then, when there has been a nuclear breach, the term is used." "I don't understand. The only person who has the missile launch codes is the president. You know, he has that guy who has the football or something like that," Jim said. There was laughter all around the table. John spoke up. "You watch way too much television. The president does not have the launch codes; no one has the codes per se. The launch codes today are encrypted cyber files that are kept on ten laptops around the world. It is true that the president has case number one, or the 'football' as you call it. However, there are other commanders in the field, either on land or sea, who have the same case. Their access to the case and codes is supposed to be restricted by executive order. The government has spent billions on technology to encrypt the data, so that no one can access and launch any missiles without the order from the commander and chief. All that changed in 2001 after the nine-eleven attacks.

"The Pentagon, the joint chiefs, and the president realized that the codes were not safe with the 'football' guy. He could be kidnapped or killed. Any number of things could take place. So, in o-one, in the brilliant minds of our commander and chief and his idiot advisors, everything went cyber. The codes went into what has become known as 'the cloud.'" Jim's mouth fell open. "Are you telling me that the launch codes for every nuclear missile in the United States is in cyberspace?" The faces around the table were grim. "Yes. Bolton wasn't after the codes; she was a disgruntled employee who is very, very effective at her duties. She is working for someone else who has or is going to hack those codes using what Bolton has done as cover to access the cloud and the codes, and the most effective way to do that is to do it from Los Angeles and west coast operations, which means that we have to get to the command center before they do."

Jim sat silent. It was Barbara who was sitting in a chair next to him who, with a doe-eyed haze, said, "So, there is a mad person out there, who, after this psycho woman and her people burned down and destroyed the City of Los Angeles and killed possibly millions of men, women, and children, is going to exploit our weakness and access these unknown bases in order to take over the country?" John put his finger on his nose. "Sara, we need to sedate our guests while we travel." "How long do you want them out?" "Twenty-four." "She walked out of the room as the men began to pack up gear in duffle bags. Jim sat in his chair looking at the action. "I don't have gear or a duffle bag. I don't know what use I'm going to be to you." John laughed and said, "You are going to be of great use to us; you're going to be bait!" Barbara spoke out at John in anger, "The hell he is. He's been through enough. We're going home." There was a pause. No one said a word. John went to speak, but Jim interrupted him. "There is no home, Barb. It's gone, and if I don't do this, this motherfucker could change our lives even more. I have to do everything I can to stop this, even if it means dying."

John called out the time. Five p.m. "Lance, call the air base at Point Mugu. Give them our clearance code, and tell them we're going ancient. We need a C-119." "The flying boxcar?" "Yes. We're going to have to parachute in and take the station under cover of night. We have to drop in before our guests arrive." The men all shook their heads. Ricky and Philly said it together, "So, we get to drop in from the flying coffin? Thanks John!" "Load our gear, Blake. Lance and Jim follow me to the armory." "You've got a fuckin' armory?" Jim asked with a bewildered look on his face. John just nodded his head as the men went with him to gather weapons and artillery. He pressed his hand against a glass screen on a steel door then placed his eye over the scanner, and the lock clicked. He opened the armory, and every one of the men was impressed. "What the hell, John? Did you knock off Fort Campbell?" Blake asked. "Yea…let's pull the mechanics list. We'll need all of it," John said as they pulled and loaded all of their gear and weapons into two trucks in under fifteen minutes. He kissed Sara; she kissed him back but didn't say anything. Barbara kissed Jim and hugged him and looked at John and said, "I want my husband back alive." "I'll do my best, Barbara." "Do better than your best. We just got each other back. I'll be goddamned if I'm going to start over and try to break in a new model." It was nervous levity to break the moment, and in a matter of seconds Sara and Barbara were standing alone in what had now become affectionately known as the war room. Sara looked at Barbara and asked, "Would you like some tea?" Barbara shook her head. "I want a bottle of scotch!" "I can accommodate that. Follow me." They left the room, knowing that there was nothing left for them to do but wait for whatever was to come next.

CHAPTER NINE

"He knows what you're going to ask of him.
He also knows he won't be coming home!"

Steve had calls into every staffer of President Hernandez that he could find, but the president wasn't taking calls. He grabbed his coat and jumped in his car at Quantico and decided the best thing he could do was make a run for the White House; he knew he could get in, but he didn't know if he could get to the president with John's instructions. He jumped onto Interstate 95 north headed for Washington. He merged off the 95 onto George Washington Parkway and crossed into D.C. by way of the Arlington Bridge, passing the Lincoln Memorial on his left as he headed down Constitution Avenue. Traffic was unusually heavy for eight-thirty in the evening, so he cut up 17th Street north until he got to the Eisenhower National Office Building next door to the White House and parked. He ran through the grounds to one of several Pennsylvania Avenue entrances. He scanned his credentials and was buzzed through and onto the grounds. When he finally made it to the entrance to the West Wing, he was out of breath and dragging his ass through the doors. Secret Service okayed him, and he was given the highest level security ID, which he flung over his neck as he made his way to Daly's office.

Carl Daly was wrapping up a meeting with his staff when his secretary buzzed him to let him know that Special Agent Hoffman needed to see him. Daly was a young oafish guy and how he ever became Hernandez's Chief of Staff baffled even the best political minds. Squat heavy with a significant beer belly and standing a mere five feet six inches, he was clearly obese by any medical standard. His blond hair was dirty, and his clothes looked like he had not had a change in days. At forty four, he was a walking talking mess, and Steve had to somehow convince this moron that he needed time with the president, that it was a national crisis. "Mr. Daly will see you now, Special Agent Hoffman," his secretary said with a smile. He walked into Daly's office. Daly was sitting behind his desk with a burger in one hand and a brief in the other. "What's the crisis, Hoffman? You've left messages with everyone but the Pope…" He looked at Steve, his coat over his arm, and sweat under his arm pits. "Shit, man, have you been working out?" He laughed. Steve shrugged. "I need to see the president!" Daly put the burger on his desk and called out for his secretary. "Marsha…Agent Hoffman needs to see the president. Can we just barge into the Oval and holler at him?" There was no response. "Well, there you have it, Hoffman. I guess we can't do that. If you have a message for him, leave it with me, and I will see that he gets it." Steve was getting pissed, and Daly could see it in his face. "Look here, you little shit, I don't give a goddamn if you're the chief of staff to the president, you show me some goddamn respect, or I'll kick your ass all over this office." Daly shrugged his shoulders and picked up his burger. "I'm going to let that slide. I'm guessing you're emotional because all your shit probably burned up in LA." "Is this some kind of fucking joke to you? Are you really as stupid as people say? Based on our conversation thus far, I put your IQ at twenty points below dull normal. People are dead and dying, and we don't know if the worst is over, or if this is just the beginning. And you sit there with your fat ass in a chair eating a fuckin' hamburger and belittle me? I am a special advisor to President Hernandez for the FBI. He appointed me to that position, and I need to see him relative to the events of today in Los Angeles. Now, get off your fat ass and get me in to see him. I need only say three words to him, and I'm gone."

Daly ignored Steve's words and went back to his brief and called out to his secretary, "Marsha, Special Agent Hoffman is leaving my office now. See him to the Roosevelt Room; he can wait there until the president has time for him." Marsha came to the doorway. Steve started to walk out. He turned to Daly, who was ignoring him, eating his burger and pretending to read his brief. Steve said, "If the nightmare I perceive that I have been sent here to talk to the president about comes to pass, it's squarely on your head, and I will be the first one to call the DOJ and have the U.S. attorney seat a grand jury to make sure you're indicted and held accountable for your reckless actions here tonight." "Yea, yea. Get the hell out my office, Hoffman, before I have the Secret Service revoke your credentials, and I tell the president that you're an insubordinate son of a bitch." He followed Marsha to the Roosevelt Room. He went in to sit down and Marsha asked, "Is there anything I can get you while you wait, Agent Hoffman?" "Yea…a direct line to the president." She had a half-hearted smile on her face as she closed the doors behind her.

Ryan called for John. The call rang through to his cell as the men headed up PCH for Point Mugu Naval Base. "Swenson." "John, it's Ryan. I'm at Reagan National en route back to Santa Barbara. I will meet up with you and the men at your home." "Okay, sir. We will be waiting for you." The line went dead, and John called out over the radio to his men that Skillen was on the move.

Ryan Skillen wasn't at Reagan National; he was at Dulles Air Force Base in Virginia. When he arrived on base, he was taken to a secure location and met up with his men. He walked in in full uniform and said, "This is a black op mission, men. If you are captured or killed, no one will know about it, and no one will care. You will get no sympathy from me. I will curse your name and piss on your grave. We are in the throes of a revolution, and we are the revolutionaries who will bring about that change through the use of merciless brute force. You will kill deliberately and cruelly. No man not under my command is to be alive after we access the base at Oat Mountain. Once we have taken control and secured the complex, we will be in control of twenty-two LGM-30G Minuteman III intercontinental ballistic missiles, and make no mistake, gentlemen, we will use them if necessary on targets foreign and domestic. By this time tomorrow, I will be the supreme commander of what was the United States, and you will be my cabinet. We will take control of the military; the rest of the government will fall like dominos. On my signal, Operation Nero begins." Thirty men stood side by side in camouflage gear, faceless in hooded masks, M16s slung over their shoulders, standing at full attention. "If you want out, now is the time to speak." A hand went up at the far end of the room. "Speak, soldier," Ryan yelled. "Sir, I don't see how twenty-two missiles are going to bring the United States to its knees." "Are you doubting the success of the mission?" "Sir! I'm just using logic, sir! What about their countermeasure?" Ryan began to walk the line between the men, heading toward the speaker. "Operation Nero has no countermeasure, soldier. We created it." "No, sir, that's not correct, sir!" Ryan spoke as he walked, "Explain, soldier."

"Operation Nero was created during the cold war, sir. It was intended as a measure to ensure that if any of our weapons of mass destruction fell into enemy hands, foreign or domestic, the traitors would be called out to black ops special units as insurgents or Operation Nero, sir!" Ryan stopped in front of the soldier who had been speaking. "That means nothing, soldier. No one knows that we are embarking on this mission. By the time they know we have the base and the missiles under our control, any countermeasure will be rendered useless, and the government will fall." Ryan put his hand on the nickel plated forty-five on his hip and pulled it from the holster and started speaking, "If there is a countermeasure to Operation Nero, if called out prior to our completing the mission, we will meet with disaster." A shot rang out in the room as the soldier's body hit the floor. "Anyone else have reservations about our mission?" "SIR, NO, SIR!" was the response in unison from the other soldiers. "Good. Operation Nero is now underway. We have a C-130J Hercules on the tarmac; let's roll."

The men all picked up their gear and headed out of the building to the tarmac and loaded into the back of the plane. Once inside and airborne, Ryan called out the orders to the men. "We have a five hour flight, gentlemen, so relax and enjoy it. I don't expect to meet any resistance when we drop onto the base." The men sat in their jump seats conversing, while Ryan and two others sat behind the cockpit, preparing their strategy for an America post Operation Nero. "So, what's it going to be, Ryan?" "What's what going to be?" "Your title, man. King, Grand Master, Grand Poobah." There was laughter. "I think supreme commander will be enough. As soon as we take power, we will order marshal law and then burn the flag and the Constitution on the steps of the capitol for all the world to see. We have already had the new flag of the Socialist States of America designed, and we have a box with us on the plane." "Socialist States, really?" came the response from one of his commanders. "You're not a Socialist; you're a dictator, man. We should call the new nation The People's Republic of America."

Ryan smiled. "Oh…that has a great ring to it. We could sell the shit out of that on the propaganda machine," said one of his commanders. "Yea, we sell the people on the fact they are one people with one voice. They don't need the dictatorship of Washington bureaucrats digging into their lives. We're the liberators. We have risen to power, so that the people's supreme leader, Ryan Skillen, can lead the new republic of the people for the people to prosperity and strength." The speaker with the idea was Johnston Bushnell, a Harvard Law School graduate and constitutional scholar, who had been elected to the Senate at the same time that Ryan was. "You're now the assistant to the supreme commander, Johnston. You have a hell of a good idea there. When the coup is over, we will execute all of the government leaders on national TV. We'll start with Hernandez and work our way through the executive branch, all the way to the courts. We will have three channels dedicated 24/7 to the executions until the last of the old government is dead, and we will raise a new government that the people will love … well … will grow to love … after we take all their shit!" There was laughter all around as the plane flew on its westerly course to its target in the Santa Susana Mountains.

John and his men were greeted at the main gate of the naval air station by Colonel Roy Belker. The men gathered inside the gates at attention as he called out for them to be at ease. "What do we have here, John?" Roy and John ate a lot of the same dirt in many covert black operations including the government's nine-eleven scrub of their mission to stop the hijackers. Of all the men he knew, John knew that Colonel Belker was loyal to the United States and to protecting its citizens. "'Rome is Burning,' Colonel." He walked the men to the C-119 that was already running on the tarmac, ready to take the men in. "I see. So, Nero is en route?" "Yes, sir!" "I'm really, really thin on men and resources, John. I have all my resources deployed in LA and Orange County fighting the fires." "I understand, sir, that's why I asked for the old timer C-119." Belker laughed. "Yea. We had to really scrape the mothballs off of this one. It hasn't seen the sky in several decades. Is this all the men you have to take and hold Oat Mountain and Rocky Peak?" John nodded. "Well, at least you have the best of the best. I know every one of these men; they are a hell of a formidable force. They live up to the nickname 'devil dogs.'" He looked around and saw Jim. "Who's that?" Belker asked, pointing at Jim. "That's LA County Sheriff James O'Brian, sir." He started laughing. "No shit. O'Brian is going out there, huh?" "Yes, sir." "I didn't recognize him. I haven't seen him since we were buck privates when we entered the Corps."

John waved to Jim to come over to where they were standing. The roar of the propellers on the plane made it hard to hear. Jim recognized Roy immediately and started laughing his ass off. "They made you a full bird colonel?" "The people of Los Angeles were stupid enough to elect you Sheriff?" John thought there was about to be a fight when Jim reached out and hugged Roy. "How the fuck have you been, man? The last time I saw you we were face down in a rice paddy in Cambodia running for our lives from the Viet Cong." "Well, you got your ass out of there. I wasn't so lucky." "No shit…Roy, I'm sorry. I had no idea. I thought you got picked up at one of the extraction points." Belker laughed. "It wasn't your fault, Jim. You look good, so I'm guessing that John here is going to be using you for something other than military service?" "He says I'm bait!" Belker looked at John with a strange look on his face. Jim caught it but nothing more was said. "Well, you men get moving. I have the coordinates you left, and I will send in my black ops unit to back you up as soon as I have them here. They're on another mission right now, but it was successful, and they are en route to base." John handed Belker a piece of paper and a flash drive with the coordinates on it as well as silo contents and the cargo each missile carried. "It's encrypted. The information is on the paper. This has to be surgical, Roy. Don't release the dogs until you get a code green from me or my men." He looked at the men and said, "'Rome is Burning,' gentlemen. Go put it out, you devil dogs, Godspeed."

They all saluted and ran for the plane. Jim followed, and Roy grabbed John's arm and asked, "Bait? You really told him you're using him as bait?" "His wife was standing there. I couldn't tell her that he's going to be the target." "Does he know?" John shook his head. "I haven't told him yet." Roy watched as Jim threw some gear on the plane and looked back at him. He could see it in Jim's eyes. Roy looked at John and said, "He knows what you're going to ask of him. He also knows he won't be coming home!" John saluted Roy and said, "I've got to get going, sir. I made a promise to Jim's wife that I intend to keep. Jim will be coming home, even if that means I don't." Belker saluted John and said, "Who's running Operation Nero?" "Ryan Skillen." Belker got a serious look on his face. "Of all the people to pull this. Does that fucker know about Operation 'Rome is Burning?'" "I don't think so, sir. I believe he thinks that there's no countermeasure." "Well, let's hope you're right because the only way you're going to stop that fucker is to be ahead of him and kill every man he has with extreme prejudice." "We plan on leaving a lot of corpses on Oat Mountain, sir, and an America still intact." "Does the president know?" "I don't know, sir. I was unable to reach him. My commanding officer at the FBI, Steve Hoffman, is trying to get the message to the president as we speak, sir." "Get going. I will make some calls. I'll get the message to the president." "Thank you, sir," and with that John disappeared into the aircraft as it taxied down the runway for the short flight to Oat Mountain.

CHAPTER TEN

"... and with all due respect, sir, shit explodes when you're in battle..."

Steve sat in the Roosevelt Room at the White House trying to figure out how to get the message to the president. Marsha came into the room and said, "Agent Hoffman, you have a call on line two." He walked over and picked up the line. "Hoffman." "Special Agent Steve Hoffman?" "That's correct." "I understand that you have a message for the president." He drew back before he spoke, "Yes, and...?" "And you're getting stonewalled by that nimrod that Hernandez calls a chief of staff." "Yea." "The president is going to give a briefing in the press room there in the West Wing in five minutes. Get to the room any way you can, interrupt, and just say the three words you were told to say. You will be ushered from the room, and then you will have the president's full attention." "Who is this?" "A friend of a friend. Do as I say." "Okay." The line went dead. Steve called Marsha and asked where the bathroom was, and she showed him to the restroom just outside the press briefing room. He went in and waited until he heard them announce the president. As soon as he heard it, he rushed the room. The press was clamoring with questions on the events of the day in Los Angeles. The president was just getting ready to answer the first question when Steve bolted to the front of the room and said, "Mr. President, 'Rome is Burning.'" Hernandez froze, and the Secret Service had Steve out of the room and ushered into the Oval Office in seconds. "Wait here, Agent Hoffman. The president will be with you right away," one of the Secret Service agents told him as he left the room. Steve was paralyzed. He was standing in the Oval Office of the White House. He'd never been in the room before. He had been in the Situation Room several times, but he had never been invited into the inner sanctum of power.

The door burst open, and Hernandez and several aides including Carl Daly were on his heels. Daly saw Hoffman and ordered him removed from the room. Hernandez spun around on his feet. "Are you out of your mind?" asked Hernandez. Daly said, "Agent Hoffman was in my office over an hour ago asking to speak to you, Mr. President. I told him you were not to be disturbed. I had him moved to the Roosevelt Room, but I promise I will have his credentials revoked, and I will call FBI Director Tutts about his insubordination." Hernandez was pissed. "Carl, I'm going to speak to Agent Hoffman right now and try and understand what he just told me, and then if it's true, and you kept him from me, you're fired. Now, get the hell out of my office!" Daly walked away with his tail between his legs, snarling at Steve the whole way back to his office off the Oval. Hernandez sat down behind the presidential desk and invited Steve to sit in the chair to his right. "Okay, Special Agent Hoffman. Please repeat what you told me in the press briefing room and who told you to tell me." "I was told by one of my special agents, John Swenson, to pass on this secret statement to you. 'Rome is Burning,' that's all I know. He told me that you would know what it means and would take it from there." Hernandez got up from the desk and walked over to a window and stood staring out for a few moments. "Mr. President, what's going on? What does this code word mean?" Steve asked. The office was empty except for Steve and the president. "It means that someone is working to stage a coup on the nation, Agent Hoffman. It means that we are at war with our own people. Do you know where Agent Swenson is now?" "I'm not certain, but knowing John, he's on his way to stop whatever is happening." "Do you have his cell number with you?" "Yes, sir." Hernandez passed him a note pad across his desk, and Steve wrote it down.

Hernandez called the number. "Swenson," came the reply from the other end of the line. "Special Agent Swenson, this is President Hernandez." "Good evening, Mr. President. I take it that Agent Hoffman was able to get you the message." There was a lot of background noise from John's end of the line. Hernandez asked, "Where are you?" "About five minutes out from our drop point, sir. We are dropping in to try and secure missile command for Oat Mountain and Rocky Peak in Chatsworth, California." "How many men do you have with you?" "Five former black ops and one civilian." "Who's the target?" "You mean, who staged the whole situation here to try to take over the country?" There was a moment of silence. "The two are connected?" "That's affirmative, sir." "Who's heading your way then?" "Senator Ryan Skillen, sir." There was a look of disbelief on Hernandez's face. Steve caught it right away. "Okay, Agent

Swenson, you and your men hold the area. I'm dispatching a Delta strike team to your location. How will we recognize friendly from enemy?" "That's a good question, sir. I've never had to deal with that situation. In all of my missions, they have always been hostiles. How long will it take to mobilize and dispatch Delta Force? I assume you're sending them out of Pendleton, and I'm sure that those men are in the firefight in LA and Orange County." "I will order a meeting with the joint chiefs. I'm certain we can mobilize them and drop them into your area in the next few hours." "Okay, sir. I was able to get a C-119 from Colonel Roy Belker. He said he has a black ops unit that is en route back to his base at the naval air station in Ventura County, sir, and he said he will dispatch them upon my order. We will kill all of Skillen's men; whoever you choose to send in behind us will know we were there. We will leave a sign. This is going to be over in a matter of minutes, sir. We will be in and out before Delta team can get here; however, we will leave the area secure." "I want Skillen alive, Agent Swenson." "I'm sorry, Mr. President. We will do our best, but there is no way we can guarantee that. If he picks up a weapon and joins the fight, we will take him out, sir." "Then, I want the body!" "I can't guarantee that either, sir. It depends on what kind of fire power we're dealing with, and with all due respect, sir, shit explodes when you're in battle and that includes bodies. We'll do our best. We're over our drop, sir. Swenson out."

Hernandez put the phone down and called his chief of staff. "Get everyone in the SIT room at once." Daly walked out more contrite than he was when he was kicked out of the office earlier. "You don't know what this is about do you, Agent Hoffman?" "Well, sir, I didn't before that conversation, but I have a pretty good idea now. You do know that John Swenson is a former black op in the Marine Corps?" Steve said. "I haven't seen his file." "I have, sir, and he is a highly decorated member of the Marine Corps; he was also the leader of a MARSOC unit and joined and lead several joint missions with Delta Forces as well as SAD and SOG units." Daly came in and said they were ready for him in the Situation Room. "Follow me, Agent Hoffman. We'll both get an education." The three men were escorted by four Marines into the SIT room. Everyone stood, and Hernandez told them to sit. "This is no time for formalities. Ladies and gentlemen, this is Special Agent Steve Hoffman. He's a special advisor to my office, and one of his agents in Los Angeles has uncovered a military coup. Agent Hoffman, please tell the room what you told me in the press briefing room and in the Oval Office. "I was told by one of my agents to tell the president that 'Rome is Burning.' I have no idea what this means." The room became somber and Hernandez asked that John Swenson's military file be pulled up. They all sat reading over his history. General Mick Adams of the Marine Corps spoke up when Swenson's name was first mentioned and said, "If this is what John is calling it, and he's on the ground with the men I think he is, Skillen and his men are going to walk into a buzz saw." As they were briefed, Steve sat silent, listening to the backgrounds on the men that were believed to be with John, not to mention John's history.

The president spoke up as the chiefs were briefing him on John and his men and asked, "What does the acronym MARSOC stand for?" Adams spoke up. "Marine Corps Forces Special Operations Command. It's a counterterrorism unit, sir." Amongst other things, Agent Swenson excelled in special operations and graduated to Marine Corps MARSOC's deeper intelligence and operations unit, code named MAD…the acronym stands for Marine Adaptation Destroyer." "That unit is a myth," Daly said." The president looked at Carl and said, "Mr. Daly, you're dismissed." There was no argument, and there were no glaring stares. He simply stood up and left the room. Hernandez continued speaking when Daly was gone. "After I was sworn in, I met with each of you, and we discussed all operational units of the military. Now, you all know I'm not some wet behind the ears guy. I served my country in the army and ate some dirt in Operation Desert Shield and Desert Storm. Even as an army officer, I heard rumors and ghost stories of covert super secret military units that were so secret only the president knew of their existence. I am now the President of the United States, and gentlemen, I've never heard of this Marine unit…why not?" General Adams spoke up, "Plausible deniability, sir."

"So, I have secret military units that I send into covert operations, and I don't 'officially' know they exist?" "That is correct, sir. It has been that way since the dawn of the republic. You order us to strike an area. It's our job as the joint chiefs to advise you on the best possible military option; however, we don't have to tell you what units we are using. In this situation, sir, if it weren't for the fact that we have MAD-trained Marines and Delta Force fighters already on the ground at the location, we would be recommending what is happening right now – only we would not discuss the units that we are using, sir." Hernandez groaned. "So the bottom line is these men are expendable." "Yes, sir." "And they're okay with that?" "Yes, sir!" "What's the situation with MAD out of Pendleton?" "I have put in orders for two squads of fighters to be dispatched, sir, but they are having problems reaching the men because they have been dispatched into the field assisting local and other federal resources in the Los Angeles fires." "How long before you can get them on the ground at Oat Mountain?" "We don't know, sir. We are in uncharted territory here. We've never had a disaster of this proportion taking so many of our resources on every level." "That's what Skillen is counting on. It appears that Skillen has been planning this for some time. So, the bottom line is, we pin the hopes of a nation on these men?" There was silence in the room. "That's correct, sir. And moreover, no matter how this turns out, no one can ever know that it happened, assuming Skillen doesn't get the silos. This is national security – world security on a grand scale. These men must accomplish their self chosen civilian mission, and the government can never formally acknowledge what they did…ever!"

The president shook his head. "These men are putting their lives on the line for a country that can never know they existed. It doesn't seem fair." "It's not fair, sir." Adams said, "these men swore an oath, and I can assure you that they have no desire for any attention no matter how this turns out. They are machines that have been clicked on with the government's special training. When the mission is complete, they will shut off again unless called on by us, or God forbid, something like this happens again." "Well, let's get men in there who are being paid by Uncle Sam to do this job. I don't want the blood of civilians on my hands because we had a rogue senator with an insane plot." "Yes, sir." Hernandez went to stand, and everyone else stood. As he went to leave the SIT room, he stopped and looked at the chiefs. "There will be no communication with these men on this mission will there?" "No, sir." "How will we know they accomplished their mission?" There was a moment of silence, and the national security director spoke up. "The leader of the counter operation can contact you through the silo central communication center once they secure the silos. However, we'll most likely know they accomplished their mission when we have boots on the ground who confirm it back to us from whatever sign they will leave behind, or, if it failed, by the launch of one or more of the ballistic missiles from the mountain range." Hernandez shook his head as he walked out of the room and said, "Oh good, I thought it was going to be a boring night."

The C-119 was over the drop location, and John yelled out orders. The men put on their headsets and did a final safety check of their chutes as they prepared to jump. "We're jumping low, gentlemen. We need to come in under the radar." There were head nods all around. "We're dropping in at four hundred feet, and we have no static lines. Deploy your chutes as soon as you clear the aircraft; we can't lose a man." The pilot called back to the crew that they had ten seconds to drop. They perched in the side jump door of the plane and began jumping in succession. John had Jim strapped to him for a tandem jump, and Jim cried out as John threw their bodies out of the plane, "I'm too damned old for this shit!" His voice echoed through the darkness and into the valley below. The pilot radioed to the station that all jumpers had cleared the aircraft. They blacked out after that. The C-119 flight plan wasn't on any tower chief's log; the flight never existed. The men were on their own. The military dropped them in, but it was up to them to complete the mission and find their own way back out.

They all landed within a few feet of each other. They engaged night vision and stowed their chutes in the rocks and brush of the canyon. They met up on a ridge outside the missile field, and John gave orders of direction and attack. "If Skillen and his people haven't hit the ground yet, let's be careful not to kill innocents. Subdue and then stow them in a secure location." He showed the men a map of the base on his tablet along with the complexes and where they could put the minimal staff for safe keeping. "You have your assignments. Let's execute them and meet at the mess on the base in ten minutes. There should only be three guards posted, so we should be able to move quickly. If you run into Skillen and his men, engage the enemies. We'll know from the open gunfire that we have company." The men broke off in different directions. Jim stayed with John as they moved across the rocky field toward a small guard shack. "This is all that guards our national defense systems and missiles? Three lackeys?" John laughed. "Hardly, these are very well-trained men; fortunately, not as well-trained as us. The real security comes in if you try to access the silos and the infrastructure of the base." "What fuckin' base? It's a couple of crumbling buildings. I don't see shit that would tell me that we were on any type of base." John slid over against a rock and put his fingers over his lips for Jim to be silent. He moved around the guard shack and disabled the man inside. He hog-tied him and sedated him, then picked him up and told Jim in a whisper, "Follow me." It didn't take five minutes, and all of the men were together in the mess hall.

John sat down with his tablet and said, "Okay, we've got the drop on Ryan. He won't be expecting any resistance." "What about the guard shacks?" asked Patrick. "They won't have a count. Jim is going to go into one of them. Jim looked over at John and said, "I'M WHAT?" His eyes as big a saucers. "I told you; you are bait. Well, here you go." "Wait … if these guys are killers, they're going to kill me." "Don't worry. Ricky and Philly will be on you. As soon as they make the men, they will take them down." "Then what?" "Well, assuming all goes right and you're alive, they will hand you a weapon, and you will make your way back to the mess," John said in a casual voice. Jim was pissed and said, "This whole thing is a fucking mess!" There was some laughter but none of it came from Jim. John continued. "C4 and Blaco will work the second station, and Lance and I will cover the main entrance." They heard the distant sound of an aircraft propeller. C4 said, "It's a C-130J, and it's flying low." "How long before they jump?" John asked. "They don't know the area and terrain like we do. I figure they will make three to four passes using infrared to see what they're dealing with. We have a half hour," said C4.

John called out to sync their time pieces and to start setting booby traps along the perimeter and the outbuildings. "We have the advantage men. We know this area; they don't. Set as many explosives as you can. Set perimeter mines and proximity mines every five yards, working your way out to in. Let's kill as many as we can on their initial drop in and their advance. Set perimeter mines in all of the outbuildings, backing out the way they will enter." Cosmo said, "The second they hit the first mines, they're going to shit their pants. We need to take up sniper positions, so we can start picking them off as they enter. That way we'll get a stampede, and they'll hit the mines running from the gunfire. We also need someone in a recon position to radio back enemy counts. It's not like Ryan's coming in with other senators; he's coming with mercs, and I would bet a hell of a lot of them." John smiled. "No matter what, Skillen is mine. Capture him. Don't kill him. He will need to be interrogated." "You're going to turn him over to the government?" Jim asked with a confused look on his face. "Oh, no. He's mine." "But you promised the president that you would turn him over to him." "I will … when I'm finished with him." There was a little laughter as the men started out to set the trap lines. Jim looked at John and said, "I know what that means. They will get to see him on DVD. The Iron Eagle is going to make him a movie star."

They could hear the C-130J circling as they moved in stealth, setting the booby traps. When they were done, Philly, Cosmo, and Ricky took up sniper positions, crossing rounds so that Skillen and his men would run right into an ambush. There was only one way in, but they made sure that any back way or side way out was armed, too. Ryan and his men were coming in, but only Ryan would be coming out.

CHAPTER ELEVEN

"Oh, fuck! We're dead!"

S killen got word from the captain of the C-130J that they were low on fuel, so they needed to jump or abort. Ryan called his men together and said, "We're about to make a jump into history, men. Fifteen seconds to drop." The back of the plane slowly opened as the men hooked up to the static line and began to move to jump position. The aircraft was at 800 feet when they began jumping. John's team watched from their sniper positions as the chutes opened. Cosmo radioed to John that Skillen and his men had begun deploying, and he counted the chutes as they opened. "We have thirty confirmed open chutes." Jim heard the number of men coming and said, "Oh, fuck! We're dead!" John smiled. "Are you kidding? This is great news. I was expecting fifty to a hundred troops. Twenty-nine with Skillen will be like shooting fish in a barrel." Jim stared at John for a few seconds and said firmly, "I'm not hanging out with you anymore." John called out as he moved into position, "Philly, Cosmo, Ricky … what's Skillen's position?" Cosmo radioed back the coordinates on their landing. "Perfect! Wait until they are within fifty yards of the rear guard station; the silencers on your weapons are going to cause confusion. Give me an estimate on how many you three can take out before they hit the mines."

"They are moving in skirmish lines, ten across three deep, but there are only twenty nine men," Cosmo said. "Skillen won't move with the units. He's held up in the hills," John replied. Philly radioed that he had a lock for quick kill on five in the back.

Patrick radioed he had a kill on the other five in the back." John looked over the map on his tablet. "Cosmo, how many can you take out?" There was a second of silence, and Cosmo came back, "I can take out five to ten, depending on reaction." John's tablet started to make a beeping sound, and Jim put his hands up in a 'what?" position. "They tripped the first remote sensor; they are within fifty yards. On my command begin firing. Mark…fire!" Jim looked around but heard nothing. "What's the problem? They aren't firing?" John motioned for Jim to put his head down with him outside the line. "They have silencers. The longer we don't hear return fire, the better off we are. Even better if the first sound we hear is a mine exploding." Just as John said it, the first remote mine detonated. John peered through his night vision binoculars to see that a unit of twenty-nine men had been reduced to six. He knew that Skillen was hanging back from his men and hiding out in the boulders of the Oat Mountains while his men secured the area. He watched as four men ran for cover, only to hit another set of mines. "Two left, John," came Cosmo's call over the radio. "Correction. All enemies have been eradicated." John ordered Jim back to the mess hall to meet up with the men. He had to find Skillen before he could get any further backup. He scanned the rocky hillsides with the field glasses until he saw movement a hundred and fifty yards dead ahead. "I'm killing the mines. I've got a beat on Skillen. I'm moving in. You men collect the bodies of Skillen's team, pile them near the mess. When I return with Skillen, we will create our sign to the forces that the enemy has been eliminated."

Ryan Skillen was hiding in a rock outcropping with an advantage to see any approaching men. He watched through night vision goggles as his elite team was meticulously gunned down by an unknown force. He withdrew now in a panic when there was no more movement of his men. He was in shock and looked out over the countryside to see lifeless bodies dotting the landscape. A movement caught his eye, and he watched as a lone body moved in his general direction. It was low to the ground, and at first he thought it was a coyote or bobcat, but as he watched it moving closer he realized it was human. He picked up his M-16 and led the target and fired; he saw it fall. The shot rang through the valley. All of John's men and Jim were gathered in the mess waiting on him and heard the shot. "That's not us," Philly said. "There's only one body missing, and that's Skillen. John's down." Jim looked around. No man was moving. "What the fuck are you waiting for? There's one man left, and John is out there on his own. Now, you're saying he's down? We need to save him." No one moved. "We have to hold and protect this position." Jim got irate and started yelling at the men. "This is a fucking block building with a couple rusted out old steel tables. There's nothing here to protect. John is out there; at worst dead, but probably injured. We have to save him." Cosmo put his hand on Jim's shoulder and said quietly, "We have to hold this position; John knew what he was getting into, Jim. If we hear nothing in ten minutes, we will move to kill Skillen." Jim grabbed a weapon and ran out the door. "I'm not leaving a fallen man behind. This is bullshit." No one moved; they just held their positions as Jim ran blindly through the darkness in search of John.

Although Ryan saw a body fall, he couldn't make it out against the terrain. He started slowly moving down the side of the rocky ground when he caught movement in his night vision goggles. He saw a man running in his general direction without any gear. He was in street clothes and carrying a weapon. "This just might work out after all," he said to himself as he watched the man move through the rocks. Jim was quietly calling out John's name. There was only starlight, no artificial light for Jim to see by. He could make out shadows and forms, but he had no idea where John might be. He moved slowly, calling out to him with no response. He heard rustling in the hills just ahead of him, and he moved toward the sound, calling out John's name. He made his way to the bottom of the rocky hill when a man moved out from behind the rocks and ordered Jim to drop his weapon. He froze and recognized the voice right away. "Ryan fuckin' Skillen. You murdering asshole." Ryan moved slowly down from the rocks with his weapon trained on Jim. "Drop your weapon, sheriff. I would hate to have to kill you when I need you alive." Jim complied and dropped the rifle to the ground. "So, it's John Swenson that I shot?" He walked closer to Jim and said, "Good. The Iron Eagle is dead. He was an asshole. Where are the rest of the men?" He didn't answer. Skillen pulled and pointed his nickel plated forty-five at Jim's thigh and pulled the trigger. Jim went down, howling in pain.

"Look...I don't want to be an asshole here, but I'm not getting my head blown off because of you. Now, you tell me where the other men are, and I will let you live. I'll do even better than that. I will allow you to serve in my administration when I secure the silos. You can be my jailer – only on the other side of the bars. You will be my first public execution. Get to your feet!" Jim pulled himself up, holding onto some rocks. Skillen was so close to Jim he could smell his breath. "Where are the others?" Jim pointed in the direction of the mess hall. "Let's move." He jammed the barrel of the gun into Jim's side. He limped in the direction of the mess hall. "I have your sheriff friend, gentlemen. Swenson is dead. Now, if you want Sheriff O'Brian here to keep breathing, you will drop your weapons and come out with your hands up," Skillen yelled. There was no response from the darkened mess hall.

"You took an oath; you are federal and local law enforcement as well as firemen and paramedics. Are you going to let a fellow officer die? Come out and join me, and we will mold a new nation in our image." Jim was limping along and said, "You don't get it, Skillen. It's over. You're a dead man whether you kill me or not. You've been exposed. Those men in there will let me die because that's what they have to do to protect America, then they are going to kill you." He pushed the muzzle into Jim's back and pushed him forward. "As soon as I can get a radio or phone signal, I will call for backup. They will be on you in seconds. You don't have a choice. Join me, and let's usher in a new age in world politics."

Cosmo looked at the other five men and said, "Skillen's off his nut. Who wants to shoot him?" Blake raised his hand. There was no reaction from the others. Skillen's behavior became more and more erratic the closer he came to the mess hall. "Swenson is dead, you assholes. There is no more Iron fuckin' Eagle. The days of the vigilante killer are behind us. We can make a new world, shaped by our ideals and our desires. Just one of these missiles will change the world for all time! Join me and usher in a new era." He hollered out again and silence met his call. "Get on your goddamn knees," he yelled to Jim as he stood behind him with the gun pointed at his back. "The blood of the innocent is on your hands. You have to the count of five to come out with your weapons dropped, and your hands on your head, or I paint the sand and rock with this man's brains." There was no response. Skillen raised the gun to the back of Jim's head and said, "Now you die for the sake of a new nation." Jim knew he wouldn't hear the shot. He waited for what world was after this one when he heard a thud behind him. He turned slowly to where Skillen had been standing to see the silhouette of John standing over Skillen's body.

"Sorry about that, Jim. I tripped and hit my head." John called out, and the rest of the men came out of the mess hall. They were milling around laughing at John, who had his hand on the back of his head. Cosmo pulled a first aid kit and put a cold pack on John's skull and worked by flashlight to stitch a small laceration on the back of his head. "You tripped?" He nodded. "Do you have a headache?" "What do you think?" Cosmo laughed. "Jim was certain you were dead; he ran out to save you." John got up and walked over to Jim sitting on a rock while Patrick worked on his leg. "Thanks, Jim. If it hadn't been for you distracting Ryan, I would be dead. How is he, Patrick?" "The bullet grazed his thigh; he'll be fine." Jim looked at John and said, "I got fuckin' shot saving your ass. I'm shot. Shot trying to save your dumb ass from this psycho." John looked at Skillen who was unconscious on the ground near the bodies of his men.

"Well, thanks, Jim. I promise you a case of the best scotch money can buy. You name it. It's yours." "Scotch? Scotch? Fuck that. You and Sara are going to build me and Barbara our dream home. I saved your life. You have led me on too many adventures for too many years. I saved your ass, now you're going to repay me!"

John laughed, and Lance asked, "What do you want to do with the bodies?" John took out his field knife and instructed the others to do the same. Jim watched as the men worked in tandem cutting up the corpses and intertwining their flesh into a large object on the ground. They pulled the corpses up from each side and hung them between two power poles off the mess hall. John, Lance, and Cosmo pulled four high powered halogen lights from storage in the mess hall and set them up behind the hanging corpses. They ran the power together and laid the plug near an outlet in the building. "Let's make sure that Oat Mountain's secure, men." Jim got to his feet and hobbled behind all of them as they went to a small closet at the end of the mess hall. John pulled back a panel to the right of the little door and placed his hand into the black opening. Jim stood there staring not saying a word. Suddenly there was the sound of heavy machinery running, and the small black panel where John's hand had been placed lit up, and the small door opened into a bright white light. "Jesus Christ! Did you just kill us all?" Jim said half joking. "Go toward the light, Jim," Lance joked.

Once his eyes adjusted to the light, Jim could see that it was an entrance to an elevator. The men walked in, and Patrick and Cosmo helped Jim in as well. John pressed his palm against a piece of glass, and the elevator started moving very quickly downward. Jim almost lost his balance as the elevator descended; his ears were popping as the elevator rocketed downward. It took nearly three minutes for it to reach its stopping point. "All out!" John said as the men walked into the open white room. The room was filled wall to wall with electronic equipment. There were monitors showing the entire facility, and the ground above it. There were three seats, but there was no one in the room. "Where the hell are we?" Jim asked in amazement. John walked over to the bank of monitors and said, "This is the control room of Oat Mountain Minuteman Missile Operations." John pointed to a wall of TV monitors on the other side of the room. There were twenty-two monitors, each showing one of twenty-two missiles in their silos. A deadly, life changing sleeping giant. The titans of the modern world ready to emerge from their slumber at a moment's notice and wreak havoc on the world. "It's REAL!" Jim said in total wonderment. "Yes, Jim. It's real. This whole mission is real, and everything is secure. I need to make a call."

John picked up a red phone as the other men went to work stations. Some sat in seats; others worked standing at computer monitors. They didn't say a word to each other; they just knew what to do. John stood with the red phone to his ear, and for a moment Jim was transported to another place in time like a scene from an old movie when Russia and the U.S. were in the cold war, and the president's red phone with direct contact to the Kremlin sat silent waiting for a call. He thought these places were nothing more than urban mythology, but here he stood in the belly of the beast. He asked Cosmo, "How deep are we?" He never looked away from the keyboard he was typing on and said, "We are a little over a mile beneath the earth." "Mr. President, this is Special Agent Swenson. Nero has been beheaded, sir. Rome is safe." There were a few moments of silence between John and the president. "Yes, sir." John flipped a switch and put the phone onto the receiver; they were on speaker phone with the President of the United States. "Gentlemen, I want to thank you and commend you on a job well done. I wish that I could yell the accomplishment of your mission from the highest mountaintop, but you know that I can't. I can't even acknowledge that you exist. I wanted you to hear from my lips to your ears, thank you. The American people thank you; the world thanks you." The room was silent, every man still typing away on his assignment. John spoke up, "Sir, we appreciate your accolades, but we're a bit busy here making sure that we secure all of the launch codes and send that data back into the cloud." "What of Skillen?" "He didn't make it, sir." "He's dead?" "We haven't located the body yet, sir, but we believe he might have been vaporized by a mine." "I will have Delta Force secure the location and search the area. They have been dispatched and should be on the ground in ten minutes. You won't be there, will you?" "No, sir. We're out as of now, Mr. President. Good night." John flipped the switch closed as the men logged off. They entered the elevator. Jim watched the emotionless looks on their faces like their minds and emotions had been wiped clean. "You guys have just received a huge commendation from the President of the United States. He thanked you and me for saving the country and the world, and you have no reaction?" Ricky spoke up. "We don't exist, Jim. That's all you will hear of us, this mission, or of what happened. It will never see a newspaper or anything else. We're not impressed with accolades. We just did our job."

When the elevator hit the surface, the men moved quickly to grab their equipment, and John plugged in the lights. As they ran out of the building into the darkness, Jim looked back and saw what they had made from the bodies of the dead soldiers. There, displayed in the hot white halogen lights, was the emblem of The Iron Eagle. The further away they got, the more pronounced the image became. Jim looked at John and said, "That's one way to make a statement and get attention!" "Delta force now has an easy target to spot from the air." The men heard the distant sound of Blackhawk chopper blades cutting their way through the night sky. Nothing more was said as they entered vehicles that John had stowed at a property he owned. The area was still smoldering from the fires that had roared through earlier in the day. John had several vehicles parked in steel cargo containers near a burned out building that was lost in the fires. "Whose place is this?" Jim asked. "Mine. I inherited it from a long lost relative several years ago. It used to be a place for me to escape the world and relax." Jim looked around the land as the trucks started driving down the dirt road toward Topanga Canyon Boulevard. "Not anymore, huh?" John shook his head. "You won't rebuild?" "No…I have new prospects and a new life. This is an area and stage in my life and career that is best left in the past." Jim sat with a thoughtful look on his face and said, "Onward and upward for The Iron Eagle!"

He noticed Ryan's feet sticking out from under a blanket that John had thrown over him when he threw him in the back of the pickup truck. "And what are you going to do with him?" Jim asked with a smart ass tone. "What do you think I should do with him?" Jim got serious as he took a cigarette out of his top pocket and put it in his mouth. "I'm not like you, man. I can't even begin to imagine what he deserves as punishment. That's what the courts are for, John." "Seriously? You think the animals we see deserve a cent of taxpayer money or even the recognition of the courts?" Jim had the window rolled down as they approached the windy road of Topanga, heading into the canyon and leading down to PCH. "I'm a lawman, John. I'm paid to hunt down the bad guys and turn them over to the courts. I'm not saying what The Eagle does has no merit. It does, but if you ask me what I think should be done with another human being no matter how heinous his crimes, I can't be judge and jury." John never took his eyes off the road. Jim looked out over the San Fernando Valley. As the truck climbed the winding road toward the village, Jim looked down where there would usually be a sea of lights only to see blackness and remnants of fire.

The canyon was burned and smoldering as they drove in, and for a few seconds he was afraid that they were going to drive into the fire. John broke his silence when they crested the hill and entered the canyon headed to PCH. "There are people who have committed crimes so heinous that the justice system and the penal code, even the death penalty, is too good for. There are those who deserve to be dispatched in a manner consistent with their crimes. They must suffer as their victims suffered." "I don't know, John. There's a part of me that sees what you do to your victims as inhumane." "Inhumane? Inhumane? Just how humane were Cruthers, Marker, Statler, Billy the Kid, Barstow…and so many others?" Jim sat silent as John continued to speak. "Do you think that they deserved more media attention by parading their victims again in the courts and causing their families more suffering? Letting these sick animals relive their crimes while forcing the public and the families to relive the nightmare? There are lines, Jim, in every society. In our society, the line of judicial prudence and timely execution of sentences went away years ago. These men should not be allowed, after making a mockery of our judicial system and been made idols by the media, to sit on death row for decades only to die of natural causes, comfortable with three hot meals, a warm bed, medical care, and civil rights. Who was there for their victims? Where were their rights when they were being tortured, raped, terrorized, and eventually allowed to die when their captors were bored with hearing their cries and pleas? Those victims forced to pray unto profanity, to endure sadistic cruel and dehumanizing treatment, all for the chance to breathe another moment? I've seen the terror in their eyes; I've heard their screams of pain and their pleading for mercy, and none was given. I'm sorry, Jim, but I've looked into the abyss, and it has looked back into me."

Jim took the unlit cigarette out of his mouth and with his elbow resting on the window of the truck asked, "And what came from that abyss, John?" He never took his eyes off the road, carefully navigating the burned and burning landscape. "The Iron Eagle, and all the hell that follows him." "So, now The Eagle has Bolton and her men as well as Skillen. How do you measure suffering for them? Hundreds of thousands dead. How do you make them suffer the pains of hell they inflicted on an unsuspecting city?" A smile grew across John's face. "Slowly, meticulously, sadistically. To make death not just welcomed and prayed for but to make the pain so unbearable that they forget that death is even an option, that they lose themselves in their agony and feel the pains of hell here and now. Their minds warped to the point that they no longer know where life ends and death begins. Then, and only then, will justice have been extracted and death allowed to follow."

Jim sat staring at John's emotionless face; it was cold, dark, and terrifying. He knew that he was not looking at the face of his friend and law enforcement colleague. He was looking into the face of death, the face of retribution, the face of suffering. And when he allowed death to enter his realms, it asked permission of him to take its victims. Death was not proud or feared in the world of The Iron Eagle. He controlled it, embraced it, and tamed it to do his bidding. For the first time in his life, Jim was truly afraid. Not of John Swenson, but of The Iron Eagle, driving him back to his lair. The face of controlled and unleashed anger that held the scales of justice in its talons and the weapons of war, too. A fear for his own mortal soul and what it would mean to die at the hands of this beast. The conversation ceased, and they drove on to the Malibu residence, and Jim felt a sick feeling of pity for those monsters that started this situation, for he knew what they didn't. Death was their friend, and they would call on it long before The Eagle would ever let it have them.

CHAPTER TWELVE

"It's our fault; it's the military's fault. We started this rolling!"

The sign left behind by John's team left the pilots of the Blackhawk speechless. What had started out looking like a pinpoint of light upon approach became a glowing beacon with an image set against the lights behind it. Captain Mark Chapell ordered his team to ready for a ground invasion as the two Blackhawk helicopters went to silent mode and swooped down three hundred yards ahead of the lighted figure in the distance. "Well, they were kind enough to leave us a perfectly lit LZ," Chapell said as the choppers hovered 40 feet off the ground. He ordered his men to repel down and spread out. When the two choppers had dropped their cargo, they moved back to the 118 Freeway where the military was using the westbound side as their temporary landing zone. The men moved slowly toward the light and the image that it illuminated. They could see from a distance that the ring and its inner circle that made up the symbol of The Eagle appeared to be dripping as if hosed down with water. As they approached, the two twelve man units cleared the mess hall and the rest of the base and sealed it off. Chapell's men stood in stunned silence staring up at the structure erected before them. The sculpture had been created with the tangled nude bodies of men. And not just any men. Many of the soldiers in the black op units sent in to stop Skillen, and his men recognized the distorted faces in the heap as fellow Special Forces operatives. The liquid they saw dripping was the blood of their comrades.

Lieutenant Paul Oberman was standing before the human sculpture when Chapell walked up. "I know they were terrorists, but they were brothers in arms, too. Who would do something like this?" Chapell looked on. "A black ops team that's a myth! We have orders. Let's start looking for Senator Ryan Skillen. Cut these men down. They will all have their dog tags on." Oberman stood staring at Chapell. "Yes, sir. Men, remove these bodies from the posts. Lay them side by side, so we can get IDs on each. Also, we have instructions to seek out Senator Ryan Skillen. He's believed to have been with this party." One of his men hollered out, "Sir, what are we to do with Senator Skillen?" Chapell called out and said, "Bring him to me dead or alive." As half of the team broke out in search of Skillen, the other men cut the bodies down from the posts. When the last piece of rope had been cut, the bodies came crashing to the ground. There were moans and calls from the pile. "Sir, some of these men are still alive." They got more light onto the bodies to see human savagery beyond their own imaginations. The men in the sculpture had been stripped nude, skinned, and the skin used like rope to intertwine one to the other. All had been disemboweled; their intestines used like string to create the image that the killers desired. The men left behind that were used to create the sculpture, while critically injured even before the torture they endured, were still alive with their skin and entrails used for the killer's artistic piece. "Get medics up here. Let's try and save a few of these men. We can interrogate them if they survive," Chapell barked as he walked into the mess and entered the elevator to secure the silos.

When the medics got on scene, they advised the Captain that there was no way to save the men. They were intentionally left the way they were and to try to separate them would result in instant death. The medics advised that if they wanted information from the living before death, they would have to do a field interrogation as the men had been and were losing blood fast. Chapell's team members were able to interrogate a few of the men before they died, but they got no answers on who did this to them or most importantly why. By the time the sun crested the eastern horizon, only two of the twenty plus men were alive, and they were fading fast. The sunrise brought the true nature of the brutality into focus. Even Chapell, a hardened seasoned veteran of multiple international conflicts was both sickened and speechless.

"We have IDs on all of the men, sir!" one of his corporals called out. "Are any still breathing?" A few moments of silence followed, "One…" But a few seconds passed, and the corporal came back and said, "I'm sorry, sir. None. They're all dead." "Bag the bodies and leave their dog tags on them. Call out to Edwards and tell them we're going to need a C-130J. They can land it on the 118 Freeway. Give them a body bag count." "Do you want flags, sir?" Chapell's response was quick and forceful, "Fuck no… these men were traitors to their country. They deserve no military honors, and they sure as fuck aren't going to lie under the flag they betrayed." Oberman approached. "There's no sign of Skillen, sir. There are several detonated mines; however, the mines were incendiary mines. There's nothing left but blood." "Have the men do a mop up." "What are we doing with the bodies?" Chapell took a cigar out of his pocket and bit off the end. "For those fuckers, we have orders to return their bodies to D.C. The president wants them cremated, and the remains will be gathered into one container and dumped into a landfill." "That's one way of dealing with them." "Hey, I talked him out of putting them into the Baltimore sewer system." Oberman let out a laugh. "I would guess that there's now an open senate seat. Skillen is a blood spatter." Oberman walked off, and Chapell looked on, lighting the cigar and murmuring to himself, "Skillen isn't a blood spatter. I've got a pretty good idea where he is, and in the end he will be wishing he had been incinerated by one of those mines."

He puffed on the cigar, looking on as the C-130J approached to land. Three trucks were driven up to Oat Mountain, and his men threw the body bags onto the trucks like one would throw roadkill into the bed of a rendering plant truck. By noon, they were done at the site. Chapell ordered the men to secure and lock the scene, and he left a detachment of ten men to stand guard over the base. Oberman jumped into a Humvee with Chapell and said, "Well, sir, I thought I'd seen everything in war, but this one takes the cake." When they got back to the 118, they left the Humvee to be loaded onto the C-130J and jumped into one of the Blackhawks. As the chopper raised over the Chatsworth hills and headed out over the San Fernando Valley, the scope of the past forty-eight hours was overwhelming. Chapell said, "Look!" He was pointing out over what was left of the San Fernando Valley. "Look at this small section of the city of Los Angeles. This is something I thought I would never see, an American city destroyed. There are hundreds of thousands of bodies unaccounted for, Oberman. Civilians. I have seen high body counts in war, and they never fazed me. But this…this is a tragedy without measure. This city will never be the same." Oberman looked out over the valley as they flew southwest toward downtown Los Angeles. "There aren't even any looters." Chapell took a drag off his stogie. "You can't have looters when everyone is dead, and all the shit that could be looted is burned up!"

They crested the hilltop over the Griffith Park Observatory overlooking downtown Los Angeles. Chavez Ravine and Dodger Stadium was to their right and what was left of Los Angeles was below and ahead of the slow moving chopper as it moved on to LAX. It was all burned. There were no houses. The streets were crowded with burned out cars; there were bodies on the streets and hanging out of cars. The smoldering remains of the nation's second largest city was passing below the chopper as it headed for the airport, which was now a temporary military base and morgue. The skyscrapers of downtown Los Angeles remained though there was little movement on the streets below. A few fire engines that had survived the inferno were dousing hot spots with dazed crews not knowing what to do. "All of this set by a few lone wolves to punish the government," Oberman said. "It may have been the work of several men and women to start the flames, but one woman did it all," Chapell said as they flew on. "Bolton?" Oberman asked. Chapell nodded. Oberman looked out over the devastation and destruction and said, "It's our fault; it's the military's fault. We started this rolling!" Chapell just nodded his head slowly as he looked down at the city. "A brilliant tactical commander who used her training and the tactics we taught her to destroy the lives of innocent Americans. I don't know where she is if she's still alive, but I will say that she got her point across."

Oberman didn't react right away but when he did it was somber and honest. "I was there at her court martial. I knew Colonel Bolton very, very well. She was an excellent commanding officer and was loyal to her country. I warned them when they decided to go down this road that they were toying with forces they could not imagine." "Shit, man, you describe the woman like she's some kind of supernatural being." "She had a way about her; she knew how to read people. What the government and the military did to her was wrong, and the country and innocents have paid for our error with their lives." The chopper was landing at LAX when Chapell responded, "It makes no difference now, does it?" Oberman shook his head. "She did her worst, and we must pick up the pieces, and the American people will be told yet another spook story. This will be spun and blamed on foreign terrorists. Government will exploit the situation for a greater power grab, and those things the founding fathers gave us – the Constitution and the Bill of Rights – will be extinguished all in the name of 'National Security.' A nation will give up the last of its rights to be protected, never knowing that it was their own government that brought this upon its people." Chapell said, "September eleven all over again!"

Oberman responded, "No…most of the commanders who could have saved this nation that day are here in LA. They saved Oat Mountain and the silos, not for the government but for the people. They now have targets on their backs. The government can't let them live, or let them tell the truth about all of it. They kept them quiet all of these years; however, I have a feeling a new war is brewing, and it won't be fought with a foreign government or even with the people. I see a war coming, and it will be fought by one or two men against the government, and the outcome of that war will be the difference in whether this republic remains or a dictatorship rises from the ashes of this attack." Chapell nodded. "And when the CIA, NSA, FBI and all other silent but deadly forces can't put it down or kill its movement, the commander and chief will call on us to take off the rebellion's head. Will we do it?" Oberman opened the chopper door to head to the C-130J with Chapell behind him. They stood together near the rear of the aircraft as the body bags were being thrown onto the plane. Chapell said, "Your last question is one for the ages. We are commissioned officers and subordinate officers at that. I respect those few men who tried to save this nation and its people, now twice. I guess two was a charm for them in a sad way. I can say that if the order comes down to take out those men or a single one of them, it is an order I will disobey." Oberman nodded. "Agreed, sir. I will not allow those men to go through more of what they have endured after the sacrifices they have made to the republic." "We'll be branded as traitors," Chapell said casually. "Then, I say we start to think about how we prepare for this likely scenario, Lieutenant, and where we send our men." He nodded, salutes were exchanged, and each man went his separate way.

What no one knew, not The Eagle or his team, or the government that had walked in on a civilian black op scene, was that a lone outdoorsman and survivalist named Charlie Baxter had survived the fires by dodging flames and winds in dugouts, natural dens, and other natural environments to follow the flames back toward civilization. He had been sleeping in a ravine on Oat Mountain when John's team dropped in, and he was an eyewitness to the whole event. After shooting thousands of photographs and video, his camera hung down from its sling in front of him as he watched the choppers and other military aircraft take off from the 118 Freeway. He stood on the top of a clearing overlooking the base in stunned silence. He was the only civilian survivor of the nighttime battle and had become a war correspondent without even knowing it. He pulled out his laptop and put the memory card into the computer slot, and the images began to download to a file he called, 'The Oat Mountain Offensive.' When he was done, he uploaded the data to all of his social networks. It would take only milliseconds for the events of that night to go viral in the world of social media.

CHAPTER THIRTEEN

"Now, I've removed your pride."

John and his men arrived back at the house in Malibu near noon. They had to snake their way through the Topanga pass again as fires were still raging in the hills. Jim and John pulled in to park, and John took Skillen, who was now alert, from the back of the truck, and threw him over his shoulder, and he and Jim made their way to one of the holding rooms. John threw Skillen down on the floor, locked him in, and entered the war room. Sara was sitting with Barbara; they both had a scotch in their hands and were staring at one of the television screens on the wall. The scene on the TV was one of horrific death and destruction. The fires had burned nearly every structure from Palmdale to Long Beach in LA County; the fires were burning out of control in Orange, Riverside, and San Bernardino Counties. The media coverage was from the air, with most of it from military aircraft. The winds were making it nearly impossible for firefighters to make a stand anywhere, and water dropping aircraft weren't making a dent. One meteorologist who was being interviewed from the National Weather Service in Las Vegas was telling viewers and reporters alike that the fires were so large that they were now creating their own winds.

The interview was being relayed over the Internet via VOIP through satellite as most of the power sources and hardwire phone communications had been knocked out by the fires in Southern California. Some local news crews had set up near the beaches in LA and Orange County and were doing their best to report the news in any way that they could, but misinformation was the hot topic of the day. The million dollar question on the minds of those left alive and the rest of the nation was who did this, why, and would it happen somewhere else? The White House had no comment on who or what had caused the disaster; they focused their media and propaganda on the people of California, and the military and civilian efforts to save lives. The rumor mill was churning, and one of those rumors was right on the money. John asked Sara to do some channel surfing, and she came across an NIP broadcast and a live interview with a retired three star army general named Fergus Markinson. General Markinson retired from the military five years earlier and was being interviewed because someone at NIP had him as a friend and contact. All the men were present as they heard the audio feed of the interview live.

This is Lori Sparks reporting for NIP. I'm speaking with retired three star army general Fergus Markinson, former head of intelligence at the Pentagon. General Markinson, can you repeat for me your theory on what has and is happening in Los Angeles and Southern California?

Of course, Lori. What the government is not telling the American people is the truth about what's happened and is happening in LA and other areas of Southern California. What's happened here is a top secret plot that the government hatched post nine-eleven. You see, the nine-eleven attacks had been discovered by special operatives within the government nearly three years before the first plane was hijacked. What the government won't tell the American people is that our operatives had the flight information and the names of all the hijackers and were set to be on those hijacked jets on nine-eleven.

So you're saying that the government allowed the attacks on the World Trade Center and Pentagon to happen?

That's correct, Lori. High level executive administration officials were briefed on the situation, and on the morning prior to the attacks, the president and his closest staff, including the vice president, ordered that the military black operation to stop the attacks cease and desist. They were ordered scrubbed.

Scrubbed?

The operation was canceled the morning of the attacks. Out of the six teams trained for the mission, only one of them got onto one of those flights that morning.

Which flight was boarded by one of those teams?

Flight 22 out of Philadelphia. The black op team boarded the flight and was able to overpower the hijackers almost immediately.

If that's the case, what was it doing heading back in the direction of Washington, D.C.?

The hijackers moved on the cockpit fast. The team was able to kill the hijackers, but the pilots had been incapacitated. All of the men were commercial airline pilots, and multiple scenarios had been worked out depending on the movements of the hijackers. In this case, the men secured the plane and advised air traffic control that they had the aircraft and were turning to land at JFK International. Two F-16 fighter jets had been scrambled to intercept the flight with what the men on the commercial airliner thought was to escort them to JFK. Instead, the vice president gave the order for the flight to be shot down over an unpopulated area.

The government shot down the plane?

Yes, Lori. The government shot down a civilian airliner.

Why in God's name would they do that?

The government had scrubbed the other missions, and those men had been detained to make sure they not only missed their flights but could be 'dealt with.' The men on Flight 22 knew too much. They were aware that the other three planes had struck their targets, though the Pentagon was not an intended target. Flight 5 was intended for the White House, but the hijacker couldn't see the White House from the air, so he struck the nearest recognizable object of military significance, which was the Pentagon.

How does all of this play into the events in Los Angeles?

Shortly after the thwarted efforts of the special forces to stop the attacks, the men involved in the scrubbed mission disappeared.

Disappeared? As in killed?

Let's just say that a lot of men died in a very short period of time, and no one knew about it. Several of the commanders of those troops were high ranking officials, and several others dropped off the radar on their own after the events of that day. Six months after the nine-eleven attacks, word started running through the intelligence community that there was a plot to target Americans in a major city. While the concepts were vague, the code name of the project was Operation Nero.

In all honesty, General, this sounds too much like the conspiracy theory stuff you read about in books!

Well, Lori, it doesn't get any more real than this. Several high ranking military personnel were disgraced and stripped of their ranks and released into the private sector. Six months ago, the NSA, in one of its eavesdropping sessions on American citizens, picked up some chatter with regard to Nero. Two weeks ago, it was confirmed that Operation Nero was being deployed, and two nights ago it happened. That's what's happening in Los Angeles and all of Southern California right now.

There was a pause.

So, this was about burning down the city of Los Angeles and killing American citizens?

Half...the fires were a separate act of domestic terrorism that was the result of military personnel to distract from Operation Nero. I can only speculate that the commander of Operation Nero felt this was the best way to use up resources and create a distraction while they worked to fulfill their primary objective.

What was the objective, sir? Lori asked exasperated.

Taking control of nuclear missile silos in and around the Los Angeles area.

There was a long pause before Lori blurted out,

Was there a countermeasure to Operation Nero?

Yes!

Can you tell me and our listeners what the name of the countermeasure is or was?

'Rome is Burning.

The faces of the men in the war room with John were stone cold and emotionless. Jim piped up and said, "What the fuck? This guy knows everything, and he's talking about it on a national radio program." Barbara put her hand on his shoulder to settle him. Markinson continued.

The problem is that there was no way, at least that I knew of at the time, for our military to affect a response. Unlike the attacks of nine-eleven, where our special operations teams knew when, where, and how the attacks were to be carried out, it was pretty much agreed in military and intelligence circles that if Operation Nero started, then Operation Rome is Burning would be an assault on an already enemy-controlled missile base. We had no idea of when, where, or how!

Lori lost her composure as an interviewer and asked,

So our second largest city is burning because the government pissed off former military personnel?

Yes.

And, obviously, if what you're saying is true, then the government's countermeasure didn't work.

That's not altogether true, he said so casually that it caught her off guard.

I'm sorry, General, but millions of people are presumed dead. How you can say such a thing is beyond me!

There was a second scenario to this attack that was not directly related to the attacks, but that could exploit the weakness of local and federal resources for something much, much worse.

And what would that be, sir?

There was silence on the other end of the line. Lori called out to the General two or three times before she got a dial tone. There was confusion on the radio, and then the station's signal was lost. Barbara looked at the men and said, "What the fuck just happened?" John turned to the room full of people and addressed Barbara's question.

"The government just killed the General." He said it calmly and so nonchalantly that she thought he was kidding. "You're kidding me?" He shook his head. "All right, men. I think we all know where this is going. You all need to go back under your rocks. Sooner or later, the government is going to put hits out on each of us." Cosmo spoke up. "What a fucked up deal. We save the nation only to be killed by the very government that we helped to preserve." John nodded. The others were somber as they packed their gear and prepared to depart. Lance asked, "What about Bolton, Skillen, and the rest?" John was putting some things away in a cabinet with his back to the room. "The Iron Eagle will deal with them." "Will he allow any to live for the public to see?" Lance asked. Jim popped in before John could respond. "It would make no difference; if The Eagle doesn't take care of them and turns them over to the government, they will never see the light of day. The government will just kill them. They don't dare let this hit the mainstream media."

There was a quiet consensus in the room. Ricky spoke up. "I want to kill Saj!" John nodded and said, "I know you do; however, you know I can't let you do it." Ricky nodded his head slowly in agreement. "How long before they pin this on us?" he asked. John looked around the room and said, "They already have. There will be black op teams dispatched to eliminate us as soon as the fires are out. We will be demonized in the media and hunted like animals." Jim laughed. "You're a special fucking agent with the FBI. You're not exactly hard to find." John didn't show any emotion in his response. "The government and this administration will start kill teams to hit the lowest profile targets first. Forget about getting back under your rocks. All of you need to get your names in the papers ASAP. Do interviews; spread conspiracy theories like crazy. However, under no circumstances tell the truth!" The room erupted in laughter, even John laughed. Phillip spoke up as he laughed, "Tell the truth? Fuck man...you can't write this shit. If we dared tell the truth, it would be more outlandish than the shit we're going to make up." There were a few goodbyes, and the men departed. The only people left were Jim, Barbara, John, and Sara. Jim took a cigarette out of his pocket and handed one to Barbara. "So, what now, John?"

Jim poured some scotch into a glass and swigged it down. "Sara will show you two to one of the guest houses. It's best that you and Barbara remain out of this area of the house going forward." "So, what, now I'm a social pariah?" "You want to stay alive, Jim. You want Barbara to stay alive. The only way that that is going to happen is if you're as far away from the next events as possible." "They killed people we love, too, John. They destroyed our home, our city. I want to extract my revenge." Jim looked at John with a determined look on his face. "I know you mean well, Jim, and I know you think that is what you want to do, but you can't. You told me yourself – you're a lawman. You catch the bad guys. It's up to the courts to deal with them from there. Here, The Eagle is judge, jury, and executioner. He metes out justice in the manner he sees fit. You don't have the stomach for this type of work." Jim started to speak when John interrupted him. "It's one thing to watch a killing on video; it's a whole other to be actively engaged in the act. This isn't your area, Jim. Go with Sara. She will make you comfortable. Let The Iron Eagle deal with this." "Are you going to kill Valente?" "Just go, Jim. The less you know the better."

Barbara and Jim followed Sara out of the room. John sat down in one of the chairs with his head in his hands. Sara came back a few minutes later and said, "You're tired of the killing?" He lifted his head from his hands and said, "No...those who did die, and will die here today, brought their punishments upon themselves." "Then what?" Sara asked, sitting down across from him. "You're not safe. None of you are safe, Sara." "What do you mean? What are you going to do?" John let out a sigh and stood up. "I don't know yet. Let me deal with these animals first, then you and I will discuss where we go from here." "Do you need my help?" He nodded. "What do you want me to do?" "Prepare the operating room. I'm going to start with Bolton and work my way through them. Skillen will be the last to die." Sara walked out of the room. He grabbed the remote and changed the channel. One of the local news stations was working out of the Santa Barbara area. The newscaster had tears in his eyes as he read the report.

We now have a preliminary death toll in Los Angeles County. The estimate being given to us by state and federal authorities is two point six million people dead in the fires. That death toll is expected to rise significantly.

John turned off the television and started for the operating room. "Well, it's time for a chat with Ms. Bolton and the others."

Colonel Colleen Bolton was stretched out on the gurney just as The Eagle had left her, seemingly unfazed by her situation. Sara walked in and pushed the gurney into the operating room, placing it under the bright surgical lights. "You're a pretty woman, kid. What's say you and I have some fun before The Eagle gets here?" Sara didn't respond nor did she look at Bolton. She just prepared the equipment that The Eagle would need to administer her punishment. "What's wrong? Um ... I don't know your name," Bolton asked in a sensual voice. Sara didn't respond. She finished setting up and walked out. Bolton called out to her and said, "We could have had some fun, you bitch!" Bolton was looking around when her eye caught The Eagle standing in the doorway. "Oh, man. You're a stud. What's say you fuck me to death?" He moved into the room and over to the gurney and the equipment laid out by Sara. "Two point six million people dead, and the death toll is going to rise." Bolton looked away. "Oh! Now you don't want to look me in the eye, Colonel. Two point six million innocents dead. For what?" Bolton shot right back at him. "To prove a point!" "And that point would be?" Silence met his question.

"Colonel Bolton …before I inflict your punishment, I thought you should know that your killing spree was used by a high ranking government official to stage a coup on the American people." She looked off into space as he spoke. "He used thirty mercs to help him take Oat Mountain and the twenty-two missile silos up there. He was able to access the cloud and penetrate the base." Her face grew grave and angry. "Then, I WIN! I am triumphant. Our plan worked." "While your body count is impressive, his would have made yours look like a bad holiday weekend of drinking and driving." She screamed at The Eagle, "THAT'S NOT FAIR! THIS WAS MY LESSON TO TEACH. MY TEAM DID A GREAT JOB! FUCK!" "Have no worries, Colonel. You will be happy to know that me and my men stopped Ryan Skillen and his men. I have you and your men, and Mr. Skillen will occupy this room in a while."

He reached over and took a syringe from the table and injected Bolton with a high dose stimulant, agitating her instantly. He pulled another syringe from the table and injected her in the sternum. "That's cold!" "I know." He pulled the restraints on her wrists and ankles tight and then put a restraint across her lower abdomen to completely restrict her movement. He took a scalpel from the table and said, "Let's get started. As I recall, you are very, very proud of your breasts and use them to seduce men and women to get what you want. You make sure they are prominently displayed as your first point of seduction, correct?" "Fuck you. I get what I want, and men see my tits before they see my face." He took her right breast in his hand, and she giggled. "It's nice, isn't it?" "Yes, it is, Colonel. It's a very soft, supple, and quite large natural breast. Too bad you don't need it anymore." He moved the scalpel left to right under the breast cutting away the tissue. Bolton screamed as the blade incised the whole of her breast until it was nothing more than a large piece of meat with a nipple. He cut away the last of the tissue and laid the breast on her stomach. Her screams could be heard echoing down the halls into the chambers where the others were being held. He took the blade and removed the other. "Now, I've removed your pride."

She was screaming unintelligibly as blood ran down the sides of her chest. "You're bleeding pretty heavily. I don't want you passing out. Let's cauterize those wounds." He grabbed the logo of The Eagle, held the handle of the branding iron tight, and as he did the end of the emblem began to glow white hot. "You burned millions of Americans today, Colonel. Do you know what it feels like to have your flesh burn?" She glared at him, and tears began to run down her face. "You got your point across. For God's sake, have some compassion and just kill me." "Not just yet, Colonel. You haven't paid even a small part of the price for your crimes." He pressed the branding iron into her flesh, and her screams were deafening. He pulled the branding iron away after he had burned the second symbol into her chest. Only a slight trickle of blood came from the wounds. She was screaming and crying, gnashing her teeth, and fighting against the restraints, writhing in agony. "Oh, God. What have you done to my beautiful breasts?" There was no response as The Eagle spread her thighs, exposing her vagina and anus. He held the branding iron in his right hand and pointed a finger in her line of sight to her genitals. "Here is your second weapon. Here, you took your prey inside of you, and in the throes of their passion, you extracted your desires, sexual and ambitious. This is where you got what you wanted." Bolton began to shake her head wildly and screamed, "No more, please, no more…let me die!" "Well, I know that you never used the words 'no more' when it came to using your body to get what you wanted, and you will die when I allow it." He took the branding iron and pressed it into her genitals. Her screams were followed by the smell of blood and urine filling the room. She was panting and out of breath; her body was starting to look like a cooked piece of meat. He kept to his work, saying nothing. She screamed with each cut of the blade or burn from the brand until the combination of pain, blood loss, and exhaustion took over her body.

The Eagle put the instruments down on the table and walked to the end of the gurney. He picked up a remote and pressed a button to record on the video units in the room. Bolton saw her nude body appear on multiple screens around her. The Eagle smiled and said, "For posterity," as he moved back over to the table. "I don't deserve this. I was wronged. They had to be taught a lesson." She was slurring her speech from the drugs and the pain of what she had been through. "I agree that you were wronged, Colonel. You were treated disgracefully by the very military and government you served. But that is no excuse for killing millions of innocent Americans." Her face was contorted, her hair dripping with sweat. "There are no innocents, asshole. Don't you get it? There was no way to exact my revenge without taking out civilians. Their death opens a door for dialogue and for a public apology. Those animals raped me, and when they weren't raping me, I was giving them my body to do with as they pleased to advance my career. I am better than them, but I couldn't show it in combat. I had to show it in the bedrooms and barracks to get what I wanted, and then those same men took it all away from me." "So, killing civilians is getting back at them? I don't see it. You killed the men who raped you, now that's perfectly reasonable to me. Hell, I would have helped you. You killed Provost. You ate three victims, and you served Provost's body to his family…now that's twisted. However, I understand your anger there. I would have hunted you in my official capacity as an FBI agent, and you would have gone to prison … but this? To add insult to injury, you leave behind as your calling card the fleur-de-lis; your message of betrayal? Come on, Colonel. Then you hatched this twisted plot with Ryan? You have killed and continue to kill innocents; people are burning in their homes and cars on their own streets. These people didn't harm you, and you harmed them. There's no way that I could ever inflict on you the pain and suffering you have inflicted on the people of this state and this nation. All those victims who are still suffering and dying even as I deal with you ..." As The Eagle spoke, she saw two large objects out of the corner of her eye where there had been a large canvas covering, and she began to scream.

"I had these items retrieved from your home. I thought they would make a nice addition to my torture devices. You enjoyed feeding the machine as I recall!" He walked over and pulled the cover off revealing Bolton's worst nightmare – the industrial meat grinder she used on her victims. He rolled the unit to the middle of the floor and began to prepare it for operation. "Please, please, as your superior officer I command you to cease and desist with that unit." He continued putting the blades into place in the hopper and moving the receiving tray in front of the machine. He finished the prep and plugged the unit in. He pressed the start button, and the unit whirred to life. The screams from Bolton reverberated off the walls. The others in the holding rooms could hear the sound of the meat grinder as its metal blades started to spin faster and faster. "Well, Colleen, you asked to die, and I'm going to allow it; unfortunately for you, it will not be a quick death. You don't deserve that; however, I do plan to watch." He made some adjustments to the unit and said, "I have several of your men to deal with, so I'm afraid that I'm going to have to cut this short. I can assure you, however, that your death is going to be very long and very, very painful." She screamed at the top of her lungs as the gurney was rolled over to the machine. He released one arm, and she tried to fight, but she was too injured to do anything. He wrapped her wrists in heavy leather straps and put the hook of a small cherry picker between the restraints. He used the cherry picker to slowly lift her body off the gurney. He left her feet untied to make her battle with the machine that much more terrifying. Once he had lifted her body high enough above the hopper of the meat grinder, he set the picker to its slowest automatic lowering level and let the machine do the work of lowering Bolton's body into the grinder.

She screamed and cursed as her feet began to lower closer and closer to the spinning blades of the machine. She kicked out her right leg to keep her foot out of the unit as well as her left, and she was able to brace herself against the stainless steel sides of the machine. The picker continued to lower her, and her own body weight and her hands over her head made it impossible for her to keep her footing. The Eagle stood watching her battle with the machine as her left foot slipped and went right into the turning blades of the grinder. She screamed as blood started to fly up over the edges of the hopper. Her right foot followed, and in a matter of seconds, her feet had been consumed by the steel beast up to her ankles. Her screaming became louder, and her cries for mercy fell on deaf ears. When she had been ground up to the top of her knees, The Eagle stopped the machine, and she glared at him with blood foaming out of her mouth. "You're no better than me, you sadistic bastard. You were trained to be a KILLER! Damn you, damn you to hell." He hit the switch again, and the machine continued to consume her body. The unit was up to her waist. Blood and other bodily fluids were frothing out of her mouth.

She was weak, in agony, and most of her words were unintelligible. There was one sentence that came out clear, however, as the machine was taking the last bit of her life. "I'm not sorry for what I have done." "I know you're not. That's the difference between you and me. I mete out justice based on the actions of people; you just killed for the pleasure of killing. You will meet your maker soon, if you believe in that sort of thing, and then you can answer all those nagging questions about your actions in life." As the unit ground into her chest and lungs, she let out a final howl. She looked down at the hopper and then to the receiving tray. She saw her body like hamburger rolling out the end of the grinder onto the tray. The Eagle watched her watch her body until her neck and head were just above the blades, and her eyes closed as her skull split open and her brains splattered on the inside of the grinder.

With Bolton now dead, Saj and Cathy met the same fate. The meat tray was nearly full when he brought in Valente, who didn't say anything. The Eagle could see in his eyes he knew his fate was sealed. He had heard the screams of the others, and The Eagle knew there was no need to rehash what had already been said. Valente looked at the hopper as his wrists were being tied. The cherry picker started to lift his body and moved until he was above the grinder. He looked down into the spinning metal blades but didn't say a word. The Eagle looked at him as the machine began to lower his body into the unit and said, "Such promise snuffed out by the ignorance and arrogance of others." Valente remained quiet until his feet were being consumed by the grinder. He screamed the entire time. No pleas for mercy, no last minute bargaining as his counterparts had done. He died with a quiet dignity that The Eagle found refreshing.

When it was over, he threw a sheet over the meat, rolled it out the doors to an incinerator, and shoveled the remains into the furnace until the last bit was gone. There were pieces of hair, teeth, and bone as he hosed down the hopper and the table. All the killers were incinerated – a fitting departure for the arsons of Southern California. He turned his attention to the closed door at the end of the hall and one final piece of the puzzle … Ryan Skillen … and how he was to die.

Jim received a call on his cell asking where he was. The people needed to see the leaders of the police forces in a united front. He told the caller that he didn't have a dress uniform, all had been destroyed in the fire at his home. "We don't care about that Sheriff O'Brian. Be in street clothes. The media is starting to get up and running again now that the fires are fading, and they need to know we're here for them." "What time are you planning the news conference and where?" He wrote the information down on a notepad that Barbara had handed him and told the caller he would be there. "I don't know what kind of dog and pony show they want to put on, but I have to go to Santa Monica for a news conference." She nodded. She was too tired to argue or get into a question and answer session. "They're going to call you too, Barb," he said as he put on his suit coat. "Yes, I know. We've been cut off from the world. I really have no idea what to expect outside of these walls." Jim was adjusting his tie as he responded. "Hell, Barbara. Hell is what we can expect. The gravity of that hell is yet to be seen, but hell it will be, and there's a pretty good chance that we won't see much of each other for a while." She nodded, kissed him, and said, "We'll get through this. Right now we have to earn our money and do our jobs. I will watch the news conference, and I will wait for your call. I'll send you a text message." "Tell John and Sara that I have been called away on official business. I will call John later to discuss where we go from here." She nodded and said, "Jim…" He turned and looked into her eyes. "Be safe!" He smiled as he took a cigarette out of his breast pocket. "I'll be as safe as I can be, my dear; you do the same. I love you." She reciprocated the sentiment, and Jim disappeared out the door heading for the garage. Barbara went into the bathroom and started the shower. She knew that she would be needed, too. She also knew that there were going to be a thousand questions about where she had been, assuming that her coworkers had survived the fires.

CHAPTER FOURTEEN

"We didn't see this coming?"

News made it back to Washington that Senator Ryan Skillen's body was not recovered and was believed to have been incinerated in the gun battle between his team of mercs and Swenson's team. Daly had been asked to resign after the events of the past several days, and Brian McMillan, one of President Hernandez's closest advisers, was promoted to the role of White House Chief of Staff. McMillan didn't waste any time when word came back from Delta team that all of the men that Skillen had recruited were dead, and that Skillen himself was missing. He advised the president of the situation and convened a meeting in the Situation Room of the White House to discuss options. McMillan was well liked by all members of the joint chiefs. He was a former Marine Corps full bird colonel and would have been promoted to general had he not decided to enter politics when Hernandez ran for office. The SIT room doors opened, and all in the room were called to attention as the president and McMillan entered. Hernandez told them to stand at ease and looked right at CIA Director Tom Yarnell and asked, "We didn't see this coming?" Yarnell said no. "Skillen was the supervising special agent for the FBI in Los Angeles until his fame after the Barstow case catapulted him into the limelight, and he ran for the senate. His military, personal, and FBI file didn't show any signs that he would make a move like this. Mr. President, Skillen, much like Colonel Bolton, had axes to grind with the government; however, Ryan Skillen turning traitor is nothing anyone would have expected."

Hernandez sat taping his long, thin brown fingers on the conference room table. All sat quiet as he rose and paced the room, all six feet two inches and two hundred and fifty pounds of him. "Okay, so we have containment of the situation. What about Skillen's staff?" FBI Director Jennifer Tutts responded. "For the moment, Mr. President, they are under the impression that the senator went to California to visit some old friends." "Well, that won't hold very long. We know he won't be coming back." "We can terminate the staff with little notice and place our own people in the office, sir." Hernandez laughed. "You mean execute them?" There was silence. "Sir, it would be best if we spun this as a terrorist attack committed by foreign nationals. We can easily pin this on any number of Islamic fundamentalist groups or radical extremists. If you ask me, sir, we have a great opportunity to get even tighter legislation passed in the wake of the Southern California fires and convince the people it is for their safety." Hernandez sat down in his chair. "And what about Swenson and his group?" Tom Yarnell fielded that one. "Swenson's group left only one marking behind at Oat Mountain…they killed Skillen's men and contorted the bodies into the mark of The Iron Eagle. The public knows nothing of this as it is now classified. However, someone in his group is either The Eagle or knows The Eagle!" Hernandez sat back in the chair and took a breath. "We've stayed away from the whole Iron Eagle situation. I've never approved any operations that involved the CIA or NSA or any other government office to get into it."

Yarnell pointed a remote at one of the screens in the room. On the screen was a camera shot of Delta team arriving at Oat Mountain. "This footage was taken by Delta team, Mr. President. This is what Swenson and his men left behind as both a marker for the team and a warning." Hernandez watched the film as the Blackhawk choppers grew closer to the lighted object and the clear symbol of The Iron Eagle shown in the camera's eye. "The image was made with the bodies of Skillen's mercs, sir. They were torn to pieces to create the image." "You said warning. What is the warning?" William "Bill" Stamford, head of the NSA, spoke up. "We think it is a warning to all of us not to go down the roads of the past." "Roads of the past?" Hernandez shook his head, clearly frustrated. "Explain!" "This team includes the only surviving team members from the ill fated nine-eleven strike team that had the intel ahead of time to stop the hijackings. It's likely that these men stopped Skillen to avert another catastrophic event, since they could not stop the fires." Head of the joint chief's, Admiral Mike Wallace, chimed in. "Mr. President, no one knows about the black ops operation that the former administration thwarted in order to allow the September o-one attacks to happen. That operation was a black op, and the only reason the men we suspect were involved in this operation are still alive is because we haven't been able to find them."

"So, the men who served their country could have stopped the nine-eleven attacks and just saved America from an overnight coup are slated to be killed?" The room fell silent. "Why?" No one wanted to respond. Each looked at the other. Hernandez was pissed. "You don't kill soldiers who saved a nation; you commend them. You don't punish men who could have stopped the worst act of terrorism on American soil because the last administration was a bunch of sick fucks who took the opportunity to make a power grab. These men are heroes, and they live in the shadows knowing that the government that they swore to serve and protect is trying to kill them? What kind of sick twisted shit is that?" Yarnell spoke up. "There's a lot more to it than that, sir." "Really? Enlighten me!" "They know the truth, sir. Not just of the nine-eleven attacks but of many, many operations they conducted on American and foreign soil. If they ever leaked the information to the press, it would destroy everything we have achieved over the past decade." "Yet, there is no evidence that these men have ever told anyone about their missions, thwarted or otherwise," Hernandez replied. Larry Green, the Commandant of the Marine Corps, interrupted the conversation. "And they never will."

Hernandez looked at him and asked, "How can you be so sure?" "These are Marines, sir. They took an oath, and they went deeper and darker into the bowels of the secrets of our government than even most of the people in this room know about. The warning was a simple one. 'Leave us alone.' These men are in the private sector and a few are working in the government like Agent Swenson and Jim O'Brian. These men are trained killers, and they know that we're having this conversation right now. They are also prepared, if we target any of them, to bring war against the government, and they will terminate every person in this room with extreme prejudice." Hernandez leaned in on the table staring into Larry's eyes and asked, "Are you telling me that you think that these men could take out the head of government?" He nodded. "That's what they were each trained to do, and they have done it many, many times. If we start to actively hunt these men, they will turn and come after us." "I can't believe we're even having this conversation." Hernandez had a look of disgust on his face. "Ah, but we are, sir," Tutts said, looking over at the image of The Eagle frozen on the screen. "Well, the conversation ends here. These men are not to be touched. If I learn that a hair on one of their heads was touched, and I learn that the order came from the people in this room, you will be brought up on charges of treason, and I will personally sign your death warrant. Am I clear?" There were weak 'yes sirs' all around the table. Hernandez stood up and said, "We have a city in a disaster. Let's focus our energies on helping those Americans first. We can let the media spin its own tales for a few days while I think about how I want to handle this."

They all rose. As he left the room, the door closed, and they all sat back down. There was silence around the room when the doors opened again, and Vice President Oren McNeil entered. All stood at attention, and he told them to stand at ease. "We have a problem, Mr. Vice President," Yarnell said. "Brief me on where we are," said McNeil. Brian McMillan got up from the table without not so much as a word. He knew where this conversation was going, and he wanted no part of it. The conversation was getting heated as the doors to the SIT room closed behind him. He pondered how he was going to tell the president that his own cabinet and trusted advisors were going to work around him, and that there was no way he could stop them.

CHAPTER FIFTEEN

"You've been neutered."

ohn walked back into the common area in the command center where Sara sat alone with a glass of scotch. "Are you finished?" she asked, looking out over the sea. "No." "Who's left?" "Skillen." "Are you going to kill him?" There was momentary silence. "Yes." "Do you need my help?" "Only if you want to assist." She took a sip of her drink and sat it on one of the end tables in the room. "That son of a bitch was going to take over the country. I think it's only fair that he have a doctor present for his treatment." There was no emotion in either voice. John turned and walked back down the darkened corridor with Sara right behind him. "Do you think he has any idea what's about to happen to him?" Sara asked. "No…he has no idea, and that's the way I want it. Were you able to get the brachy containers from the nuclear medicine department?" Sara was still behind him as they walked into the operating room. "I was able to get five. I also was able to get gamma radioactive isotope seeds for the brachy sacks, so you can control the amount of radiation you want him to carry and absorb." "How many grays do we have?" Sara kept her distance. She knew she was talking to The Eagle not John. She pulled out two radiation suits she had recovered from the lab. "I was able to get my hands on several different dosing options of gamma isotopes. We can dose the brachy sacks accordingly." They put on the suits, and Sara pulled out three cylinders made of stainless steel. Each cylinder was lined with lead and concrete to keep the radiation from being released into the air. They worked together to dose the brachy sacks with the isotopes through a mobile nuclear medical incubator that allowed them to work in an environment that kept the radiation under control. Sara had an excellent understanding of the medical applications, while The Eagle had been trained in nuclear containment and material handling. Together they made a swift safe team, preparing each of the sacks that would usually be used in cancer treatment to turn Skillen's body into a silent suicide bomber. When they had finished, The Eagle went to the room holding Skillen to retrieve him.

The Eagle was dressed in the radiation suit. Ryan saw him enter the room and said, "I know it's you, John. I swear to God, if you release me I will never tell a soul about your alter ego or identify you as The Eagle." The Eagle moved toward him, and Ryan shuddered. He cut the ties on his wrists and hands and ordered him to his feet. "Follow me," he said to Ryan as he got to his feet. "Don't think of running in any direction; you will be killed immediately." He knew that Ryan was sizing up his escape. They walked to the doorway of the operating room, and The Eagle ordered him inside. He walked in to see another person in a radiation suit standing next to the operating table. "Lie down on the table, Mr. Skillen," The Eagle said in a calm monotone voice. Ryan's eye's started darting around the room. He saw a large piece of equipment covered in a tan tarp and several steel tables with surgical instruments. The lights from the operating lamp over the table were blinding, and he begged them to release him. Sara said nothing; she pointed to the operating table. He shook his head. The Eagle grabbed him with both arms and lifted him and threw him down onto the table. In a matter of seconds, Sara had restrained his hands and feet. The Eagle didn't say a word as he began to cut off Ryan's clothing. Skillen began screaming as the cold steel of the scissors was pushed against the warmth of his flesh. Sara started an IV and gave him a heavy dose of sedative, knocking him out.

"How long before he starts to exhibit symptoms of radiation poisoning?" The Eagle asked Sara. "He will be dead in two weeks. He will start to exhibit symptoms only in the last two days, and the symptoms will be typical of the flu. No one will realize it's radiation until it's too late," Sara said and then asked, "how much shielding are you going to use internally to keep the radiation from his vital organs?" "I have cut enough lead-inlaid fiber wire to make the leak of radiation very slow. As the sheeting breaks down over the next two weeks, he will get higher and higher doses, while those around him will have less and less exposure." The Eagle made four incisions into Ryan's skin, one under his left armpit, one in his abdomen, and two others in his right thigh and pelvis. He opened the muscle with his scalpel, and with the help of Sara, set the sacks and sheathing in place. Once done, Sara sutured the incisions in such a way that they were undetectable. "He will be sore," Sara said coldly. "Wake him!" Sara injected stimulant into Ryan's IV, and he shot awake.

"Please, I'm begging you. Let me go, please." The Eagle pulled out a small cauterizing tool and began to burn Ryan all over his body with special attention to the incisions. Ryan screamed in agony as the burning kept going for what seemed like hours. The Eagle put the tool away and pulled out a small hammer with a blunt end that was padded. He began to beat Ryan about the body with it, and his screams filled the room. Sara walked out, closing the door behind her. Her work was done. It was now time for The Eagle to exact his punishment on Skillen. The Eagle took out a circumcision tool and slid the bell over Ryan's penis. He screamed as a quick flick of The Eagle's wrist removed the head of his penis. Blood began to pool on the table, and he used the cauterizing tool to stop the bleeding. Ryan was screaming and begging as The Eagle grabbed his testicles and made two quick incisions in the scrotum. The testicles flopped out onto the table, and The Eagle quickly grabbed each and pulled with quick force, removing them. Ryan lost consciousness before the first one had been removed. "You've been neutered," he said to an unconscious Ryan Skillen with satisfaction in his voice. He closed the scrotum, and in a final blow gave Ryan a shot of adrenaline that woke him right up. The Eagle showed him the brand he used on his victims. He held it right up to Ryan's face, the emblem of The Eagle glowing white hot. "And finally, one last little thing to remember me by!" The Eagle pressed the brand into the center of Ryan's chest holding it with a great deal of pressure. Ryan screamed in agony, unable to move under the strength of The Eagle and the pressure of the branding iron. The smell of burning flesh and hair permeated the air, and steam rose in the cold room.

"Now, let's get you back to your friends." He struck him hard across the face knocking him out. The Eagle walked out of the operating room and closed the door. Sara was in the foyer sipping her scotch, still in her radiation suit. "Mr. Skillen is ready to be released to the authorities." She nodded and poured a second glass of scotch and handed it to him. He removed the hood, sweat dripping down his face. "Thank you," he said. She nodded, and he sipped the beverage looking out over the sea through the giant windows. He knew that in a few hours his plan to destroy his enemies in government would begin, and that the countdown to the man hunt for him would be set in motion.

Jim returned from what he described as a 'bullshit news conference.' He said what remained of local, county, and city government wasn't much. He told John that the city of Los Angeles was under martial law, though with nearly half the population dead and another third seriously injured, there was little need. Jim was pacing in the foyer of the main room with the girls and John just talking. He wasn't talking to them; he was talking to the air. He was talking to somehow get the smell and taste of death out of his mouth and lungs. He was talking in the hopes that what he had witnessed and continued to witness was somehow a nightmare that he was going wake up from. It was Barbara who brought him back to reality with a cigarette and a glass of scotch. He took the two from her and said, "Jesus fucking Christ…what have we done?" The Eagle had dressed Skillen, and he was wrapped in a silver blanket with a helmet on his head. "Is Ryan a pilot now?" Jim asked, swigging down the scotch and lighting the cigarette. John threw Skillen into the back of his truck and said, "We don't have a lot of time. We have to get him into the hands of Tutts and her team." Jim nodded. He put down the empty glass, took a deep drag off his smoke, and then kissed Barbara. He gave a peck on the cheek to Sara and followed John to his truck.

John was pulling out his cell phone while Jim was leaning on the passenger door where he had just placed Skillen. "You might want to stay as far away from there as possible. Mr. Skillen is hot with radioactivity." Jim jumped back. "Jesus Christ, John. What the hell did you do?" John dialed a number and listened as it rang. "Hoffman." John's voice was disguised, and Hoffman recognized immediately that it was The Eagle on the other end of the line. "Agent Hoffman, Senator Ryan Skillen can be retrieved from a dingy in the port of Long Beach in the harbor near the bow of the Queen Mary. I'm certain that FBI Director Tutts will want to have this information." The Eagle hung up, and Steve immediately called Tutts's office. He was on hold for only a few seconds when her secretary came on the line and said, "Special Agent Hoffman, I have you patched through to Director Tutts. Go ahead." "Director Tutts, I received a call that Ryan Skillen is in a dingy off the bow of the Queen Mary in Long Beach." Tutts was in a car headed for the airport. "When did you learn of this?" "Just minutes ago. Do you want me to get the local field office in Los Angeles to retrieve him?" There was a moment of silence, and Tutts responded, "No! I'm en route to Los Angeles. I will have one of our teams from Edwards do the extraction of Skillen. We need to make sure he can be interrogated. Who gave you the tip where Skillen could be found?"

Steve looked at the phone and thought carefully before responding. "There was no name, just a male voice telling me where Skillen was. He did say that I should contact you, that this would be of interest to you." "I will take it from here, Agent Hoffman. Have you been able to organize anything with the Los Angeles and other field offices?" "It's been very difficult, director. We have suffered a massive loss of life. The fires ripped through whole cities in minutes in the early hours of the morning. So far, I have only been able to get verification of fifty agents in the whole of Southern California that are alive and on the job." "What about Los Angeles?" Tutts asked. "Our communications were knocked out by the fires; communication is sketchy. I haven't been able to contact the LA headquarters, and I've been getting mixed reports from different agencies on manpower, but it's a mess. I'm planning on jumping a plane this afternoon to get out there." "NO!" Tutts said quickly. "You're needed in Washington. The president is going to need our guidance. With me out of town with the bulk of my staff, I will advise the White House and the president that you will be the Bureau's point man for the White House. You will take my place in the Situation Room. I will relay information to the administration through you on our findings in LA. This is going to be a long and intense scene to process and to deal with. Once we have Skillen, I will advise." The line went dead, and Steve sat in bewilderment as to what just happened. His office phone rang within minutes of the call ending with Tutts. It was the White House operator requesting that he come right away by order of the director and the president. He grabbed his jacket off the back of his door and headed for 1600 Pennsylvania Avenue.

CHAPTER SIXTEEN

"Poison the rats then send them back to the nest."

Tutts's own extraction team arrived on scene at the Queen Mary within ten minutes of Steve's call. They hovered in a rescue chopper over a small black dingy tied to the ship and lowered two wet team members to the boat. They radioed back that he was alive, and a basket was lowered and his body placed in it and pulled up to the chopper. John was across the harbor in his condo watching with binoculars as they whisked Skillen away in the unmarked chopper. He pulled his phone from his pocket and called Jim. "The first team of dead men have retrieved Skillen. They'll move him to FBI headquarters in Washington for interrogation." "Okay. Where's Tutts?" Jim asked. John put the binoculars down and walked into the kitchen. "She will use divisional protocol and set an itinerary for LA publicly. But knowing that they have Skillen, she won't leave D.C. She will have him brought to FBI headquarters for interrogation." "So, The Eagle just detonated a human nuclear bomb on the federal government?" There was a moment of silence. "If they move him the way I think they will, yes. They will bypass all of the building's detectors for radiation and other hazmat situations and take him into a secure underground interrogation room." Jim laughed, "The water boarding rooms?" "Yea. I'm sure Tutts is on her way there as well as most of the highest ranking intelligence officials." Jim cleared his throat, "What's the kill rate you expect from Skillen?" "Hard to say. Anyone who comes within ten feet will be affected. The closer they are, and the longer they are exposed, the more concentrated the radiation. They will carry that out of the interrogation rooms to anyone they come in contact with. He could potentially wipe out the entire executive branch, as well as most of the leaders of the CIA, FBI, and NSA in D.C." Jim laughed. "Poison the rats then send them back to the nest to kill the rest. Shit, are you going to warn the president?" There was a pause.

"In a few days, the president is going to order us wiped out. I'm going to let them do their thing." "So, what…do we leave our lives?" Jim asked with a worried tone in his voice. "No…we are going to be proactive. This is the first step in the process of eliminating the enemy." "What's the second step?" "Bring the fight to them before they have a chance to get a foothold." Jim was being called for a news conference. "So, do I meet you back at your place tonight?" "Yes. We can discuss our next move. I will get word to the rest of the team that POTUS will be putting out a hit on us." "I just don't see it, John. The man praised our efforts after stopping Skillen. Why would he want to kill us?" John opened the refrigerator and took out a bottle of juice. "It's not that the president wants to issue the order, or that he will even know that the order has been issued. This has been coming for a long time, Jim. We knew too much after they stopped us in o-one. The conspiracy theorists abound, but the government knew that they had our silence, and those they felt were a threat were neutralized." Jim was getting called again for the news conference; John could hear a female voice in the background.

"Why now, John? Why would they want to kill you all now?" He took a drink of the juice and walked back over to the window looking out at the harbor and the empty dingy floating next to the ship. "We know about Skillen. We know about his efforts to take over the silos in the Chatsworth hills. We know about the silos, the missiles, and most importantly, all of the government's cover ups for the past two decades. We're a liability. They can't spin the propaganda machine with us in the world. The order for the kill on us will come from Tutts and Yarnell." "But the radiation is going to kill them," Jim said with frustration in his voice. "That's the tipping point. That's what will force our elimination. When they're dead, the government machine will work to kill us. We'll be branded traitors and terrorists, justifying their actions. The CIA and FBI will use their counterterrorism units to try and take us out, that's why we attacked first." There was silence on the other end of the line. "The real mastermind behind the terrorist attacks the world over is alive and well and living here, isn't he?" asked Jim. "Yes." "And the government is protecting him?" "Yes." "Do you know where he is?" There was no hesitation in John's response. "Yes." "Then why don't you take him out?" "Because he's already moving in his grand finale through the ports here in Southern California. Because he's a ghost, a spook story. But most importantly, the intelligence agencies and the government's police force, the FBI, are protecting him. They are helping him launch the final great assault on the nation, the final blow that will give the government what they couldn't get after the o-one attacks and now Skillen's failed coup." "What's that?" "Total and complete control of the people, the destruction of the Constitution, and ultimate power over what was America." "This is insane. I'll speak to you tonight. I have to get to this conference." Jim hung up, and John walked out onto the balcony of his condo. "Killing the commanders of the intelligence community is only half of the mission. I have to find Ali Abdul Shabad before he puts his next plot into action; a plot that if executed will change the world."

Sara tried to call the hospital, but the phone lines were down. What news she could get was still sporadic, and the death toll from the fires was still climbing. The freeways were impassable because of the truck bombs used by Bolton. The news that the media was able to get out showed practically every major freeway overpass destroyed. There was no way to get police, fire, ambulance, or any other service to the city. Los Angeles looked like a war zone, and the dead outnumbered the living. She called John and asked if he had seen any of the news coverage. "No...I've been distracted with other things." Sara was exasperated. "Jesus, John. They aren't calling you and your team in on this?" "No." "Why the fuck not?" His voice was calm. "There's no need to at this point. The government knows who did this and why. They are trying to figure out how to make it look like a foreign act of terrorism." "I can't get a hold of the hospital. All the lines are down. The streets and freeways are impassable, even police and fire can't get around the area." "We neutralized the rogue element that committed this atrocity. There is little that I or anyone else can do but let the people and the government pick up the pieces." "You are a part of the government; it's your job to help pick up the pieces." There was a pause.

"Not anymore." Sara's face became riddled with panic. "What do you mean?" "I'm outside government now, Sara. They are going to come after me as well as the rest of the team." "Are you out of your mind? You saved the nation. You're heroes." "We're liabilities, Sara. There is so much I need to tell you. This isn't about this situation. This is a culmination of things over the course of nearly two decades. I and my men know the truth about many, many things the government has been able to spin their own way. They are about to unleash on this nation a catastrophe of devastating proportions, and they are going to use the most notorious terrorist mind in the world to do it." She held the phone tight and said, "Are you talking about Osama Bin Laden? Because he's dead." John chuckled under his breath. "Bin Laden wasn't the terrorist mastermind that the government led the American people to believe he was." "He wasn't?" "No, Sara. He wasn't. He was the government's scapegoat. They stuck a label on him and used his face as the face of terror in the world. He and his family were close friends with one of the presidents of the United States. He was the leader of the Afghan rebellion against the Russians in the Russian Afghanistan war. We fed weapons and military training to his freedom fighters to defeat the Russians. Bin Laden was involved in the nine-eleven attacks, but he wasn't the brains behind them or other worldwide attacks before and after." "Are you telling me that this is all a government conspiracy?" "Yes." There was silence. John said, "I will be back at the house in a few hours. We can discuss it more in depth then."

Sara hung up the phone in utter shock. The past few years had uncovered some of the most horrific things she had ever seen, and now her husband was telling her that those things were only the tip of the iceberg to what was really happening in the country and the world. She walked out onto the back patio and stood looking out over the ocean. For a moment, a look of regret came over her face. She watched and listened as the waves crashed on the beach. "What have I gotten myself into?" she asked as she stared out into the cold green Pacific. One of the house staff asked if she would like lunch. She nodded. "Can I get a side of comfort and security with it?" There was no response. She followed the woman to the dining room where she sat down to lunch and to wait for John to come home and explain what was going on, and what was going to happen to her and her life now that all she had worked for was gone.

CHAPTER SEVENTEEN

"The country is very likely fucked though
...how about that sandwich?"

Ryan Skillen was in full restraints as the Boeing 747 touched down at Andrews Air Force Base. There wasn't any gabbing on the flight. Ten soldiers sat with guns trained on him for the whole five hour flight back to Washington D.C. He knew he had already been condemned to death; it was the information that they needed from him that could stay his execution. The plane taxied to a far out runway where it was met by several black SUVs and a black cargo van. Skillen was removed from his seat and lifted and thrown into the back of the van. There were no windows, just a dim dome light and the shine from the black cold steel of the rifles still aimed in his direction. "No windows?" he asked casually. "I wonder what you don't want me to see?" There was no response. After twenty minutes, the van stopped, and the rear doors opened. Light flooded in blinding Ryan. He was grabbed yet again and thrown onto a gurney and wheeled to an interrogation room in the sub-basement of the FBI headquarters in Washington. Ryan looked around and said, "Well, I see we're not at 935 Pennsylvania Avenue NW. This isn't the Hoover Building." The door was shut, and he was left alone, lying on the gurney looking up at the ceiling. He didn't have time to think before the doors burst open and Jennifer Tutts and Tom Yarnell came walking in.

"Well, it's so good to see you again, Senator," Tutts said in a sarcastic voice. "I wish the feeling was mutual, Jenn, but it's not. What can I do for you?" There was a row of chairs against the wall of the room and a large one-way glass mirror behind it. Tutts and Yarnell grabbed chairs and sat down next to Skillen. "We were told you were evaporated in the gunfight at Oat Mountain," said Tutts. He smiled and moved his hands in a gesture of 'oh well.' "It seems someone wanted to keep you in the dark about my earthly existence." "Where have you been?" Yarnell asked. Skillen looked at their faces. Clean and healthy. He felt sick inside, and he was in agony. "Where have I been? I've been in hell!" Tutts called a guard over and had him press on Skillen's chest. He cringed in pain. "Where have you been, and who have you talked to?" His voice was labored. "I told you...I've been in hell for the past twenty four hours." "You were tortured?" Yarnell asked. Skillen looked at the two of them as if they had three heads. "Look at me! For God's sake. Are you two retards? What the hell do you think?" A hand appeared out of nowhere, striking him in the solar plexus. "Answer the questions, Ryan. Don't be a smart ass. Who had you, and what did you tell them?" Yarnell asked. He winced as he tried to move against the pressure on his chest and the restraints that were pressing on the brand. Tutts saw the pain in his face as did Yarnell, and they quickly ripped his shirt open to reveal the brand of The Iron Eagle on his chest.

"Did you see his face?" Tutts asked. He shook his head. "Was he working alone?" Yarnell asked, glaring at him. He was confused by that question. It was all a blur. He thought he remembered two radiation suits with two different people, but he wasn't sure. "I don't know...it's foggy. He was doing so much damage to my body and inflicting such agony. It's hard to remember. I can tell you that he's a big fuck!" Yarnell moved in close to Ryan's face and asked, "What the fuck does that mean?" "It means that he's tall, strong, and mean." "Did you get a look at his face?" He shook his head. "So, he was in disguise?" He nodded. "What did he do to you?" "The question is, what didn't he do to me? I can tell you that I will never have sex again...not that that's news to you two. You're planning on killing me as soon as you get what you want from me." Tutts and Yarnell looked at each other. "Well, then ...," Yarnell said, "now that we have that out of the way, tell us what we need to know, and I will dispatch you quickly... or delay. It's your call. I can guarantee you that if you screw with us and don't tell us everything we want to know, I'll make you live so long and torture you so hard you will be begging to die."

He couldn't help it. Ryan started laughing hysterically. "I've already been in that situation, Tom. Is the CIA so feeble as to think that I don't already know your tactics? I'm a dead man. If I know the answer, I will tell you." Tom turned to Jennifer and motioned for them to step away from Ryan. They moved into a corner of the room. "What do you think? Do we lean on him, then kill him, or do we lean on him and hold him?" Tutts asked. "We will only get what he knows in the interrogation. We lean on him, and when we feel we have our data, we kill him," Yarnell said with a smile. They walked back over to Ryan, still breathing hard from the brand on his chest and the lack of testicles removed earlier by The Eagle. Tutts started the interrogation. "Were you involved with Bolton in the California fires and truck bombings?" "Yes." "Do you know where she is now?" He looked at their faces looking down on him. "She's dead!" Yarnell looked into his eyes hard. "How do you know?" "The Eagle had her and her men. I heard her screams as he tortured and killed her." Tutts moved the chair closer to the gurney and sat down. "Did you see her body?" "No." "Did you see her die?" "No."

Yarnell was getting pissed off; he motioned for one of his men to move a table of equipment over to the gurney. Yarnell took a pair of jumper cables off the table and clamped them onto Ryan's nipples. He yelled out. "Feel good, asshole?" Yarnell asked as he turned the knob on the battery charger. Skillen screamed as the voltage ran through his body. "How do you know Bolton is dead?" He was seizing and unable to respond. Yarnell turned off the electricity, and Skillen began to breathe again. "I told you. I heard her die. I heard her yelling obscenities at The Eagle. I heard him ask her questions." "What kind of questions?" "He asked her about the attacks, and the men she killed. He told her that he had no problem with the fact that she killed the men who raped her but that was not an excuse for killing innocents." "Then what?" He looked around the cold, sterile room and the few men that remained, his executioners. He knew that Tutts and Yarnell didn't have the balls for the job. Plus, they had to have deniability when it came to his demise. They had a great cover story because as far as everyone was concerned he was dead. He felt a sudden wave of nausea come over him and started throwing up. "Side effects of the beating he took from The Eagle?" Tutts asked. "Probably. We need to get this moving."

He called out, and they moved Skillen from the gurney to a two by eight inch board. As they carried him over he said, "Waterboarding? Come on. I thought we were past this crap." There was no comment. One of the men placed a black hood over Ryan's head and strapped him to the board. He was still talking as they worked. Tutts and Yarnell looked on. At one point, Skillen, who could no longer see, said, "So, you have contracted this out." Yarnell laughed. "It's better this way. I don't want to get my suit wet." The men placed a bucket at the end of the board where Skillen's head was and took a plastic gallon jug of water and sat it next to the board. Two men stood at the end of the board, and once Skillen was strapped in, they placed a towel over his masked face and lifted the board raising his feet and lowering his head. One of the men began to pour water down over the towel and Skillen began to jerk and thrash. After several minutes of this, they uprighted him, and he coughed and screamed through water-soaked lungs. "What the fuck do you want to know? I've told you everything." Tutts responded, "I don't think so, Ryan. How did you get the access codes for the silos and the missile launch codes?"

He was still coughing and not responding when they lifted the board a second time. This time the water ran faster, and his struggles and coughing became more erratic. They lowered the board; he wasn't able to speak right away. They raised his head to allow the water to go down his throat, and for him to cough up the water in his lungs. "Answer the question, Ryan, or I'll have them lift that board and do this for an hour, bringing you to the brink of drowning before reviving your ass," Yarnell shouted. "Access was easy; the codes are in the cloud. I learned it while serving on the Senate Armed Services Committee. I got briefings every day. When I learned that the whole 'football' deal with the president was crap and only for show, I hired a group of freelancers to hack into the Pentagon." "That's where you got the codes?" Yarnell asked. "I have no fucking idea. Hackers are spooks. I never met them. I don't know any of them. I used a contact through a contact to start the mission. When they were done, they created a backdoor into the control center, and I had access to the codes." Skillen was coughing as he answered. "Does this control center have a name?" Tutts asked. "It's a black box site. No identifying it. They used fingerprint and retinal data to allow access. Once in, I was able to see all missile sites in the U.S. and abroad." "Through the site, could you see our air, sea, and moving ground missiles?" Tutts asked. "Yea, I could see everything." "Did that give you access to the launch codes?" "No…the hackers created a backdoor to the backdoor, so to speak, that allowed me to access the nuke codes, but they were only able to break the encryption for the Oat Mountain site." "Do you still have access to the hackers?" Tutts asked. "Yea, I suppose so. Unless they think I'm dead." Skillen started laughing. "You can't kill me. You need me. If they broke the encryption on Oat Mountain, by now they have probably gotten most, if not all, of the codes. Hey, does someone want to get me off this board and get me some lunch? I'm starving."

Tutts and Yarnell shared a look of disgust. They knew he had them. "Not so fast, slick," said Yarnell, "if you're dead, then they won't know what to do with the codes." Skillen started laughing hysterically; it was a combination laugh and cough from the water in his lungs. "You really are a moron, Yarnell. If they think I'm dead, what's to stop them from selling the codes to the highest bidder on the software black market? They themselves can't use the codes, but they could most certainly find a foreign or domestic buyer with the ability to use the codes against America or other countries. I can think of a half a dozen Middle Eastern countries that would give their last nut to get control of an American nuke and send it careening into Israel compliments of the United States." "You fuck!" Tutts said. "We did that, remember Jenn? In all honesty, you weren't that good. The country is very likely fucked though…how about that sandwich?" Ryan asked while laughing.

John got back to the house before eight. Jim was already there when he arrived. The girls were in the kitchen with the house staff fixing dinner. "What's the body count?" he asked Jim, putting his coat on the back of a sofa. "Four million and counting." "I see that the bulk of the fires are out. The infrastructure is going to take years to rebuild. If there is any consolation, there won't be very many cars on the road." John's attempt at humor wasn't a good one, and Jim just rolled his eyes. "Out of a population of 22 million, plus or minus, from Ventura County down to San Diego County, we've lost a significant number of people. We don't have time to ID the bodies because we have no storage for them. All branches of the military have been mobilized to dump bodies at sea as quickly as possible. The next big hurdle will be disease from rotting corpses, not to mention the animal population that survived the fire feeding on the dead." John sat down on the couch, and Jim sat down across from him. "So, Skillen is in the hands of the government. You think that son of a bitch is dead yet?" He shook his head. "They will torture him and learn about the hackers he used to get the launch codes." "I thought we took them out in the firefight in Chatsworth." "As best I can understand, we did, but there are rough folks out there who have bits and pieces of the project. It's unlikely that they knew each other well enough to coordinate and piece the information together, but it's likely that Skillen will buy himself some more time once they know." Jim took out a cigarette and put it in his mouth. "So, you think they will move him and expose others to the radiation?" "Yes. He has about a week before he starts to show the telltale signs of radiation poisoning. By that time, he will have exposed most of the inner circles, at least in the intelligence community." "Do you think he will get to the president?" "No...they will want to keep Skillen and anyone he comes in contact with away from the Oval. This is about containment now. First, they will try to get information on The Eagle, which Skillen won't give up." "How can you be so sure?" Jim asked with the smoke in his teeth. "His best chance for survival right now lies with the hackers. If he gives The Eagle up, he knows that they will think that I was in on it, and they will kill him. He will use the hackers and send the government on a wild goose chase before he gives up The Eagle." "And when the goose chase is over?" Jim asked, lying back in one of the living room chairs. "He'll be dead. My secret is safe, but we still have to find Shabad."

"What's your obsession with him? He's probably dead." John stood up and walked toward the window overlooking the now black sea. "Only a handful of high level intelligence folks know he exists. He got away clean after the nine-eleven attacks. If Skillen didn't give him access to one of the warheads, I'm certain that he has contact with one of the hackers that we didn't kill, and through that source he can get to one of our missiles overseas." Jim coughed. "So, you think he's going to launch one of our missiles at us from overseas?" He shook his head. "He will gain access and take the warheads. He will pack them in a cargo container and send it to the port in Los Angeles or elsewhere, where he can get them and disperse them throughout the U.S." "Are you going to share this information with anyone?" "Not a chance. The last time we shared information over three thousand Americans died, and four U.S. jetliners were used as missiles ... and the government let it happen. No. This is under wraps. Only you and a few of the other guys will know about this mission." "Mission?" John nodded. "We're going after Shabad. He's here in the U.S., and we're going to find him and do to him what we should have done over a decade ago." Jim shrugged his shoulders and asked, "Do what?" John turned to face him with a serious look of anger and frustration. "Kill him. Take out his network and try to save a nation." Jim got up as the girls were entering the room to call them for dinner. "Look, John, we're not in the military anymore. We are in law enforcement. I think it's a bad idea to start hunting down old terrorists. If he's in the LA or surrounding area, he's probably dead. And even if he isn't, the country has been rocked enough by what's happened here. They will be watching the ports like a hawk. We need to do our jobs, sort through this mess, write our reports, and try to get life as we know it back to some semblance of normalcy."

Barbara cleared her throat from behind him. "If there is a mad man who can do even more harm to our country and our people and we know about it, we have a responsibility to do something about it. I can't believe I'm hearing words of defeat coming out of my husband's mouth." He pointed to his leg. "I got shot. I got fuckin' shot saving this fool's life just a few short hours ago, and you support me getting into another rocking adventure with Thor and his battle team? Jesus Christ! When does it end? I just want to have a smoke, enjoy a glass of scotch, and relax. But no...I have to have Ms. Voice of Reason behind me and The Iron Eagle in front of me telling me I have to risk my life again to save the country." He threw his hands in the air as he lit the cigarette and walked out onto the balcony. "No one's going to be fucking happy until I'm dead. I GOT SHOT...what's next? Is The Iron Eagle going to cut my nuts off? Oh wait...he just did!" Barb smiled at John as the door closed behind Jim and his rant. "He's in." John smiled. Sara was standing behind Barbara, and he could see in her eyes that she was tired, and her whole world was upside down. He didn't say a word. She had heard the whole conversation. She walked over to him and wrapped her arms around his mid section and put her head against his chest. "Please tell me that when you get the man that we can at least take a vacation before you go back to doing what you do?" He smiled and hugged her, leaning his head down to kiss her on the top of the head. "I promise, Sara. I promise." Jim was standing on the deck pounding his fists on the railing, screaming words that were unintelligible, though everyone knew there was a string of profanity.

Barbara laughed and said, "I'll get Mr. 'I GOT SHOT' to come in for dinner, then I will get him drunk and let him have his way with me. That will calm him down. You guys want to join us?" They looked at Barbara's pretty little face and smiled while turning down the invitation. "You might be surprised, big guy. I know stuff!" John laughed. "I bet you do. Sara knows enough stuff for me but thanks for the invitation." She shrugged her shoulders as she walked out onto the balcony to retrieve Jim. "Your loss. Maybe another time!" John and Sara stared at each other as the door closed behind Barbara. They shook their heads no and walked on to the dining room for dinner.

CHAPTER EIGHTEEN

"I think you're inviting the devil to dinner,
and you're all going to be the main course."

yan Skillen made the rounds for almost two weeks, being debriefed by nearly every secret level of the intelligence community. He was scheduled to brief the joint chiefs in a secret session when he fell ill. He died less than three days later. Tutts and Yarnell died a few days after Skillen. Members of the intelligence community and their families and friends were getting sick, and as the death toll rose, a reason was sought. Three weeks after Skillen's death, an autopsy revealed that he had been implanted with a lethal dose of gamma radioactive isotopes. It explained how the radiation had been screened to send the gamma rays out of his body while he slowly was contaminated by them internally. The vacancies in the two top investigative and intelligence communities were filled quickly. Deputy Director Brian Smalls was made interim director of the FBI, and Steve Hoffman was promoted to deputy director. The next in line to Yarnell at the CIA was Harold Cantos, who was promoted to interim CIA Director. Both men were interim directors until they could be confirmed by the Congress, but there was little concern of their confirmation as both had been in their respective fields for decades and were well respected. Smalls called a meeting with Cantos, Hoffman, and the rest of the intelligence community in secret at CIA headquarters to discuss the situation and how to contain it. When all the invited guests were assembled, they sealed the room, and Cantos started the meeting.

"There's no reason to recreate the wheel here. We all know what has happened up to this point. This meeting is about containment before the president calls us into the SIT room, which I expect to happen at any moment. Here are the facts. The Iron Eagle and his team of black ops took out Skillen and Bolton and their men. Oat Mountain missile range in Chatsworth, California is secure. Skillen and The Eagle showed the vulnerability in our missile defense systems. Through our interrogation of Skillen, we learned that he sold the encrypted data to a foreign operative. The Eagle booby-trapped Skillen's body with enough gamma-laced radioactive isotopes to kill dozens of people. The Eagle released Skillen back to us instead of killing him as retribution for our shortcomings. The Eagle is very, very educated in all of our intelligence community and law enforcement's measures and countermeasures. He knew that we would not run Skillen through our regular facilities where the radiation would have been picked up because we wanted to get the information from him and then kill him before he could tip our hand on what he and we knew. The Eagle has been labeled a vigilante serial killer, which I will have Assistant Director Hoffman discuss in a moment, and President Hernandez idolizes the men that The Eagle used to stop Skillen but doesn't know that it was The Eagle who targeted internal intelligence agencies here in Washington for death or why! So … what we need to do now is figure out a way to pin this all on The Eagle and his men." He pointed to Hoffman and asked, "Agent Hoffman, would you please bring the room up to speed on The Eagle, and what you and your men know of him?"

Steve stood before the room and explained that everything he and his staff knew of The Eagle was that he meant no harm to anyone but the worst of the criminal world. That there was no record of The Eagle ever killing anyone who had not committed or had been committing heinous crimes. "Our profile of The Eagle is of a man obsessed with ridding society of the evilest of elements. He has brutally murdered several serial killers, killers that were brutal beyond measure." One of the others in the room spoke and asked, "Isn't it true, Mr. Hoffman, that The Eagle is even crueler to his victims than his victims were to the people they killed?" "Cruel is subjective. In all of the cases that I and my offices have been involved in, the 'justice' that The Eagle inflicts upon his victims follows closely the same manner of killings as his victims performed. He has a tendency to hold his victims longer and to inflict punishment on them in the same capacity that his victims did to others." "So, you're saying that he not only tortures and kills his victims, but that he does so in the same manner as they killed their victims?" Hoffman nodded and continued. "However, The Eagle has departed from his typical killing pattern with the terrorist attacks in Los Angeles and the surrounding area. In this case, The Eagle and men who he knows and worked with in his military life …" There was an interruption from the group.

"How do you know he had a military life?" a male voice with a thick Middle Eastern accent asked. Hoffman looked to see the face of the man asking the question but couldn't make him out through the darkness. "We know based on The Eagle's first kill, which involved a Marine Corps Corporal who raped and sodomized young boys at Camp Pendleton. The manner in which the victim was executed, and the unfettered access that the killer had to the base and the barracks of the corporal, indicate that The Eagle is former military." Smalls spoke up. "We know he's ex-military; get to the rest of the profile on this guy." "Our profilers have him as a white male with excessive strength and above average intelligence. Early to late thirties; he's a loner who spends a great deal of time hunting for his victims. He has an axe to grind with someone other than his victims, but it's not clear with whom. Our profilers believe that The Eagle wasn't always this way. We believe that he was created. Possibly trained in special operations by the military. He is extremely cunning, extremely dangerous, and, though we don't have direct proof of this, will kill to protect his identity." Smalls walked back to the front of the room interrupting Steve. "Thank you, Agent Hoffman. Okay, we know The Eagle is a spook, we know that we trained him, and we know that his attention is now turned to the government as his new target. We need to know why. We also have to figure out a way to put this mess on his shoulders, then hunt him down and make a public spectacle of him. It's the only way we can cover our asses."

Carl Daly was sitting in the back of the room silently listening and got a lot of attention when the lights came back up. Smalls had invited him as he knew the inner workings of Hernandez's White House. "Mr. Daly, do you have anything to add to this conversation?" He rose from his seat and walked slowly to the front of the room. All eyes were on him as he walked past the powerful room full of military and intelligence people. He stopped in front of a whiteboard on the wall at the end of the conference table that filled the room, now fully seated with people. He picked up a marker and in bold red letters wrote, OPERATION RED ALERT! The room had been abuzz with sidebar conversations but fell silent when Daly put down the marker. "This, gentleman, is why Skillen was sent back to Washington as a human nuclear bomb and not killed by The Eagle. Skillen is a warning shot across the bow. This is about Operation Red Alert." Steve had no idea what Daly was talking about and, for a moment, could feel the air leave the room. Steve could tell from the look on every face that they knew what Daly was talking about, and for the first time in his career, he was afraid for his life. He had a bad feeling that he had just been inadvertently let in on a secret. A secret so large that, with the exception of the men in the room with him, everyone else who knew of this operation was dead. Cantos stood up and walked to the front of the room, looking hard at Daly. "Does the president know about this?" Daly shook his head. "But you do because you were his chief of staff. You were briefed?" Daly nodded. There was silence, and Steve wanted to slip out a back door, but there was no place to go. So, figuring his life as he knew it was over, he asked, "Excuse me, but what is Operation Red Alert?"

All heads turned his way, and Cantos hit Daly in the arm as they looked over at Hoffman. "Assistant Director Hoffman," Cantos said, "it is both fortunate and unfortunate that you are here for this." A lump grew in Steve's throat. "Jesus Christ, Carl. Look what you've done!" Daly addressed Steve directly. "This was a top secret operation that was being carried out to stop the nine-eleven terrorist attacks. Operation Red Alert was the code name of a top secret team of black operatives that knew every detail of the attacks of that day who were deployed to intercept the terrorists, but who, at the last second, were called out of service so that the attacks could happen." Now it was Steve who sat in stunned silence. But not for long. "We knew in advance about the attacks and could have stopped them?" "Not could have. The plan was in place. The operatives and their teams knew the whole plot. We were ready to stop the whole thing until the plug was pulled at the last minute by the president and the vice president." Steve's face filled with rage. "What on God's green earth would make the president allow that to happen?" Smalls and Cantos laughed as did others in the room.

Cantos replied, "Absolute power. The executive branch of government wanted absolute power, so they allowed the hijackings to happen." "The revolution law?" Steve asked. "And so much more, Agent Hoffman. We couldn't stop Bolton, but our guys stopped Skillen. The American people are in the dark, and this is a chance to exploit their fear even further and take away the last of their civil rights. Or should I say 'allow the American people to give up their constitutional rights in the name of safety?'" Cantos had finished talking and sat down. Smalls looked to a small thin Middle Eastern man in the back of the room and said, "Well, Al, I think you have seen and heard enough. Do you have the information that you need to do your work?" "Yes," he said in a thick Arab accent. "Then, you best catch a flight back to Los Angeles or what's left of it. I will be in touch; you have a package to collect." The man nodded and left the room.

"Well, Steve. You know the big secret. The conspiracy theorists had a lot of the information right. To be honest, we started those conspiracies and have helped to fan the flames of hatred and intolerance. The man who left this room a few seconds ago is the true head of the terrorist group that worked for years to bring down those buildings. He works in secret and doesn't claim responsibility for these things when they happen. He stays off the radar, which allows our government and other world governments to use his services. When he has fulfilled a contract, all of those involved are dead. A secret is only good between two people if one of them is dead. He makes sure that all of the loose ends are tied up, and that there is no way to connect him to the acts of terrorism he has masterminded." Steve was in shock. His government, in the end, was ultimately responsible for the terrorist attacks in the U.S. and abroad. He looked at Smalls and asked, "He didn't clean up everything, did he? The Eagle knows who he is." Cantos jumped into the conversation, "Yes…and Al knows who The Eagle is!"

Steve got a perplexed look on his face. "If that is the case, then why haven't they tried to take each other out?" Daly responded. "Because they need each other." Steve looked at all three men and said, "What the fuck…that makes no sense at all." Cantos was closing up a briefcase as he responded. "The Eagle gets messages from Al, and Al gets messages from The Eagle. The reason the two are both alive is that we keep them apart. Neither knows where the other is, and we plan to keep it that way." "But you want to put the actions of Bolton and Skillen on The Eagle. That's certainly not going to go well with either of these men. What if it backfires? What if they come after us like Skillen did … only to take out government all together?" Smalls laughed. "These two men aren't into politics. They have their own personal agendas and none of that has to do with any government." Steve sat down as he spoke, "That's not true. The Eagle put together a team to save the country. Now, I'm no political expert, but that rises to the level of protecting his country and the American people. I would call that a political cause."

Cantos and Daly were getting frustrated. "Look, this guy got involved because he got caught up in the heat of the moment. One thing leads to another, and he got a team in there to stop what was happening. I think this was just dumb luck for us that he discovered the plot that Skillen was hatching. In the end, there's no politics involved with The Eagle." Steve sighed. "Until you make it one!" Cantos knew what he was saying. "We will capture or kill him before he even knows he's our scapegoat." "I don't think so, Mr. Cantos. I think you're all wrong. I don't know who The Eagle is, and I know from this conversation neither do any of you. But I can tell you, I have been trailing and profiling him for over a decade. If you use the government to pin him as a traitor, blaming him for what Bolton and Skillen and their men did, I think it will backfire on you. I think you're inviting the devil to dinner, and you're all going to be the main course." Steve had his hands folded in front of him as he finished his talk. Daly and Smalls spoke off in a corner of the room when the phone rang in front of Cantos. He answered it. There were only three words spoken by him. "Right away, sir." And he hung up. "That was the White House. They want us in the SIT room now."

Hernandez called an emergency meeting of his cabinet and the joint chiefs. The SIT room was packed when Hernandez entered. "At ease. Can someone explain to me how it is that we had a traitor in our midst, a human nuclear reactor, and no one knew about it? Half of the intelligence community is dead or dying, and I'm just learning that Senator Ryan Skillen was found alive in Los Angeles and that he was here for weeks?" His questions were met with silence. He stood up and took a briefing manual the size of a phone book and hurled it across the room. It smashed into a monitor at the far end of the room, and he said in a thundering voice, "I'm getting goddamn tired of this shit. You are my advisers; you serve at my pleasure as the President of the United States. At this moment, what I have is a group of people I either inherited or appointed, or who were elected and are making executive decisions that are only mine to make. Now, I want to know who the fuck did this, and how we didn't know that Skillen came back here to kill even more of us, or I'm going to call in the FBI and the DOJ and have them arrest the whole bunch of you for treason." The Acting CIA Director, Harold Cantos, spoke up. "Mr. President, there are a lot of us who are new to our positions, sir. You promoted me through attrition after Director Yarnell's death. I have been working very closely with FBI Director Brian Smalls, who was also promoted by you to fill the vacancy left by FBI Director Tutts. We know that this was a rogue operation, sir. We know that several units of the government were working in deep secret on Skillen in the hopes of learning if he divulged any of the information that he obtained and how he got the information." Hernandez sat down in his chair. "Then, for the love of God, tell me why the fuck this has happened." Cantos stood up and asked that the lights be dimmed for a slide show presentation. The room went dark, and the black screen came to life with the emblem of The Iron Eagle and the words *'The Iron Eagle'* emblazoned above it. "This, sir, is who we believe is responsible for everything that has happened in the last three months."

Hernandez looked at the emblem on the screen before him. "That's not a person, Cantos, that's a photograph. What is The Iron Eagle?" "The Iron Eagle isn't a what; it's a who, sir." There was tension in his voice, a nervous tension as Cantos spoke. "Then, who is The Iron Eagle?" Smalls piped up, "The Iron Eagle is a serial killer, sir, or so we thought. We have reason to believe now that The Eagle is, in fact, a former military operative who works in a high level government position." Hernandez had a thoughtful look on his face and said, "I remember seeing this image at the Oat Mountain silos. Those men who left this mark are heroes. I was told that they left this image both as a sign to the Delta strike force that the traitors were gone and to send a message to others who might try this again that this is what will come of them." "You were told that by Tutts. Is that correct, sir?" He nodded. "The men who carried out this mission with The Eagle are the best of the best that this country has ever trained, sir.

They make our military black operatives look like kindergarten teachers, sir. I'm sure it was explained to you that you were never told about this elite unit because of the ramifications it could have on your presidency." "'Plausible deniability' is what I was told." "Yes, sir. That would be correct. We believe that The Eagle and the men who worked with him in this operation were using it as a cover. We believe that they were in on this with Skillen as well as Bolton. We believe that The Iron Eagle is actually the head of a secret terror organization and that Skillen and Bolton were working for and with him and those under his command."

Hernandez looked around the room. "You're trying to tell me that this man used a group of elite trained former or current military personnel to stop a plot to take over missile silos? He did this to endear himself to us?" There was no immediate response. Hernandez continued, "So, what do you group of thinkers advise that I do here?" Smalls spoke up. "Go on national television denouncing this man who calls himself The Iron Eagle. Announce that he is responsible for the deaths in Los Angeles, that he is the terrorist mastermind behind this whole situation, and offer a large reward for his capture." Hernandez looked around the room at the nodding heads. "You want me to put out a contract on a person we don't know that just saved this nation?" "Ultimately, Mr. President, it is our opinion that it is The Iron Eagle who caused this situation. We also have reason to believe that he is planning an even bigger attack on U.S. soil." Hernandez kept looking around the room. "Where is Deputy Director Hoffman?" Smalls responded. "We did not invite him to this meeting, sir." "I want him in the Oval Office in the next ten minutes. He ran the Los Angeles FBI headquarters. He knows this killer. I want his input." Smalls and Cantos spoke in unison, "I don't think that that would be advisable, sir!" "Give me one good reason!" Silence fell over the room again. "I didn't think there was one. Ten minutes, gentlemen. I want Hoffman in the Oval."

Hernandez stood up and walked out of the room. Cantos and Smalls spoke quietly together off in a corner. Cantos said, "We get Hoffman in with the president and let him talk." Smalls smiled and said, "Ah...and have him tell the president that he feels that The Eagle is no danger to the nation?" Cantos smiled. "Yes...Al is working on our next attack...we can pin it on The Eagle and ultimately Hoffman for supporting him." There was a pause, and then Cantos asked, "If we do this, then we have to find The Eagle. You tell me just how the fuck are we going to do that?" Smalls slowly shook his head, "We don't find The Eagle. He will find us. When the president addresses the nation denouncing The Eagle, the nation will rally around the president and all of us. We flush out The Eagle, we capture him, and then parade him before the public as the demon who tried to destroy the nation." "And when Al sets the next attack in motion, how do we explain that to the president and the American people?" Cantos laughed.

"Who cares? We will finally get the last piece of legislation through the Congress to strip the people of their rights all in the name of security. We will also get our guy into the White House in the next election, and once that happens, we can roll back term limits and the rest of the laws that have kept this nation down. We can get our guy in the White House permanently. We can widen manipulation of the Electoral College with more manipulation of redistricting in our favor and win elections based on voting districts. Without knowing it, America has a supreme leader." Smalls put a hand on Cantos's shoulder and said, "Slow down there, big fella. You're putting the cart before the horse." Cantos settled down a bit. "Yea…but we can do it; we can see the light at the end of the tunnel. We just need to get Hernandez to set the nation against The Eagle; the rest will fall into place."

Smalls called Hoffman and told him to meet him in the Oval Office at the White House immediately. "So, you're going to let Hoffman tell the president all the crap he told us?" Cantos asked. Smalls nodded. "You bet. If there is any way to sway Hernandez, it's to make The Eagle look like a saint, and Hoffman is going to do that. Then, we'll show Hernandez the work of The Eagle and his killings, out of context of course, and Hernandez will do as we have asked." Smalls walked into the outer office of the Oval and waited for Hoffman. Cantos went back to CIA headquarters to set up a false report on The Eagle to present to the president.

Steve showed up at the Oval as demanded and spent nearly an hour with the president. When he was finished, the president thanked him and sent him out. Hernandez ordered Smalls and Cantos to the Oval, and they spent another two hours showing the president the work of The Eagle, out of context. When they were finished, the president set a news conference to speak to the American people at nine p.m. Eastern Time. He would outline a goal to capture and prosecute the man calling himself The Iron Eagle and all those who worked with him as traitors to the nation. He would praise the work of Smalls and Cantos as well as Hoffman, and by six-thirty p.m. Pacific Time The Iron Eagle would be the most hated and hunted man in the world.

CHAPTER NINETEEN

"Pal, we don't have no fucking time machine."

fter dinner, the four went into the media room to watch the president's address to the nation. Jim had heard when he was out and about earlier in the day that the president was going to address the country on the terrorist attacks in Los Angeles. The group sat down to watch as one of the national television stations in New York aired the broadcast. The president came on the screen sitting behind his desk in the Oval Office.

My fellow Americans, over the last forty-eight hours we have seen a terrorist plot unfold that is without measure in the history of this great country. We have seen American bloodshed, civilian and military, that based on our best intelligence sources has pointed to a single homegrown American terrorist. While he has not claimed formal responsibility for the horrific loss of life and property, we feel it is only a matter of time before he does. This traitor of the American people is known only by his nickname, and that name is The Iron Eagle.

The four sat in front of the television as Hernandez laid out the case and responsibility for the deaths of innocent Americans on the rogue serial killer, and he set a reward for the capture and prosecution of The Eagle at fifty million dollars. At one point in the speech, Jim leaned over to John and said, "You're worth a shitload of money, man. Who do you think will turn you in first?" John just watched the television as did the others until the news conference was over. Tears were running down Sara's face as well as Barbara's. Sara couldn't hold the raw emotion in, and she screamed at the television, "He saved the country. He saved lives, you bastard, and this is how you repay him?" John had no reaction. He looked at Jim. No words were exchanged, just head nods. Jim left the room, and Sara and Barbara were left alone with John. "What are you going to do, John?" Barbara asked. Sara just sat staring at him with tears running down her face. "First, I have to make sure you two are safe. You are going to take a vacation immediately. You're going to Europe where you will remain until I call you back." "I'm not leaving you in this mess, John. I'm going to stand by you no matter what. I love you. I want to help you," Sara said while crying. "If you love me, you will do as I ask. I can't protect you and do what I have to do in this situation with you here. I can have no distractions, and if you two are here, Jim and I will be distracted from the mission." Barbara looked around the room. "What do you mean 'you and Jim?'" "He knows who I am. Sooner or later, they're going to figure it out, and then he will be the next casualty in this. He and I have to set a military mission with precision to eliminate once and for all, all enemies." Jim walked back into the room, a cigarette in his mouth.

"John wants us to go!" Barbara told him. "Yes, you have to go, Barb. I can't protect you here. You both have to do whatever John tells you. Things here are about to get very messy and very confusing." Barbara knew things about Jim that Sara didn't. She looked at Sara and said, "Let's pack some bags. We need to be ready to catch the first plane John tells us to get on." Sara didn't want to leave the room, and she ran to John and hung on his neck kissing him and begging him to let her stay. "I can help you, honey, I can help you." He pulled her off him and with a great deal of love in his eyes said, "Yes, my love, you can … by getting on the private jet in Santa Barbara. In the mess that has followed this scene here in Los Angeles, it will take months or even years to sort out the living from the dead, and there is no way that the government, state, and federal agencies can ID all the bodies. Your disappearance won't be noticed for some time, and by that time I will have this resolved. I will not be able to speak to you until this situation has been resolved. But knowing you're safe will allow me to do what I need to do." She pulled back and asked, "What the fuck are you going to do, John? Run from the government? Hide in some lone cabin somewhere waiting for the heat to get off you?" He smiled a sad smile. "Just the opposite, sweetheart. I'm going to take the battle right to the government. I'm going to finish what I wasn't able to finish over a decade ago. The government just declared war on me and my men; I'm going to take them out." "You can't kill the president!" Sara said. "I'm not going to. He has no idea what he's dealing with. He's gotten some bad advice. If anything, I'm going to try to protect the president from his own advisors."

There was a brief struggle, but soon the girls were off to pack their luggage, and Jim and John were left alone in the living room. John looked at Jim and said, "You didn't sign on for this. I never saw anything like this coming. You put a call in to the guys?" He nodded. "You need to jump a plane with the girls. You don't want any part of this." Jim started laughing and grabbed a scotch bottle from the bar at the back of the room. He dropped a few pieces of ice into the tumbler and filled the glass. He did the same with a second glass and brought them over to the couch and handed one to John. "Jesus Christ, man. Do you think that I'm going to turn my back on your fuckin' ass now? Outside of our own men and me, everyone else who knows who The Eagle is is dead. They have no idea it's you. We are going to show up for work tomorrow morning, and we are going to begin the methodic work of dissecting government. We know who the enemy is, and they are easy high profile targets. Shit, man, this will be like shooting fish in a barrel." He handed John the scotch. "My suggestion to you is to start drinking again." They each took a drink of their scotch, and John said, "It's not the government we need to worry about. I can deal with them when the time's right." Jim took a drink and sat back on the couch with his legs spread apart. The bandage on his thigh had blood soaking through it. "What the fuck are you talking about?" "We have to go back in time…." Jim laughed and said, "I've only had two sips of my scotch, and I know you're not drunk, but, pal, we don't have no fucking time machine." John stood up and walked across the room and stood looking out the window at the sea. "Not literally going back in time. I have to find and take out Shabad before I can do anything to deal with this government situation." "And how the hell do you plan on doing that?" "By getting to his next shipment before he can get it, and then killing him before he kills me." "How are you going to do it?" Jim pulled on the gauze wrap on his leg, waiting for John's response. John stood staring out at the sea, "Carefully…very carefully!"

He heard the girls come back into the room. The house porter was ready to take them to the airport. "I don't want to go, John!" He kissed Sara's face and said, "It's the only way we are both going to stay alive." She nodded. Barbara kissed Jim and told him to keep from getting shot this time and to slow down on the scotch as she drank the last sip out of his glass. A few tears, and the girls were on their way to the airport. It was near midnight, and Jim announced he was going to bed. John sat down on the balcony overlooking the sea and started to doze. In his mind's eye, he could see Shabad standing on the jetway at Dulles International Airport waving goodbye to him as he and his team were whisked off to a holding room where the rest of his teams were waiting. As he began to fall asleep with the sound of the sea for background noise, he could see the suite at the Airport Marriott at Dulles International Airport. He could see the calendar on the desk. He could hear his team calling out the flight numbers for boarding on the eleventh and the names of the men they were to take out as soon as the planes left the ground on that fateful day. In the back of his mind, he knew that the events that led up to the nine-eleven attacks were the very thing that was going to expose the greatest conspiracy in U.S. history, and that he was going to have to relive those fateful days in his mind in order to stop Ali Abdul Shabad from helping the U.S. government do it again to the American people.

Shabad was driving home from San Diego International Airport after returning from Washington D.C. He listened intently with no discernible expression to the address to the American people. He just drove north on Interstate 5 headed for Los Angeles, listening as the president went on and on about The Iron Eagle, and how he was responsible for all the ills that had befallen the people of Los Angeles and the surrounding area. He caught the interchange of the 5 and 405 and continued north until he got to the 710 Freeway and took it down to the Vincent Thomas Bridge, straddling the ports of Long Beach and San Pedro. He had chosen to live in San Pedro because it was a small port town where everyone knew everyone, and there was a heavy Middle Eastern community nestled amongst the varying cultures. The president was giving his closing statement to the American people and announcing the fifty million dollar reward leading to the arrest and conviction of The Iron Eagle as he crossed the bridge and turned onto North Gaffey Street. He turned into the driveway and turned off the car.

As he got out, one of his neighbors hollered out to him, "Hey, Al. How are you doing?" He waved a weak wave and said, "Hi, Rick. I'm doing fine, just a little tired." "How'd it go in Washington? Were you able to get them to listen to our longshoreman's union demands?" "Oh…now, Rick, you know as union president I can't discuss that with members." "Are you going to be back in your crane tomorrow?" Rick asked cautiously. "You bet. Those containers aren't going to move themselves off those ships. Are you going to be driving your container handler tomorrow?" "You know it!" Rick had a big smile on his face as he answered that question. "Then, it will be a good day. We'll both be working. Have a great night." He waved to Rick as he went into the house. After he dropped his bags in the bedroom and had kissed his wife and two children, he walked out onto the front porch and looked at the lights from Terminal Island and the other platforms and asked himself, "Why does the CIA want to open up a weapon like The Eagle? They won't catch him; all they did was stir the hornet's nest. He'll be coming after me now, and I'll have to kill him before he kills me."

He pulled a box out from under the front porch of the house that he had hidden and opened it on his lap. In it were miscellaneous items including newspaper clippings from nine-eleven. He picked up a copy of the Los Angeles Times dated September 6th. A small article on the front page said it all, *Al-Qaeda operative arrested in Minneapolis tells of terror plot.* "Oh, how close we came to getting caught. I remember waving to John from the jetway at Dulles at five-thirty in the morning as he was being pulled back with eight other men. I was getting on United 55; my men were boarding other flights. He wanted to grab me before he started his portion of the mission that morning. It's a shame." He looked down at the photographs from the newspaper clippings and said, "John, if you hadn't seen me and ran after me, you might have made your flight, and your men theirs, and the world would never have changed." He smiled as he put the box back under the porch and sat back in his chair. "No matter what happens, it's going to be fun running from and toward you again…or I should say The Iron Eagle?"

OPERATION RED ALERT

Book Four: The Iron Eagle Series

PROLOGUE

Special Agent John Swenson stood looking out his office window at 11000 Wilshire Boulevard, the Los Angeles headquarters of the Federal Bureau of Investigation. His office was on the seventeenth floor and had panoramic views looking out over Westwood and a large portion of western Los Angeles. His desk was cluttered with files. The building had survived the fires set nearly a year earlier, and while still heavily shorthanded after the devastating loss of life, he had a job to do with what he had to work with. He stood staring out the window when an all too familiar voice spoke up behind him. "So, what are you daydreaming about, fuckface?" He turned to see the smiling face of Los Angeles County Sheriff Jim O'Brian sitting in one of the chairs in front of his desk. He had his feet up on the desk and an unlit cigarette hanging out of his mouth. John sat down and said, "Well, look who's climbed out from under his rock." There was a smile on Jim's face, and the two sat for several moments in silence. The men hadn't seen much of each other since Operation Rome Is Burning. They had been keeping a low profile, but John knew why Jim was in his office. Jim was looking over at a whiteboard that John had next to his desk with the emblem of The Iron Eagle at the top and crime scene photographs below it. He was staring at the photos, waiting for John to say something, but silence met his stare. Jim turned and pointed to the board and made a really poor attempt at making the sound of an elephant. "It's in the room, man. When are we going to talk about it? You've been ducking me and everyone else on these three cases for three months."

John sat down and pulled open a grey case file and handed it to Jim. The file was the crime scene folder for the most recent killing John's office was investigating. It was the murder of Lance Coswalski. His body was found floating in the marina in Manhattan Beach a week earlier. Jim handed the folder back to John and said, "I already know. I want to know when you're going to start doing something about this." He didn't have any words. Three of his best friends, and the best black operatives who worked with him and Jim, were dead, and John was at a loss for words as to what to do.

Jim sat chomping on his cigarette for a long time before he spoke again. "You know this shit ain't random. You also know that sooner or later they're coming for us," he said in a calm and fearful tone. John shook his head. "Not here." Jim nodded. John pointed to his office door, and the two men walked out to the elevator and down to the ground floor. They crossed the employee parking lot to John's car and entered it, neither saying a word. They drove through the streets and freeways until they got to Santa Monica, where John parked the car and got out. Jim followed close behind. The once scenic area, now a makeshift refugee camp since the fires. Hundreds of thousands of homeless people lined the coast of California from Santa Barbara to San Diego. There had even been spillover into Baja. Mexico was assisting in the efforts to help get America's second largest city back online.

John started talking through the noise of the crowds of people. "Lance's is the third death of one of our team in the past four months." Jim nodded. "Phillip and Blake are dead as well, and Ricky is missing." Jim nodded again. John stopped, and they sat on the steel tines of a forklift looking out at the sea. "We are under twenty-four/ seven surveillance." Jim nodded again. "It is only a matter of time before they try to make a move for you, Jim." "I'm not worried about it." John looked on out to sea. "Do you know where Shabad is?" Jim asked. John nodded. "Don't you think it's time for The Iron Eagle to make his move?" "It's not that simple!" Jim looked out over the seawall that held back high tide and kept the port even and accessible year round. "Well, The Eagle better make a move and make one fast, or there won't be anything to talk about. More Americans will die; a limping city will be struck again by a terrorist that a handful of people know exists, and not only will we be dead but so will our wives. How does that sit with you, Mr. Eagle?" John nodded in agreement. Everything Jim said was true. "The low profile thing ain't working, John. You said that we are at war. It's time to get off your ass and get the rest of the men that we do have together and kick some political ass!" Jim had taken a cigarette from his top pocket and was lighting it with his Zippo as he was saying it. He took a drag off the smoke, and the wind off the sea blew it back in the direction of the city that was still charred ruins.

John didn't make eye contact but said, "Shabad is waiting for The Eagle to make his move." Jim took another long hit of his smoke and said, "No fucking shit! Well, what the fuck are you going to do about it?" John stood up and said, "Meet me at my home tonight after sundown. We will go from there." Jim nodded and stood up and followed John back to his car. They went back to the federal building where John dropped Jim off. He called his office to let them know he was going to be out for the afternoon and drove down the 405 Freeway toward the ports. He knew what he needed to do, and he knew he needed to do it now. He set his frequency scanner to Al Shabad's cell phone number and set up his midi recorder to pick up any calls that Al might get.

Al Shabad was working the controls of the port crane in San Pedro when the cell phone in his jacket started vibrating. "Yes," he said as he was using one of the controls to stack one container onto the other. A male voice told him, "The cargo is ready for delivery," in perfect English. He hung up the phone, and after setting the container down, radioed he was going to lunch. The climb down from the port crane took several minutes. When he reached the bottom, he saw Ricky Park dropping a container for loading at the port's edge. He waved to him, and he waved back. Al walked over to the cafeteria and ordered some lunch then walked out of the port gates to his car with his cafeteria tray. He sat in the front seat eating his meal when his phone buzzed again. He answered with a mouthful of food, his thick Middle Eastern accent hard to understand as he spoke. "What?" he said calmly. He recognized the voice on the other end of the line immediately.

"So, the cargo is ready for delivery?" Al sat silent. "Cat got your tongue, Al?" The voice was taunting him. "How did you get this number?" There were a few moments of silence, and the caller said, "Al...you've had the same number for over a decade. You don't need to hide. You have the government to protect you... or do you?" Al looked around his car in all directions, but there was nothing out of the ordinary. "Where are you?" he asked. "Somewhere you never thought I could get, Al. Somewhere you never thought I could get." There was a look of panic on his face. "You don't want to go down this road with me," Al said, trying to sound intimidating with a quiver of fear in his voice. "Oh, Al, you spent so many years protected. It's time for you to pay the price." "Fine. Not my family." "That's all up to you now, Al. I want the cargo. You give me the cargo, and I will release your family." There was a moment's pause as Al stared out the windshield of his car. He waited a moment too long and heard the scream of his daughter on the other end of the line.

"Leave the cargo manifest at Cherry Cove on Catalina Island just off the pier next to Pike's Boat Rentals by midnight. I will tell you where you can find your daughter after I verify the manifest. If you fail to do as instructed, you will find what remains of your daughter in pieces on your crane. I've already fucked her, Al. You don't want me to dismantle her." The line went dead. He started the car and headed for his home. He pulled into the drive and jumped out of the car only to find the front door to the bungalow wide open. He ran in, and the house had been ransacked. There was blood pooled on the floor in the kitchen and chunks of long black hair that he recognized as his wife's. The rooms of the children were destroyed, and two of his daughter's favorite stuffed animals were left in a sexually explicit position. He screamed as he ran out the door back to his car with his cell phone in his hand. He jumped into his car and raced down the street and back to the freeway headed for the port.

The Iron Eagle sat parked in a corner alley watching the whole thing unfold. He had intercepted Al's earlier call. He knew Al couldn't go to the police. He could only call those he worked for in the hopes of getting back his family and not giving up the manifest. The Eagle watched as Al's car sped down the street to the freeway and listened to his phone calls back to Washington, knowing that Al was going to get no help from D.C. and that his daughter would be the first of his family to be killed and dismembered after the killer had done the unspeakable to her. Al's wife and son would be next, and then the killer would move on to Al himself to get the cargo he wanted and to stop the government's plans. The question The Eagle asked himself out loud was, "Do I really want to help you, Al, or do I wait to capture your nemesis when he's finished with you?"

About the Author

Roy A Teel Jr. is the author of several books, both nonfiction and fiction. He became disabled due to Progressive Multiple Sclerosis in 2011 and lives in Lake Arrowhead, CA with his wife, Tracy, their tabby cat, Oscar, and their Springer Spaniel, Sandy.

CPSIA information can be obtained at www.ICGtesting.com
Printed in the USA
BVOW04*1353160315

391154BV00001B/3/P